# A Cambridge Childhood Revisited

**F.T.Un**

© F.T. Unwin, 1991
First Published in Great Britain, 1991

ISBN 0 9512545 4 5
Published by F. T. Unwin, 9 Cockcroft Place, Cambridge
Tel: Cambridge (0223) 352438

Typeset, printed and bound by
The Burlington Press (Cambridge) Ltd,
Foxton, Cambridge CB2 6SW
Tel: Cambridge (0223) 870266

By the same author:

Dew on My Feet
Pimbo
What Pimbo Did Next
Pimbo and Jenny in Old Cambridge
Knock on Any Door
From Cambridge – One and All!
In the Shadow of King's
Gentle Tales of Old Cambridge
Cambridge Tales of Mystery and Mirth
The Magic Book for Cats
Cambridge – As War Clouds Roll By
"A Cambridge Childhod" – (Pimbo and Jenny in the 1920s)
Fame Costs (A true story of the author's struggle to break
into print)
More Gentle Tales of Cambridge
Cambridge Barber Shop Tales
Flicks Through Cambridge

# CONTENTS

# The Market Square

Along the busy cobbled street,
Cosmopolitan folk you'll meet.
And take a sniff of the pungent air,
Hot dogs, and burgers, smell out their ware.

Market traders lustily cry
Incite your willingness to buy.
But once they pack, the fading light,
Sets the stage for the coming night.

The shops are shut, street lamps are lit,
Homeless beings, just quietly sit.
Listening for that hoped for call,
To a cosy bed before night-fall.

In the morning, the cheerful sun,
Wipes out the memory of all that's done.
Market Square prepares its day,
For jostling crowds – and come what may!

Sarah Thomas
(Age 12 years)

# CHAPTER 1

## Pimbo's new home

"You remind me of a lovable circus clown I once knew; he had red hair, thin legs, and dimples. Pimbo, that was his name, and that's what I'll call you my boy – Pimbo." Bob Freestone, despite his chronic asthma, had a keen sense of humour. Besides, thought Bob, was it not the fashion to give a foster-child a nickname? It saved a lot of questions – and was kinder to the boy.

Pimbo aged seven and small for his age, glanced round the little kitchen of number ten Leeke Street, Cambridge. In the centre of the room stood a wooden table spread with newspaper. On a bare shelf over the fireplace, an old tin alarm clock ticked away loudly. Cheap printed oilcloth lay spread over the kitchen floor, as though anxious to cover up cracked floor boards.

Mrs Maude Freestone, Bob's wife, a stout matronly woman, turned to Mrs Bruce, her next door neighbour, who had just entered. "Well, here's my boy, my first foster-child. With Bob off sick with his chest, the money will be a godsend." Maude noticed Pimbo's wide blue eyes staring up at her.

"In any case, I've always wanted a boy", she said,

patting the lad's shock of red hair as though confirming her statement. "Bob knows all about the boy and the Holt Sanatorium – we've talked about it for some time now".

Mrs Bruce gazed down at Pimbo. "Been to Holt has he? Consumption, eh? He don't look too healthy to me, sanatoriums are all right but you can't beat a mother's love – now can you?"

Since the death of his mother Pimbo had been moved from one home to another. Dr Phillips, the Cambridge chest consultant had given him only a year to live. The Norfolk air around the Sanatorium in Holt, had given Pimbo a fresh start in his fight against the dreaded T.B.

In the morning Pimbo was allowed to explore his new surroundings. "Don't go on to Newmarket Road, it's race day," warned his new foster-mother. "Pop in now and again to let me see you're all right."

Leeke Street was a small cul-de-sac off Newmarket Road, this being a main road running through the centre of Cambridge. Leeke Street boasted fifteen houses on each side. There was a rag and bone man, a fishmonger, a boot repairer (with a shop on Newmarket Road), a coal merchant, and an escapologist. Apart from a bookmaker, the remainder earned a living by casual employment, most were more out of work than in.

At the bottom of the street, Pimbo was attracted to a pile of second-hand clothing surrounding the home of Mr Brown the rag and bone man. Through the open door he watched as Mr Brown, aided by his wife, adjusted his wooden leg. At last, moving confidently, Mr Brown swung his way out to a waiting motor cycle and side-car – proceeding to start it up. "Give us a push boy?" he said suddenly.

Proud to feel that his help was needed Pimbo pressed his small thin frame against the heavy metal at the rear of the motor cycle. To his surprise a healthy *chug-chug* ensued. Mr Brown touching his cap and winking at his wife, moved smartly away.

On the following Monday, Maude Freestone was all rush and bustle. Pimbo was starting his new school. Pimbo found difficulty in keeping up with her as she hustled him along Newmarket Road, past Godesdone Road, and into River Lane. The school, which stood opposite the gas-works in River Lane, was a small primary, accommodating mixed classes of about thirty children.

Miss Cowell, the headmistress was a tall, gentle lady. She spoke kindly to Pimbo as Mrs Freestone introduced him. The children came from the poorer homes and, owing to the inability of their parents to afford adequate diet, at nine o'clock a spoonful of Malt or Virol was given to each child.

Pimbo watched Miss Cowell as she called out the children's names. He noticed how different she looked from the mothers in Leeke Street. There, careworn faces seemed to be the order of the day. Sometimes through the thin walls of his bedroom he would hear Mrs Bruce crying – it was always something about money.

During lessons, Miss Mason, one of the teachers, called out Jennie Smith, a girl whom Pimbo knew lived in Brown's Yard, a small sunless alley off Newmarket Road. The rear of Jennie's dress was held together by a mass of large safety pins.

Miss Mason held up a dress she had fetched from the changing room. "It belonged to my niece, she's grown out of it, it seemed a pity to throw it away," she told Jennie kindly. Pimbo noticed Jennie was crying as she looked down at the pretty dress.

At playtime Pimbo stood in a corner of the playground, watching big boys thunder past as they played cowboys and Indians. Miss Meakins, the games mistress walked over to him. "Let's see, you're Jackie Thompson, the new boy, aren't you? I'm sure you'll be joining in the games, once you're used to the other boys – what kind of games do you like playing?" she asked kindly.

Pimbo, surprised at hearing his real name, paused for a second. Since Bob Freestone had

*Start of barrow race from Moss the chemist, Newmarket Road, to Six Mile Bottom. Won by Bunny Warren.*

dubbed him Pimbo, everyone thought he had no other name. Many times he'd heard Mrs Freestone gossiping to neighbours; always the word consumption cropped up, to be followed usually by something about Dr Phillips and a year to live.

Pimbo wondered whether the nickname meant that perhaps he oughtn't to be alive – it might be just a name to get him by. Then again he liked the name, after all no one asked questions about his mother, or his dad, whom he believed was killed in the war.

"Well," Miss Meakins was saying, "what games do you like playing?"

Pimbo looked up. "I like watching, Miss. I join in with my thinking; then I'm the Sheriff – I catch rustlers."

The teacher smiled and patted his head, "It doesn't matter, you can't get hurt that way – but try and join in sometimes won't you?" she asked kindly.

On Sunday Mrs Freestone, with her husband, took Pimbo along to the Salvation Army Citadel in Tenison Road. Bob carried the banner on short marches. With his weak chest he thought it a challenge although his wife had heard neighbours spitefully suggest that if he could manage standard bearer, he might do better and take a job instead of living on the dole.

Pimbo sat on the front row wearing his Sunday suit, he felt good wearing nice clothes. Every boy in Leeke Street had a special suit for Sunday. During the week they wore shabby clothes with darns and patches. Pimbo hated patches, when his trousers were patched, he sat down as often as possible to hide the patch. But on Sunday it was different, Pimbo could face any boy he met in the better off streets on the way to the Citadel.

During a lull in the fervent hymn singing Captain Woods, the leader, would call out, "Come forward you sinners and repent." Pimbo noticed that mothers with small babies were amongst those who went forward to kneel at a bare wooden form.

Mrs Freestone tried as much as possible to acquaint Pimbo with life in the Barnwell area. When not at school she took her foster-son along to the pawnbrokers, Norman Bradleys of Fitzroy Street, which did a roaring trade on Monday mornings.

The suit worn by her husband on Sundays, was handed over in exchange for enough money to 'see her through the week' as Pimbo once heard Mrs Freestone explain to a neighbour.

*Scene of fire at Barham's brush factory, Newmarket Road, 1928.*

Mr Shipp, the pawnshop manager, because of wear and tear of the garments, would often knock down the money handed over for the pawned goods. This action caused more than a little commotion in the little pledge office at the rear of the shop. Women would cry or swear, which sometimes provoked the manager into handing back the goods. On Saturday pawned goods were redeemed, ready to be worn again on Sunday.

A few weeks after Pimbo's arrival at Leeke Street, Mrs Freestone placed an application through the Children's Welfare Society for a pair of new boots for her foster-son. A week later a stern looking lady called and carefully studied the heavy steel-tipped boots. After a short argument she finally handed Mrs Freestone a ticket for a new pair.

"I'll take you along to the police station," said Maude happily, then noticing Pimbo's pained expression added "it's all right my boy, nothing to worry about – the police supply the boots for you."

Pimbo enjoyed every moment of the walk to collect his new boots. The main part of the route took him through East Road, a road leading from Newmarket Road on to Parker's Piece.

Mrs Freestone took Pimbo past the Sylvester brothers' ice-cream parlour, a firm in existence for over fifty years. Peeping into a small turning known as 'Dobblers Hole' he spotted the well-known barber shop of Chatty Collins. Bob Freestone told Pimbo during a bout of reminiscence that the barber received the nickname because of his regular use of dirty towels.

At the police station a friendly sergeant was

fitting out a queue of small boys waiting for new boots. "There you are my boy," he said to Pimbo, "no kicking tin cans about the streets – these should see you through two winters."

Pimbo felt good as he threw his worn boots on to an ever-increasing pile of derelict footwear; he listened to the metallic click of the steel tips as he walked from the police station. Outside the building, on a wall, was a large poster bearing the words 'Freeman, Hardy and Willis – for footwear'. A large arrow at the foot of the poster pointed to the centre of the town.

Pimbo was beginning to settle down in his new home. One morning a boy, Bobby Watson, who lived in Leeke Street called for him to go out and play. It was the first occasion anyone had called for him, usually Pimbo stood shyly on one side until beckoned into a game.

Bobby's father was a bookmaker, not a popular figure in Leeke Street as few people in the street could afford the luxury of a bet. Mr Watson would stand at the top of the street smoking a cigar, a fat burly figure – in direct contrast to the average resident.

Pimbo and Bobby decided to visit Coldham's Common, a favourite adventure spot for youngsters. On the way, after turning into a junction at Newmarket Road opposite the secondhand furniture shop belonging to Mr Cooper, they came to a small railway siding that supplied coal to the nearby gas works. As the horse-drawn carts, laden with coal, came from the yard, small boys would plant large stones or half-bricks in the centre of the road. This would cause the load to wobble, and as the coal fell into the road, the boys loaded up their galvanized buckets – and made speedily for home. In this manner, a poor home was provided with a bright fire on a cold winter evening.

Bobby was of a similar build to his father. As they walked along Pimbo wondered whether Bobby had chosen him as a friend because of his small thin frame – he hoped Bobby wouldn't bully him.

Taking a bag from his trousers pocket Bobby offered him a sweet from a penny lucky bag purchased earlier from Reynolds' sweet-shop; Reynolds was known in Cambridge as the Rock King, the shop was next to the gas works. It was called a lucky bag because, besides the value of the sweets, sometimes a boy might be lucky enough to find inside the bag – a penny bar of chocolate.

"We'll climb the rifle butts," said Bobby the moment they reached the common.

The butts, a huge mound of lime clay and earth, were used as a natural cushion for the local Territorial army firing range. Twice a week the Territorials placed red flags around the area, then for hours the sound of rifle and machine-gun fire would startle the neighbourhood. Large target frames were placed at the foot of the butts, stray bullets thudded into the giant mound.

The butts were very slippery and Pimbo, finding his new boots a great asset, wondered if Mrs Freestone might think the same. At last the two climbers reached the top of the mound.

Looking round Pimbo could see scores of youngsters busily picking buttercups and daisies. The entire common seemed alive with yellow and white. Bobby told Pimbo that during the holidays it

*Leeke Street, where Pimbo spent his childhood. The derelict shop on corner was Pink's the florist. (Newmarket Road)*

was a special treat for children to spend the day picking flowers. Parents would pack up their children with sandwiches and lemonade; in return children made daisy chains to be hung around picture frames, buttercups were placed in jam jars and displayed prominently on the kitchen mantelpiece.

"A load of cissies," said Bobby suddenly. "Here, I'll show you how to make a clay fire."

He showed Pimbo how to dig out clumps of damp clay. Taking a large piece of clay, Bobby moulded it into a square box. Inside the opening at the front he inserted a quantity of leaves and twigs. As he lit the ingredients the whole box seemed transformed into a smouldering inferno. Bobby then made one for Pimbo.

Snatching up the clay box, and holding it at arm's length Bobby began running in circles. Pimbo, a little nervously at first, followed suit, gradually working up a fine pace. The result for a small boy was magnificent – the tail of smoking clay gave out an impression of magic.

As they ran in circles among the small flower pickers, Pimbo felt good. It reminded him of the films he'd seen, Indians with flaming arrows encircling the palefaces. Miss Meakins would have been pleased with him. Suddenly he felt grown up, no longer a weakling – and in Bobby he had found a true friend.

## The Back of Barnwell
## (Pimbo and Jenny in the 1920s)

Echoes of voices from Barnwell people,
Vibrate against memory quirks,
Sulphuric fumes from the Gas-works,
Tint green the Abbey church steeple.
And, those voices, long since gone,
Are treasured by we that linger on.

The Cam, steals silently by, as though,
Ashamed to lose its classic pose,
Among the Gas Lanes, Brown's Yards, and
Smart's Rows.
Twinny, Baker's, Cooper, try to bestow;
An air of bustle among the poor,
Who, like Oliver – ask for more.

Buzzing of Barham's saws, cut the air,
The newly built sheds stand proud,

In his Coldham's Lane compound,
The out-of-work, stand and stare.
Such sturdy, water-tight edifices,
Shame their homes in run-down terraces.

Granny Megroff's tiny sweet-shop,
Smells, that only a child understands.
Gob-stoppers, blackjacks, liquorice bands;
Sugar mice, sherbet dabs, and lollipop.
Granny's violin plays to itching ears,
And bridges the gap between tender years.

On River Lane corner, stands Jim Hall,
His shop, catering for travelling tinkers,
Matches, laces, and cheap-jack trinkets,
Farther down, is the Ragged School,
Each child, a potential "Bisto Kid",
Destined to peep 'neath life's poverty lid!

But, the Stourbridge Fair, comes and goes,
Bringing laughter and pride to all and sundry.
Dispelling despair, for each, a fun day;
Buffeting a little of life's hard blows.
Dear Barnwell, a mixture of laughter and tears,
Changing gradually over the years.

                                        Fred Unwin

## The Pawnbroker of Fitzroy Street!

Haggling and aloof the pawnbroker peers
down at the thin, tight-lipped mother.
"The pledge, I suppose, will be wasted on beers"
he mocks as he deals with another.

The kids at her skirt begin to cry,
as stoutly to the pawnbroker, she said:
"The money you spare,I'll use to buy
some food for my living dead".
The following Saturday, she enters again,
head erect, eyes proud, and beaming.
Hubby's suit she redeems for one pound-ten,
his new job, fosters hope – enriches dreaming.

## Dooley Hall – The Windmill Man

A wooden cart, small box on wheels,
with spinning coloured whirls;
grown ups know not how it feels,
for eager boys and girls.

"For a jam-jar have a windmill boy,
hurry home and tell your Ma;
only Christmas gives you so much joy –
and this just for a jar."

In bowler hat, aged and bent,
Dooley Hall plies his trade:
back-street kids, no money spent
have now a bright day made.

Oh, jar, once proud upon a shelf
holding substance for a dinner,
for a small child – you've expelled yourself
into a bright gay spinner.

*Dooley plied his trade among the backstreets of
Barnwell – a well loved figure.*

# CHAPTER 2

## Pimbo explores

A few days after the fire-box adventure Pimbo, gaining confidence, discovered a new sweet-shop. It was on Newmarket Road a short distance from the top of Leeke Street. Catching his eye in the small friendly windows were two large posters. One, the 'Bisto Kids' portrayed two ragged urchins standing outside a posh house, their noses in the air as they sampled the smell of cooking. The other depicting the quality of Cherry Blossom boot polish, had another ragged urchin displaying – completely out of context with his unkempt appearance – a pair of dazzling shiny boots.

Opening the door of the little shop Pimbo looked expectantly inside. At the rear of a long wooden counter were shelves stocked with large glass jars containing his favourite sweets. Two very old ladies, red cheeked and smiling were waiting behind the counter – they were sisters.

"Mind the step," shouted Lucy Gray, one of the sisters.

Looking down Pimbo could scarcely believe his eyes, facing him was a sheer drop of at least two feet.

"We're getting it seen to, the builders should have been in long ago," put in Mabel the other sister.

Pimbo walked to the counter. "A black jack, please," he said, hopefully. Foraging in a large cardboard box under the counter, Lucy Gray produced the black jack; a square of hard toffee made to last – seemingly the best thing to be said of the unlikely-looking sweet.

Pimbo fell in love at once with the delicious smell of the little shop. Only small children really appreciate the fairy-like aroma. Children lived out their sweets; jelly babies weren't just masses of jelly, they had something in common with their own small brothers or sisters. Soap, powders, all the smells appertaining to babies were conjured up by the lingering smells, thought Pimbo.

Snow-balls, deliciously round and coconut topped with masses of cream inside, the smell long since forgotten by the adult world, to the small boys lingered on – Pimbo was no exception.

"You're Jackie Thompson, aren't you?" asked Lucy, who seemed the most forward of the sisters. "I've heard about you, you must come here more often, at night we have sing-songs for the older boys – can you play a mouth organ?"

Pimbo stared. "No, Miss, I'd like to though, would you teach me?"

Both sisters laughed together. "This is Mabel," said Lucy, pointing to her sister. "I'm Lucy, just call us Miss Mabel or Miss Lucy."

Mabel produced an old violin from behind the counter and started to play. Pimbo recognized the tune as one he was being taught at school – 'A north country maid'. He couldn't remember all the words but the old lady played sweetly.

"We come from the North," said Lucy as her sister finished the melody, "where do you come from?"

"I don't really know, I've been so many places – I believe I was born in London," answered Pimbo, surprised at the question.

Mabel nodded. "That's right you were, we make it our business to know all about the children that live round Barnwell, don't we Lucy?"

"Why does my foster-father call me Pimbo?" asked the boy, changing the subject. "He says I remind him of a clown."

The old lady smiled. "Pimbo was a wonderful clown, he brought laughter and tears to the world. The public knew him only as Pimbo, no one wanted to know his real name; he travelled the world over – and died young."

Pimbo nodded, somehow the answer sounded right. Moving to the door, and about to negotiate the high step, he turned to the sisters.

"Why do you put up with this step, it's very dangerous?"

Lucy looked knowingly at her sister. "Some years ago a man who loved children had a special door made in his home. It was very small, and only tiny children could enter; this way he was able to make sure of his visitors. I don't think our step was intentional, but youngsters make an adventure of it, and come again. Good-bye Pimbo, I'll bet you will come again", she finished tauntingly.

Pimbo wasn't finished. "Why do you love children – why do you stay here?"

The sisters shrugged. Lucy said, 'That's a big question for small boy – why do you ask questions?"

Undoing the wrapper of his black jack, Pimbo looked up. "I'm always thinking about things, Miss Lucy. When I was ill I couldn't join in many games. I read as much as I can, Miss Meakins said that I'm the best reader in the class. P'raps that's why I ask questions."

Miss Lucy smiled. "We have no children of our own, so we make the best of those who live around. Out little sing-songs help us understand the children, sometimes they tell us all their little problems – now for a small boy, it's quite enough for one day, perhaps you should run along."

She helped him over the awkward step and slipped another black jack into his sticky palm.

*Star Brewery, Newmarket Road.*

At the top of Leeke Street Pimbo was surprised to see Mrs Freestone hurrying towards him, her face looked set and drawn.

"I've been looking for you Pimbo. Mr Freestone isn't well, go up to his room and stay until I return with the doctor," she said quickly.

Pimbo found his foster-parent lying on the bed having a bad asthmatic attack. A quaint-looking jug with a spirit steaming away lay on a small table beside him. Bob smiling weakly, looked up at the boy. "Dr Livingstone, I presume. Hold the jug Pimbo, while I get my breath – it looks as though I'm in for a bad turn this time."

During Bob's rapid breathing Pimbo could hear the voice of Bob's wife in conversation with the doctor. "Of course you do realize that your husband must get away, this place is too damp – the whole street is a damp trap," the doctor was saying.

Inside the bedroom Dr Webb moved over to Bob and sounded his chest. "Yes, I'm afraid so, it will have to be six months at least in Papworth – you must go immediately," said the doctor firmly.

Mrs Freestone was crying. "How shall I manage? I lose his sick money when he goes into hospital. I've got the boy now you know."

Dr Webb ushered Pimbo downstairs, from the bottom of the stairs he could hear the doctor informing Mrs Freestone that come what may Bob, for the sake of health, must go to Papworth.

A little later two sturdy ambulance men carried Bob down the narrow stairs into the awaiting ambulance.

Mrs Freestone, alone with Pimbo in the kitchen, suddenly placed him in the centre of her broad lap.

"Pimbo, at the tender age of seven you're the man of the house. Those were the words of your foster-dad – tell Pimbo to look after my old Dutch."

She ran her fingers through his shock of red hair and kissed him. "Pimbo, I haven't spent as much time with you as I might have done. With you being weak like, it made me afraid, I didn't want to love you too much – then lose you. Sometimes they call and say it's time for a move – then hey-presto Pimbo gets yet another foster-mother."

Pimbo found himself hugging her tightly. It seemed years since his mother had died, somehow he'd forgotten the little things that mothers do. From then on he decided to make things as easy as possible for his foster-mother. He would earn his own pocket money, other boys ran errands, fetched coke, chopped wood; true they were stronger than he but after all, wasn't he now the man of the house?

Mrs Parker who lived two doors away, was the only person in Leeke Street who never allowed boys to run her errands. Some boys said it was because she wouldn't trust them. Her husband had been in a lunatic asylum for some years, they said it was because of his attacking her with a chopper. Pimbo was afraid to try out other neighbours in order to earn his pocket money in case boys might be done out of their regular chore. He decided to try out Mrs Parker.

The alleyway leading to Mrs Parker's back door was dark and narrow. A large wooden fence, regularly creosoted, ran the entire length of the small terraced homes of Leeke Street. Pimbo, too small to climb the fence, was told by bigger boys that a

*Removals in Newmarket Road. George Love of 15 Burleigh Street carrying out removal close to house no. 215.*

*Cook's garage on Newmarket Road. Bicycle repairs were also carried out on the premises.*

timber yard flourished the other side, sometimes he could hear the sound of saws.

The place was rat-infested. Large holes at the bottom of the fence told the unmistakeable tale. From his back bedroom Pimbo often watched great brown rats foraging amongst the dustbins at the bottom of each garden.

Walking towards Mrs Parker's back door, Pimbo heard a rustling at the back of her dustbin. Picking up a stick he pushed aside the bin. An enormous rat sprang out, rushing between his legs and through a convenient hole at the bottom of the fence. Pimbo felt relieved that the rat had not stopped for further confrontation.

Mrs Parker watching from her window moved to the back door, beckoning Pimbo into a small cosy kitchen. She was a short tubby person, tidily dressed in a coloured pinafore over a neat brown dress.

"Kind of a pied piper, eh my boy?" she asked kindly. "To what do I owe this visit?"

"Mr Freestone is ill, they've taken him away, I want to earn some money for the pictures," said Pimbo.

"Well then you're truthful, and you don't expect money for nothing. I don't usually allow boys to run my errands, my daughter says some boys are far too nosey. They run home and tell their mothers everything."

Looking round the room, Pimbo noticed how much cosier it was than his own. A proper table cloth, a pretty cloth running round the bottom of the mantelpiece. China ornaments on the shelf, rugs on the floor, and a marble clock that struck the hour.

*Arena Transport House. Junction of East Road and Occupation Road. At rear was an open bath house for truckers.*

*Newmarket Road residents on sea-side outing, 1930s.*

"Boys could only say nice things about you, Mrs Parker," he said kindly, "why do you worry what they say?"

The old lady shrugged. "You're a real one, aren't you boy. I don't think you would say anything. My husband was a master builder. We saved to get a good home, around here everyone's so poor. If they thought I had anything it would be borrow, borrow, borrow. A shilling for the gas, a cup of sugar, dust of tea; that's why I clamped down."

She stood up and picked a threepenny piece from a little mound of coins on the mantelpiece. "Here, every Saturday you can fetch my coke from the gas-works. This week's bonus week for your bravery about the rat – they call you Pimbo, I believe, don't they?" she asked, handing him the coin.

Pimbo received the coin, thankfully. He won-dered how she knew his nickname. Sometimes he had noticed a slight movement of her front room curtains as he passed her window. He guessed that Mrs Parker was a lonely person. In Leeke Street something happened all the time, he was glad he lived at number ten, it was like being in the centre of everything.

As he moved toward the kitchen door, Mrs Parker picked up two pennies from the shelf. "Here," she said handing him the coins, "put them in your gas meter, don't tell your foster-mother, or anyone else."

Pimbo called for Bobby Watson to accompany him to the pictures. The Kinema, every small boy's favourite haunt, was a small building on Mill Road. Saturday was matinée day, the money earned by running errands provided a twopenny seat and a penny ice-cream.

*Primitive Tabernacle, Newmarket Road. Once used by Finbow's removal firm.*

On the way as they passed into Gwydir Street, leading into Mill Road, they approached Dale's Brewery. On the top of the building was a huge golden cup. On a fine day the cup glinted proudly and could be seen for miles around. Bobby said it was won by the brewery for brewing the finest beer.

Alongside the Kinema was a queue of shouting, excited children. Glancing at the poster outside the entrance Pimbo saw it was a Tom Mix film, entitled, *Destry rides again*. He considered Tom Mix his favourite cowboy, then came Buck Jones, Ken Maynard, and William Boyd.

Inside the cinema the shouting continued. As soon as the operator climbed the short ladder into the projecting room, the boys and girls screamed their heads off.

"He's up, he's up," they shouted until the dimming of the lights told them that the programme was about to commence.

First came the serial. It was an Edgar Wallace story called *The Green Archer*, ending usually in a tight situation which was to be continued next week.

When the hero was in difficulties, the children shouted, "Look behind you." Boos and hisses greeted the arrival of all villains. Scenes failing to show an appreciable amount of fighting, were regarded as boring, and received a large amount of hand clapping.

Love scenes were regarded as sloppy, and woe betide any manager foolish enough to show such a film during a Saturday matinée.

Comedies usually featured Larry Semon, a pasty-faced little man, wearing overalls and a bowler hat. He performed amazing feats, climbing on to high buildings, and jumping into barrels of water. Sometimes they featured Fatty Arbuckle, or the Keystone Cops.

Bobby asked Pimbo many questions, and was told about the escapades of others such as Charlie Chase, Ben Turpin, Harry Langdon, Chester Conklin, Jackie Coogan and, of course, Charlie Chaplin.

In the interval, Bobby bought ice-cream, giving half to Pimbo.

On the way out boys practised the scenes in the film by pretending to ride horses. With imaginary reins they galloped around the foyer, teasing the girls and fighting the smaller boys. Burly attendants would then grab them by the neck and deposit them on the pavement outside. Thankfully the incidents were soon forgotten, and the same boys turned up each week. On the way home Pimbo decided that he would make the Kinema a weekly feature; in Mrs Parker and the coke, he had a regular income.

*Mr Proctor's grocery store. Mr Proctor was instrumental in seeing Cambridge United achieve success.*

# CHAPTER 3

## Pimbo at school

On the way to school Pimbo had made a habit of calling for Jennie Smith. Jennie lived in Brown's Yard, just around the corner from Leeke Street. It was a dark alley with a dozen or so terraced houses facing a large brick wall concealing the premises of Cox's bakery.

Jennie's father was rarely in work, and Rose Smith his wife suffered periodically from fainting fits. Jennie told Pimbo that the doctor said the fits were caused through lack of food. On the few occasions Pimbo has been invited into the home, he had noticed how ill Jennie's mother looked.

Jennie was wearing the pretty dress given her by Miss Mason. The morning was dull and rain was falling heavily, the children hurried along New-market Road. Jennie's shoes were very thin at the sole, Pimbo noticed squelches and bubbles coming from them as she passed through the unavoidable puddles.

Arriving at school, Miss Cowell called them both into her room. Inspecting Pimbo's boots first, she then passed on to Jennie. A frown appeared on her usually warm features. "I must look into this

Jennie," she said kindly, "otherwise we shall have you down with a cold – now both of you return to your class."

Pimbo loved school, reading being one of his favourite subjects. *Coral Island, The Swiss Family Robinson* and *Robinson Crusoe* were amongst his first read novels. Charles Dickens was his favourite author, and with the blessing of Miss Meakins he was tackling *Oliver Twist*.

Barley Newman, a class friend of his, had an annoying habit of giggling. Pimbo couldn't resist whenever meeting Barley's eye, to breakout into an uncontrollable bout of laughter. Miss Meakins promptly placed Pimbo in the front row and relegated Barley to the back of the class. During a boring part of the lesson, Pimbo would look over his shoulder and catch a glimpse of Barley's face. This would upset other members of the class, resulting in Pimbo being called out to receive a stroke of the cane. But Pimbo noticed a little twinkle in Miss Meakins' eye as she delivered the punishment and this helped him make up his mind not to slack – somehow he felt that she was on his side.

One morning as she sat at the desk in front of the class, about to read from a textbook Pimbo suddenly said, "How to make a long story short."

Miss Meakins stared straight back at Pimbo. "Can you read backwards?" she asked in astonishment.

Pimbo shook his head. "No, Miss. I just guessed – that's all."

"Then you guessed correctly, my boy. You must be a mind reader, that's exactly what the lesson is about – how to cut a long story short."

Pimbo found the incident very helpful in making friends. Most of the children were backward in reading and thought Pimbo almost a magician. Being seen talking to Pimbo developed a kind of status symbol. The teachers, too, although they had always been friendly towards him, seemed to find a little extra time in explaining his problems.

Next morning as he knocked at Jennie's door, it was opened by Mr Smith. Jennie's father was a surly man, fond of drink, and not above smacking Jennie for trifling offences.

"Come inside little Nosey Parker, I want a word with you," he said angrily. Pimbo, taken by surprise stepped nervously into the bare little kitchen. Jennie's mother was sitting at the table looking very white and sobbing bitterly.

"Don't harm the boy, Alf – it wasn't his fault," she stammered between sobs.

Mr Smith stepped forward grasping Pimbo by the jersey.

"Now then young whipper-snapper, the kids tell me they saw you take my girl into the head-mistress's room. First it's a new dress, now it's going to be new shoes – what did you tell her – I wasn't a fit father? Tell me the truth or I'll ...."

Pimbo somehow managed to blurt out everything that had happened. Between words Jennie's mother stopped crying. "There you are Alf, I told you the boy wasn't to blame – I'll get a job, they want a bed-maker at St John's College, I'll go in the morning."

Alf Smith let go of Pimbo's jersey, and stroked his head. "Sorry boy – I was het up. An official came round yesterday afternoon. Snooped into every-

thing, wanted me to sell my wireless. The neighbours get to know everything. Alf Smith's taking
charity, that would be the cry – I couldn't have held
my head up in the street."

Pimbo found Jennie holding his hand tightly,
Rose Smith was actually smiling. Pimbo felt good
again. "Are my boots charity, Mr Smith?" asked the
lad brightly, "they came from the police station, I
don't mind as long as they don't let in water."

For once Alf let go a smile. "They tell me you're a
winner, Pimbo. One day you'll understand – but for
God's sake don't change, you'll do for me any day of
the week."

On his way home Pimbo wondered about Jennie.
All the fuss, and at the end of it Jennie could finish
up with new shoes, as well as a new dress. Sometimes he'd heard Bob Freestone talk about a working man's pride. The means test came into it; he
supposed that meant getting rid of the wireless Mr
Smith was on about.

It was the first time Pimbo had ever been in a
real row. Somehow he wasn't afraid. But he would
be very careful in future. He would remember
those two key words – pride and means test. Mrs
Freestone had a very good tea ready for him. She
told him as it was Saturday next day, he could go
with Mr Brown the rag man, as she would be
visiting her husband in Papworth hospital. She
had seen Mr Brown, who would be pleased to have
Pimbo for the day. Pimbo could hardly sleep with
excitement, the thought of a day out in the country
kept him peeping out of the window at the early
morning light.

It was 6 a.m. when finally he ran round to Mr

Brown's. Already his leg had been fixed, the side-car loaded with empty sacks and Mr Brown ready to set out for the village of Histon, a few miles from Cambridge. Pimbo sat on the pillion seat and with a nice healthy *chug-chug*, they moved out of Leeke Street on to the Newmarket Road.

The first call was at the *White Ribbon* on East Road. This was a hostel run by the Salvation Army. Pimbo recognized the man behind the counter as a cornet player he'd seen at the Citadel. From 6 a.m. the hostel served hot tea and sandwiches or bacon and eggs. Mr Brown ordered a cup for both, and a rock bun for Pimbo.

"It's cheap here," said Mr Brown, "saves the missus worrying – on the way back if we have a good day – I might manage a meal."

The motor cycle and side-car although old seemed serviceable. "If it weren't for my leg I'd have had a pony and cart. With my wooden leg I can't get around with a horse – so I settled for this," Mr Brown was telling Pimbo as they reached the top of Histon Road.

"Why have you a wooden leg?" asked Pimbo, innocently.

The rag man smiled. "The war, Pimbo, good job it's something you know little about. I get a lump sum from the army – a small pension and just get by. The outdoor life suits me – but I suppose I couldn't manage much else."

A sudden sweet smell drifted into Pimbo's keen young nostrils. It was the jam and fruit factory of Chivers and Sons. Passing the factory, Mr Brown drew up on the side of a small green. "Here we are, Pimbo – take a sack and do the little cottages on the

*Medcalfe's sweet shop, East Road. Top rooms were scene of gruesome murder.*

left. Just say you're calling for Mr Brown – with the wooden leg."

Blowing hard on a large horn on the side of the handlebars, the rag man stomped off to the rear of the first house.

Pimbo enjoyed the travelling from cottage to cottage. It was threepence for a rabbit-skin, six-pence for a hare-skin. Rags usually meant tup-pence. The satisfied lady would smile and put the two coins into the gas meter. Pimbo, hated hand-ling bones, they were smelly and awkward to carry. He couldn't make out why they were bought. Mr Brown, didn't seem to know either, "Suppose they melt 'em down for glue," he would say – then laugh.

Pimbo made many trips backwards and for-wards to Mr Brown and sometimes the rag man would stand beside the side-car and wait for cus-tomers. The blowing of the horn would bring out his regulars, many enjoyed a chat and laugh – using the money as an extra bonus.

Mr Brown seemed pleased with Pimbo. "I'm doing better than I've ever done – seems you attract them like flies – if ever you set up as a rag and bone man – I'll have to retire," he said laughingly.

Some of the ladies asked questions. Was he Mr Brown's own son, or any relation? They told of other boys who had been along with the rag man. They didn't seem to like some of them. Pimbo wondered at times why they set so much store on who he was. It seemed that everything had to be neatly tied up. He didn't like to tell them who he was. If he said he had no mother or father they would stop and stare and hold him up. He wondered if Mr Brown was telling all about him. Sometimes a lady on whom Mr Brown had called would point him out to a neighbour, and give him a kind of curious glance.

Pimbo worked hard. One lady had an old stove to sell. The rusting parts were carried quite a distance by Pimbo. She received one shilling and sixpence for the stove. As he returned with the money, she gave him sixpence for himself. Pimbo decided he would give it to Mrs Freestone, sixpence would mean a lot to her – after all it was up to him, with Bob in hospital, to help as much as possible.

His jersey, now dirty from carrying the rusty stove, was viewed at some length by Mr Brown. A tear at the front, enhanced by the sharp edges, had run further down. Taking a coloured jersey from inside the side-car, the rag man offered it to Pimbo. "There boy, put this on. I've checked up on you. A lot of boys who come with me don't play the game. The money I give them to take to the house is short changed. I have lost customers that way. You're O.K. – you can have the jersey for nothing."

The jersey fitted well, Pimbo wrapped it up carefully and placed it back in the side-car. A lady standing at her gate in a house near by waved at Mr Brown. Pimbo noticed a boy his age standing next to her, it was her son, thought Pimbo. Mr Brown waving back smiled at his young assistant. "You see what I mean – honesty is the best policy." Pimbo remembered the lady, he'd taken back two shillings for her, she had given over a large sack of clothing.

*Pearson's shop in East Road. Silver Jubilee 1935, with family.*

At midday Mr Brown pulled up outside the *Barley Mow*, an old public house in the centre of Histon. Pimbo sat on a wooden form, and waited whilst the rag man went inside. Presently he came out with a stone bottle of ginger-beer in one hand and a bread and cheese sandwich in the other. "There boy, knock that back. Keep an eye on the side-car, I'm just going back for my own vittals," he said laughingly.

The open air and the running to and fro during the morning, made Pimbo thankful for this unexpected meal. He felt proud as he drew envious glances from boys passing by meekly with their parents. Somehow he didn't mind who he was, he did know that he was enjoying life – what else mattered?

Mr Brown made for home at 3 p.m. "It'll give me time to get my stuff weighed, everything sorted, and the bike filled up for the morning." Before leaving he drew his vehicle into a side turning. There he sorted out the rags, anything worthwhile was placed aside. "My bread and butter lines," he said laughingly to Pimbo. Pimbo realized that next day his wife would be bringing around the cast-offs to the houses in Leeke Street. Mrs Brown was a kindly sort, and would trust for payment until the end of the week.

On arriving in Cambridge, Mr Brown turned off East Road into South Street, at the yard of Mr Careless the rag and bone merchant. The rags were placed in larger sacks and weighed. Bones were weighed and thrown on to a large, maggoty-looking heap.

Mr Careless then walked with Mr Brown into a

*The old tram-lines' swan-song, 18 February 1914, East Road. E. O. Brown's shop in background. He was the then Mayor of Cambridge.*

small office at the back of the yard. As they came out, Pimbo noticed the rag man was smiling, he must have been satisfied with the day's work.

On the way home they stopped once more at the *White Ribbon* where Mr Brown treated Pimbo to a hot tea of poached eggs on toast. The cornet player was still on duty. "See you on Sunday, Pimbo. A special band concert by the Junior bandsmen – you'll enjoy that," he called out.

Pimbo felt it was the end of a perfect day.

## An Ode to Charlie Darler
### (the cheerful Gold Street cobbler)

My awl is bent and rusty now,
My hobiron stashed away.
Old boots and shoes, no longer see,
A cheerful dwarf like me.

They little know, how hard I slaved,
To repair down-trodden shoes.
Down-trodden people, too, I fear,
In times of yester-year!

"Gold" Street, then, an unworked mine,
No gold to pan for me.
I tacked thin leather on gaping sole,
Most men were on the dole!

A hunch-back, I may have been,
My shop, a dusty hovel.
Never much, my scanty gain,
My laughter – kept them sane!

Now, sunk in earth, my cobbler walls,
My poor frame, as any man.
Rests beneath a churchyard's sod,
As I'm given back to God!

Fred Unwin

*Charlie's little shop attracted many child visitors. The dear old shoemaker would tell them many happy stories. Pimbo, of course, being a regular visitor.*

# CHAPTER 4

## Pimbo finds trouble

On the following Monday after school, Pimbo found his foster-mother with two official-looking women awaiting him in the kitchen of their little home. Maude looked as though she had been crying.

"It's about you Pimbo," she explained as he entered the kitchen. "Someone has reported me, they say you are allowed to roam the streets at all times – and probably you're not getting enough to eat."

Pimbo stared, one of the ladies stood up. She was dressed in thick tweeds, flat heeled shoes, and was wearing thick spectacles; she reminded Pimbo of the many officials who so far had guided his life.

"We'll speak to the boy alone if you don't mind Mrs Freestone – may we see him in the front room?" she asked sharply. Maude nodded her agreement. The other lady immediately stood up and with her companion followed Pimbo into the little room at the front of the house.

"You needn't be afraid my boy," said the woman in spectacles. "I'm Miss Bragg, this is my assistant Miss Hart. We just want to ask you a few questions; it's for your own good, and it won't take long."

Pimbo nodded nervously and sat on a chair near the window.

"Now my boy, is it true that you are allowed to roam the streets at all hours?" asked Mrs Bragg, modulating her voice to appear more kindly.

"Not really, Miss Bragg," said Pimbo. "Mrs Freestone is very kind, I'm allowed out because I want to see things; I'm very happy when I'm exploring. When I read books I like to pretend that I'm in places where I know I shall never be. But being in real places is just as exciting – that's why I go out a lot. But I never get into trouble – I make friends." Pimbo paused for breath.

Miss Hart stared at her colleague, then back at Pimbo.

"At the Sanatorium in Holt everyone implied that you were a strange boy; day-dreaming and not joining in games. Here you seem different – why is this so?" her voice was warm and friendly.

Pimbo thought immediately of his foster-father. Bob's sense of humour despite his asthma, the way he struggled to carry the flag on Sundays had given Pimbo more incentive to do things, than all the officialdom, and do's and don'ts of the Sanatorium.

"I'm happy here, Miss Hart. I want to get better and never go back to Holt – that's why I've changed", he looked across to Miss Bragg and continued. "Boys in the dormitory at night used to talk together. Some of the boys' fathers had died from consumption. I felt as though my body was finished – all I had left was my thinking. A nurse once told me that I thought too much, I wasn't a normal boy, and that I ought to try and do more. But I kept thinking about Dr Phillips, who told someone I had only a year to live. It made me want to ask all the questions about living, I wanted not only to read about things – but to do them."

As he finished the two welfare workers walked over and sat by him at the window, they both were smiling. Miss Bragg had lost her air of officialdom. "You're a remarkable little boy," she said warmly. "It's unusual for a boy such as you to have been billeted with a man suffering from asthma. But Mr and Mrs Freestone are Salvation Army goers, we thought this the kind of environment that might suit you." Turning to the door leading into the kitchen she called for Pimbo's foster-mother. Mrs Freestone moved quickly, standing nervously by the door.

"It's all right Mrs Feestone, this little boy is doing well under your wing. With your husband away in Papworth I'm arranging for Pimbo to have dinners at the dinner centre. The centre is in Eden Street, and your boy will go straight from school at midday to the centre – afterwards he will return to school for the afternoon session."

Miss Bragg's words brought a sigh of relief from Maude Freestone. Somehow from the moment Miss Bragg had called him Pimbo, she felt things were going to be all right.

Following the departure of the two ladies, Mrs Freestone gave Pimbo a kiss and hug. "Whatever did you say to them? I thought they were going to take you away from me," she said excitedly.

Pimbo smiled, "I just said the truth that's all – but I can't make out who it was that reported you."

"Neighbours can be bitchy Pimbo. You never can tell, some are jealous because we go the Salvation Army. But that's something however poor we are, that no one can take from us – do you mind coming with us to the Army, Pimbo?"

The boy nodded, he had never told his foster-parent of his desire to go down to the little penitent form; how at night in his bedroom, he prayed that he might be spared until he was at least twenty-one.

A knock at the kitchen door found Jennie in a pretty dress and new shoes standing outside. "My mum's late Pimbo, my dad's not come from work yet, I'm going to meet her – will you come with me?" she asked.

Pimbo remembered the morning of the row with her father. Rose Smith had spoken about a job as bed-maker at St John's College. It was now past 5 p.m., Jennie's mother was usually at home when her daughter arrived from school.

Mrs Freestone knowing that Pimbo would take care of himself, and that Mrs Smith would likely be half-way home, agreed to allow the children to meet Jennie's mother.

St John's College was in Trinity Street. Pimbo took Jennie along Newmarket Road, through Maid's Causeway, and into Jesus Lane. At the bottom of Jesus Lane, they crossed into a narrow passage, which led into the ornamental gateway of St John's. Pimbo was surprised that so far Jennie's mother had not been seen.

Walking up to the porter's lodge Jennie enquired about her mother. A dignified porter in a top hat, bent over a little counter in front of the door. Looking at Jennie he laughed loudly.

"Why I thought you were the new bed-maker, missy – I'll put your name down – when you're a big girl, you may start right away."

Poring over a mass of keys he suddenly became serious. "G court, staircase C, room ten, here I'll take you there – your young man can come too."

As they stood outside room ten, Pimbo noticed the climb up the stone staircase leading to the room had sorely taxed the frailty of Jennie. A young curly haired gentleman answered the door.

"Oh it must be your girl, Mrs Smith. Come in both of you, your mother is having tea with me," he said brightly.

Inside the room, at a round shining table sat Jennie's mother, "I'm sorry Jennie, I didn't mean to be late, but Mr Adamson made me stop for tea – he said I'd done enough and deserved a break."

Pimbo stared at the silverware: the delicious cream buns, small pats of creamy butter lay on a college-crested dish, it seemed a feast fit for a queen. Jennie's mother blushingly sat eating a cream bun taken from a pretty gold-rimmed plate.

Mr Adamson, smiling all the time, made both children sit at the table, offering them brown bread and jam. Pimbo who had rarely tasted brown bread, found it a trifle bitter. A good portion of jam placed on by the student remedied the problem. Jennie was tucking in, as was her mother who acted still as though it were all a dream.

Glancing around the room at a large scuttle filled with coal standing beside a roaring fire, Pimbo thought at once of Coldham's Lane and how the boys of Barnwell procured their coal.

Mr Adamson looking down at Pimbo proferred a cream bun. "Mrs Smith tells me that you live in the Newmarket Road Barnwell area. I'm thinking of

*Celebrated George IV pub at top of Staffordshire Street, East Road. Famous character, Molly Hogg, was landlady.*

*Chatty Collins' Barber Shop (East Road), also, a few doors down, house of George Pope the "pram" musician.*

opening up a boys' club in Occupation Road – would you care to come?" he asked kindly.

Pimbo nodded, there wasn't much for the boys around Leeke Street. Apart from the little sing-songs in the sweet-shop belonging to the Gray sisters, most boys just roamed the streets.

After tea the student took both children over the staircase. Visiting the little gyp room he showed them where the bed-makers did most of their washing up, and kept cleaning equipment. The students' rooms were very tiny, many of them years and years old.

Bed-makers worked hard, some carried coals to the top floors, and took turns to scrub the stone stairway. The older bed-makers returned to the college at night, to turn down the students' beds and light fires. Bed-makers went home usually carrying large shopping bags, this was regarded as a bonus for working at the college. Inside the bag might be a half loaf of bread, a bottle of milk, and a few biscuits or cake. Small tips were given for extra service by the better off students.

Families such as Jennie's would have been hard pressed to manage were it not for college gra-tuities. Sometimes there would be scraps of meat, a prize catch being a basin of dripping. Pimbo re-membered seeing a notice, 'College dripping for sale', in the window of Spaxman's stores, a little shop in Newmarket Road. Bob Freestone would point it out and laugh, "There you are Pimbo, genuine college dripping – special treat for Barn-well residents."

Mr Adamson shepherded Mrs Smith and the two youngsters down to the porter's lodge. He went

*Old Working Men's Club on left, with Barbrooke's grocery store in background (East Road). Mr Barbrooke was a real character.*

inside and chatted to the porter. On coming out he handed Jennie's mother a Broth and Bread card. This entitled her to a loaf of bread and a jug of soup to be fetched at 6 p.m. twice weekly.

On returning home Pimbo found Mrs Freestone had been very busy. A new table stood in the kitchen, on it rested a real linen table cloth. The mantelpiece contained ornaments, and instead of the tin alarm clock stood a neat china timepiece. Beside the hearth lay a thick rug, and resting on a small table in the corner of the room was a wireless set. It reminded Pimbo of Mrs Parker's neat little kitchen.

"It was the two welfare ladies, Miss Bragg and Miss Hart," said Maude Freestone proudly.

"Pimbo, you're enough to melt the stoniest of hearts, after you'd gone a small van turned up – the driver said it was the compliments of the two ladies."

Maude walked over to a cardboard box, inside was a pile of books, she handed them to Pimbo.

The boy read the titles: *Tom Sawyer, Mr Midshipman Easy, Coral Island.* Among small magazines were copies of, *The Gem, The Magnet, Boy's Friend.* Some of his favourite comics, such as, *Funny Wonder, Comic Cuts, Chips,* and *Film Fun*, completed the parcel.

A note inside one of the books was for Pimbo, it read 'From the Misses Hart and Bragg – good reading and good health, Pimbo.'

In the morning Mrs Freestone told Pimbo of a letter arriving requesting the lad's presence at Dr Phillips' chest clinic in Regent Street. It stated that the Children's Welfare were satisfied with Pimbo's special progress – but his health needed checking against further exacerbation of tuberculosis.

The clinic was situated almost opposite the police station. Pimbo found Dr Phillips a huge man, with a happy knack of putting children immediately at ease. Pimbo thought how sensible it was to have such a big man as head doctor. Most patients, like himself, were very thin and weak looking. It gave confidence to see such an example of keeping well.

Stripped to the waist, Pimbo stood before a large type of screen. The room was darkened, but the boy was able to discern a man in a white coat, pointing with a kind of baton at the X-ray film of his chest. He heard the man mention something about 'a shadow' and as Dr Phillips joined him, the words 'spot' and 'chest capacity' were mentioned.

"Right my boy, you may get dressed," said Dr Phillips as the lights came on. He turned to Mrs Freestone and beckoned her into his study.

On the way home she seemed to Pimbo a little worried. "What happened, am I getting better" asked Pimbo.

"He asked if you were getting malt at school, I told him you were on Virol. He seemed pleased with you – but said you must be careful. You may have to go back to the Sanatorium and next month you must have another X-ray."

Mrs Freestone stopped suddenly and looked down at Pimbo, somehow she managed a smile. "He doesn't know my Pimbo, does he? Into everything, if there's a way out you'll find it. Do you know Pimbo, I only wish you could stay at seven years of age for ever – then nothing would matter."

On reaching Leeke Street, Pimbo smiled to himself. What a funny world it was, on one hand he was praying to be allowed to live until he was twenty-one; on the other, his foster-mother wanting his age to remain at seven.

# CHAPTER 5

## Pimbo's Easter Parade

Bob Freestone told Pimbo that Newmarket racecourse might well be the Mecca of the well-to-do; but Parker's Piece on Good Friday, was the working man's own little piece of heaven.

Pimbo called for Bobby Watson early on Good Friday morning, and armed with skipping ropes, bottles of lemonade and coppers earned from running errands, the two pals set off for Parker's Piece.

The perimeter of the Piece was alive with colour, from the Catholic church to East Road corner little stalls lined the pavements, stretching on through Park Side and Regent Terrace.

The stalls had coloured tops, streamers, funny gaily coloured hats with elastic balls hanging from the sides. Ice-cream carts were in abundance, as were lemonade stalls and 'hot peas' tents.

Everyone seemed bent on having a good time. Neighbours who hitherto had quarrelled, were now hobnobbing with each other in an all out effort to make the most of this traditional festivity. Pimbo was amazed at the sight of grown men with thick ropes made specially for skipping, frolicking together in a frenzied fandango of 'Salt, mustard, vinegar, pepper'.

Families would take on each other in skipping marathons; a 'catching' heel when the contest was close, would mean a forfeit. There seemed a mutual code of honour among the skippers, as though skipping was indeed a national sport and rules were to be abided by.

During the skipping the Piece was alive with bouncing bodies, shrieks of laughter could be heard all over Town.

Adult activities after a time would suddenly end – it was the turn of the children. Pimbo's thin rope seemed as a thread of comparison with the men's. Bobby taught him the art of timing his jumps but Pimbo found the exacting pace of a sharp 'vinegar, pepper' a little beyond him.

Then came the races, the adults arranged all kinds of events to embrace the smallest child. Shirt sleeves and slippers, was the order of dress, no one cared whether clothes were darned or patched.

During the races women spread cloths over the unoccupied parts of the grass and prepared a meal.

Suddenly all activities would cease, the entire population of Parker's Piece would be sat down. As the clock on the tower of the Roman Catholic church boomed out the hour, Pimbo felt a feeling of awe come over him. For once the poorer people of Cambridge seemed to come into their own. Cares would pass, but somehow this day was theirs. Poverty was forgotten, stresses were now calms. Pimbo could see Jennie Smith with her parents, she looked pretty, her face flushed with excitement. The dinginess of River Lane school, with its trucks and smells was left far behind.

Pimbo thought of the rich carpet in Mr Adamson's room at St John's college. Here the green grass was free, it was as though everyone owned a carpet, he thought the carpet nice – but somehow the grass seemed nicer. Pimbo couldn't believe that people could be so happy, with just a piece of rope and a bottle of lemonade.

Bobby decided it was time to look around the stalls. Pimbo almost decided to buy a novelty hat with 'Kiss me' written on it – but somehow it seemed silly. There were all kinds of novelties, but a stall owned by Mr Mansfield seemed a special stall. Somehow his goods were always a little cheaper than the others – Mrs Freestone told Pimbo it was because Mr Mansfield had six children and knew the value of prices.

The stallholder made wooden windmills, wheelbarrows, and wooden swords. He painted them all in beautiful colours, and no one could find anything in the shops to match. It was said that each evening, during the winter, Mr Mansfield's entire family would be engaged in making toys for Good Friday.

Pimbo settled for a wooden sword; it had a coloured holster and studded belt. "Try it on my boy," said Mr Mansfield, "it's just the thing for a boy like you."

At that moment Jennie, with her parents, approached the stall. Pimbo with the sword strapped on, felt big and strong; just as he did on the common with Bobby and the clay fire box. Jennie smiled when she saw him, although he wanted to show off – somehow he couldn't.

Noticing a string of pretty beads hanging on the side of the stall, Pimbo unbuckled the sword belt, handing it back to a surprised Mr Mansfield.

"I'll have the beads please," said Pimbo. Paying his sixpence he handed the beads to Jennie, who placed them around her slim throat. Her light flaxen hair matched perfectly with the beads. From behind he heard Bobby whisper, 'Cissy', but somehow he didn't care, this was his day – and part of it was Jennie's.

A sudden commotion drew the boy's attention to a lone figure in the centre of an excited throng of people. It was Mr Sanders, the Leeke Street escapologist, who was teasing the crowd with his usual banter. A wiry little man, Pimbo had often watched him in practice at the rear of his home. He would allow his small son Ronnie to jump on his stomach, and would do hand stands balanced precariously on chairs.

During the week Mr Sanders would attract a crowd on street corners. A small boy would receive a penny for watching out in case of police intervention. In the event of one being seen – Mr Sanders would live up to his reputation as an escapologist. Now, with the aid of someone from the crowd, he was being tied and bound with ropes and chains – until it seemed impossible for him to escape.

After a time Mr Sanders would wriggle and shake, sweat and turn, until in a flurry of activity he would jump to his feet – completely free. The hat would be passed round by a small boy, and the crowd finally dispersed.

Bobby then suggested to Pimbo that they go on to Christ's Pieces, where a brass band would be playing to dancing and singing.

Christ's Pieces was a fine spacious green, situated in the centre of Cambridge. It was well known for its beauty and shrubberies. In the centre was a constructed bandstand surrounded by iron railings. Coloured bulbs, placed in strategic positions, helped illuminate the stand at night. To enter the enclosure cost sixpence, but on a fine day many were content to sit outside the enclosure, where the strains of the band could be heard clearly.

Pimbo and Bobby sat on a seat underneath a tree, the band was playing and to Pimbo the whole evening seemed magical. Even Bobby, usually restless and wandering, sat and listened.

Pimbo had started on *Tom Sawyer*, the book given him by the two social workers. Suddenly he visualized himself and Bobby as Huck and Tom. Snatching a blade of grass he placed it carefully into his mouth. The band broke into a Dixie number enabling Pimbo to stretch his imagination still further. In that moment Leeke Street, and Cambridge, were left far behind. The River Cam, Cambridge's main river, could never live up to the thrills of the Mississippi, right now Bobby and he were taking a raft down that famous stretch.

As the strains of the band swung into well-known South American melodies, Pimbo conjured up visions of various shacks that Tom Sawyer and Huck played around in. Suddenly Pimbo realized that Leeke Street was a fair substitute, after all you didn't have to live in a palace to be able to dream.

*Charlie Darler's shop, Gold Street.*

Reading a book didn't cost much, you could do anything, go anywhere – you only had to think you were there. He wondered whether the two ladies realized what happiness they had given him through the books.

At Holt they thought him a strange little boy – a day-dreamer. Well if this was day-dreaming, he didn't mind. Today was one of the happiest days of his life. Glancing at Bobby who still sat listening, Pimbo realized that music and books certainly did something for people.

On the way home the two lads stopped outside
the blacksmith's forge of Mr Bloy. The forge, situated at the Newmarket Road end of East Road was
the only shoeing forge in Cambridge. Horses from
all parts of the county would be driven through the
small streets of the town on their way to the forge.
Pimbo loved the smell as the heated shoe was
placed against the horse's hoof. The metallic click
of the nails being driven home could be heard even
in Leeke Street.

Sometimes Pimbo would earn a penny by working the bellows for Mr Bloy but when the heat from
the furnace caused him to cough, the kindly blacksmith would beckon another boy to take over.

At home, whenever Mrs Freestone required a
penny for the gas, she would make a sign as though
blowing the bellows. Pimbo would pop along, and
Mr Bloy sensing her need, would allow Pimbo to
take over from whoever was presiding at the
bellows.

She told Pimbo how, on account of the heat, she
hated having to ask him to earn a penny in such
manner. But Bob would worry about knowing she
was short of money and this brought on his
asthma. Somehow Pimbo didn't mind, because
Mr Sanders said he ought to give his chest plenty
to do.

After watching awhile the two boys make for
home. Pimbo's first taste of Good Friday on Parker's Piece had given him a grand time. That
evening he was very tired and soon fell asleep.

In the morning Mrs Freestone told Pimbo about
a little job she was about to start. A friend at the
Citadel had put her in touch with a Mrs Neal, who

*Walton Terrace, East Road. "Pickle Onion" lady lived in centre cottage. Mrs Leftley specialised in pickled-onions, piccalilli and pickled red cabbage.*

*The Pelican pub, corner of Nelson Street and East Road. Bill Westley, the old one-eyed ragman lived in Nelson Street.*

lived in St Barnabas Road. Yesterday, instead of going with Pimbo to the Piece, she had visited Mrs Neal to fix up hours and pay.

"What do you think of me – really Pimbo? I would have loved to have gone with you yesterday – but the money will make up for Bob being away and help pay the bus fare to Papworth." Her voice trailed off into a tone of apology.

Pimbo smiled, "You trust me when I'm out on my own, I enjoy myself. Can I come with you to visit Bob?" Somehow he evaded the main point of his foster-mother's question. "The money I earn running errands is less for you to worry about; I'm fetching coke for Mrs Parker this morning, then I can go to the Kinema – do you mind?"

Pimbo watched as she broke into a smile, her homely features, the wisps of hair tucked inside her bonnet, the straightness of her back as she walked around the Citadel collecting the offerings, made him proud – he now felt capable of answering the first part of her question.

"I love you as a mother, you help me fight myself, if I were kept in I would feel a prisoner. In your home I'm allowed to live – one day if I get well, I shall repay you," he said softly.

Mrs Freestone hugged him tightly. "Oh Pimbo, I wish you didn't have to talk like that – you sound so old, and yet you're only a child. Somehow I think your illness has turned you into a man."

Later in the morning Pimbo called at Mrs Parker's to collect the small handcart, which was almost a trademark of Leeke Street. Almost every house owned one, it was a fair-sized wooden box mounted on a set of pram wheels. In order to allow

*White Ribbon Hotel (Salvation Army) at corner of Gold Street and East Road. Tommy Tucker, the milkman, lived in small house.*

for extra coke the box was made as deep as possible.

The gas-works where Pimbo obtained the coke, was a little way past River Lane where his school was situated; the rear of the gas-works overlooked the school.

Pimbo went to the little window just inside the gate and paid his money. For this he received a ticket, which when his turn came to receive the coke, was handed to the loader.

The loader was usually a man known by most of the boys. It was through this that sending children made sense. After filling the sack with the amount made out on the ticket, the loader would then in accordance with what he knew, or had heard about his little customer, throw into the box as much loose coke as the lad justified.

One look at Pimbo's cheeky dimpled face, carroty hair and spindly legs, resulted usually in a liberal supply of extra coke. Some boys would sell the loose coke for sweets money – but Pimbo gave Mrs Parker a fair deal in order to keep a regular Saturday morning job.

On the way home he bumped into Bobby Watson. They stopped to chatter and arranged to be outside the Kinema at one-thirty in order to head to queue.

Turning into the alleyway leading to Mrs Parker's home, Pimbo thought again of Bobby. He was such a strong boy and played football for the school. At one time he thought Bobby had only wanted him as a friend, just to be able to bully him and get his own way. Now to Pimbo it seemed the reverse, in Bobby he saw a boy whom he would very much like to be. He remembered a pair of characters from a comic, who were called Mutt and Jeff. One was small, the other large and the things that one couldn't do, the other could. It was like that with Bobby – but one day he hoped to be strong like Bobby.

Mrs Parker was well pleased with the amount of coke he had brought. She asked Pimbo to oil the wheels of the cart and for this extra duty she gave him twopence.

Copying a leaf from her book, he placed the two coins into his foster-mother's gas meter.

# CHAPTER 6

## Pimbo lands in trouble

One evening as Mrs Freestone was going to her new job in St Barnabas Road, Pimbo decided on spending a little time in the sweet-shop of Lucy and Mabel. Bobby Watson and Ronnie Sanders (son of the escapologist) went along with him.

Lucy and Mabel were in good form and the little shop was soon crowded with boys of all ages. After a tune on the violin from Mabel, Lucy called on Pimbo to do a turn; he obliged on the mouth organ with 'Molly Malone', a tune being taught at school.

A few of the boys sang, others seemed content to watch or clap. Pimbo found himself wedged in a group of boys from another area. A rough looking boy whom Pimbo had never seen before was talking to others of a similar type.

"I'll bet she's got money tucked away in the back of the shop," the rough lad was saying, "they'll not miss a pound or two." The other lads nodded, then spotting Pimbo moved away out of earshot. Pimbo thought he had heard the word 'tonight' mentioned.

On the way home he confided this to Bobby. The big lad shrugged. "It sounds like Dollar Smith, comes from the Gas Lane area, he's been in trouble before for stealing – but what can we do, they may have been bragging?"

At home awaiting Maude's return Pimbo sat thinking. He felt sure that Dollar Smith intended to try something. Writing a note to his foster-mother explaining his absence, Pimbo crept out from the back entrance. Walking round the back of Bobby's home Pimbo could see his pal through the window. It seemed his father was not at home, and his mother was sitting with her back to the window. Pimbo waited until Bobby's face was level with the window, then waved his arms violently to and fro.

After a few seconds Bobby came outside. As briefly as he could Pimbo put his fears to his pal. Bobby led him to the little gate at the rear of the garden. "Pimbo, what's come over you – this isn't your line? You must stay out of trouble – I want nothing to do with it." Pimbo hadn't heard Bobby talk like this before. It seemed that he would never give in.

"I'm worried about the old ladies – they've been good to us," said Pimbo, "surely there's something we can do – should we tell the police?"

Bobby shook his head. "Supposing it's all wrong, p'raps they were showing off. The police might even stop the sweet-shop allowing boys in at night. Then it would be worse for the old ladies," he replied.

Pimbo thought deeply. "I know, let's go and warn Miss Lucy and Miss Mabel – then p'raps they'll make sure the money is safe."

"All right, that won't take long, then you'll be

satisfied – eh?" Bobby seemed relieved to have found a way out of the situation.

Both boys made their way back to the shop. Bobby, jumping to see over the top of the Bisto Kids poster, noticed there was no light in the front of the shop.

"There you are – all peace and quiet. They must have gone to bed," said Bobby.

Pimbo thought he heard a scuffling inside the shop. They tried the door gently – it was unlocked, anyone could get in! Both lads held their breath as they eased themselves down the steep drop at the entrance. Bobby daringly peeped over the back of the counter – there was no one hiding.

The flap of the counter had been pushed back. Bobby led the way through the opening leading to the door of the sisters' flat. Both sisters slept in a room over the top of the shop. Pimbo met the gaze of his friend as they stood outside the flat door. It seemed unlikely that the old ladies would leave this door open. If the door was open – then it seemed someone must have entered the shop – or worse still, be roaming around at this moment.

Pimbo wondered how Tom Mix would have coped, then noticing Bobby's frightened face, realized that it was for real. Pimbo braced himself to be brave, this was a time when day-dreaming would be of little use. Even his pal was afraid, but somehow both boys pushed open the flat door and moved in.

In the darkness the boys could see nothing to denote a forced entry. Pimbo moving to the window, noticed it was half-open – on the sill were muddy tracks of smallish sized boots. He called

Bobby over – at the same time one of the old ladies let out a frightening shriek.

The stairs were suddenly full of action. Rushing figures stumbled from the stairs into the small living-room, where Pimbo and Bobby were waiting. Seeing the figures of Pimbo and Bobby, the boy thieves led by Dollar Smith veered away into the shop.

Bobby rushing forward made a grab at Dollar Smith who, being an old hand, seemed to be going well for himself. Soon they were wrestling on the floor of the shop. Another boy, seeing Dollar in difficulty moved forward to intercept when Pimbo, so proud of his pal Bobby, grabbed at his arms and placing his feet behind the young crook, twisted him over.

By now Miss Mabel dressed in night attire came down. The light was suddenly switched on and she stood in the centre of the room holding a cash box she must have grabbed back from the boys.

The sudden switching on of the light, caused Bobby and Pimbo to relax their grip. To everyone's surprise Dollar jumped up and shouting, "Come on make for the front door – I've left it open!" grabbed back the cash box and made for the door.

The door of the shop leading into the street was suddenly flung open. Framed in the doorway was a burly uniformed figure. Dollar stopped in his tracks looking around in amazement at the sudden change of fortunes. Thinking perhaps of a lighter sentence he sheepishly handed back the money box to a relieved Miss Mabel.

The uniformed figure moved closer into the light, almost falling down the steep drop at the entrance – to Pimbo's surprise – it was Mrs Freestone.

"I got your note – after a while I began to worry. I had changed into uniform as we have an unexpected meeting later tonight." Looking at Dollar Smith and his gang, she continued, "Your dads won't be too pleased with this night's work – if I remember rightly you're all on probation!"

The shrieking of Miss Mabel had by now attracted a small crowd. A policeman whom Pimbo reconized as Banger Day, a well-known figure around the Newmarket Road area, collected the boys of the gang and took them into Miss Mabel's kitchen.

Pimbo and Bobby, after telling all they knew were allowed to return to their homes. Mrs Freestone cancelled her meeting, and stayed back with Pimbo. "Well done! Putting your thoughts into action now, eh?" she laughed. "Wait till I tell Bob about this – he'll never believe it."

Next day coming home from school Pimbo ran into Bobby Watson. "The police have been round home for another statement," he said excitedly. "They've gone round your house, they tried at the front door – but no one answered."

Pimbo noticed a strange quietness in the street. Mrs Parker's curtains were slightly drawn, and neighbours were standing on the pavement chatting and staring at number ten.

Approaching the back door of his home Pimbo could hear the voices of two policemen. Banger Day, who had seen the boys on the night of the break-in, was talking to a younger policeman. "I suppose she's out working, we'll hang on a bit, the boy should be home from school anytime now," he was saying. The younger policeman nodded.

"Queer little street this, I've been used to a different kind of neighbourhood – they seem scared stiff round here."

Banger Day smiled, "Always fighting authority these kind of people, it's being poor that does it. Take old Sanders the escape-king, I swear every time he gets bound up, he accepts it as a challenge to escape from the law and poverty. He finishes up by dodging us, and getting paid for it."

His colleague knocked at the back door again. "Who's this kid Pimbo, he's new round here isn't he? What's he like –usual tearaway?"

Banger stiffened, "An old head on young shoulders, they tell me. Hasn't been here long, a young consumptive living on borrowed time. From what I've heard he's a regular charmer, even got Alf Smith thinking about giving his family a better do."

Edging closer until seen by the two policemen, Pimbo broke up the conversation. "Do you want me, Sir?" he asked nervously.

The policemen stared, "Nothing to be scared of my boy, routine enquiry – that's all," said Banger Day kindly. "I want you to sign a statement about the other night – and this boy Smith, can you tell me why he's called Dollar?"

Gaining confidence Pimbo perked up. Nicknames seemed to be very common after all, he thought. Bobby had once told him that Banger was nicknamed as such, because of his threat to bang naughty boys' heads together as a line of deterrent.

"It's because he's always betting people. In an argument he says, 'I'll bet you a dollar I'm right' – a dollar's five shillings, Sir."

Banger leaned back on his heels staring at his colleague. "Miss Lucy is badly shocked, it's possible that the sweet-shop may have to close. Miss Mabel, too, is taking it badly – she thinks you and Bobby Watson were wonderful."

From beneath his arm he produced a cardboard carton, handing it to Pimbo he turned the printing uppermost. It read, 'Two dozen black jacks, keep in dry place.'

Pimbo signed a document produced by Banger; as he was turning into the kitchen he noticed Mrs Freestone who had just returned from work talking to the two policemen.

Over a cup of tea his foster-mother smiled, "Been charming them again Pimbo? I've never seen Banger Day looking so relaxed – not in this street, any way. I hope they catch all the boys, then they'll get sent away, have good clothes, good food. They come home on probation looking like little gentlemen. I've seen many a boy make something of himself through what happened in the sweetshop." She paused to study the reaction on Pimbo's intense dimpled face.

"No, Pimbo, don't weep for Dollar, nor his mates – it'll either kill or cure them. That's what the Sally-Army does for you, everything happens for the best. God sends sun and rain down for everyone – we must make the best of it, eh, Pimbo?"

Pimbo stared, "Is that how Bob feels about his asthma? Doesn't he worry why he isn't the same as anyone else? He's always cheerful when I'm about – but doesn't he sometimes feel sad?"

"Of course he does, my boy. Everyone must have somewhere to hide. But that's enough for one day.

Now what about that book you were reading, *The Old Curiosity Shop?* You've just time to read a chapter or two before bedtime. Tomorrow we're going to Papworth to visit your foster-father."

In bed that night Pimbo realized why the two ladies had chosen Mrs Freestone as his foster-mother. He couldn't wish for a better home in the whole of Barnwell.

In the morning Mrs Freestone was up early. The coach taking them to Papworth was called 'The Whippet', and was based in Northampton Street. The twelve mile journey took them past an ominous looking construction known as the Gibbet.

"Caxton Gibbett," said Maude to Pimbo, as they drew level with the infamous spot, "highwaymen were hanged on the Gibbett some years ago, it was money or your life. The Gibbet stands as a permanent site – they say one day a hotel will be built in memory of the bad old days."

Papworth, known as the Settlement, was a small village on the right of the crossroads, a little way past the Gibbett. It was chosen because of its high altitude and pleasant surroundings for people suffering from chest diseases.

Industry in the shape of box making and furniture repairs, was introduced to allow the Settlement to become independent. Families moved into the houses provided by the scheme, many spent the rest of their days working and living at the Settlement. In Cambridge the word Papworth was treated with awe and neighbours admitting to having a relative or friend 'in Papworth', would be viewed with sympathy and a sense of martyrdom.

A famous establishment on East Road. Jokingly
referred to as "Stink and Whiff".

Loker's newsagent. Opposite, shop of J. Thompson,
East Road. Further down, scene of murder of young
girl by sailor on leave.

Maude and Pimbo found Bob Freestone residing in a kind of wooden chalet. The chalet, one of several dotted about at strategic points to gain advantage of the fresh keen air, was placed in a pretty glade surrounded by trees.

"They've moved me outside," said Bob cheerfully, "another month and I'll be coming home – have everything ready Pimbo."

Bob looked better, thought Pimbo. His usually thin features had broadened out. After a few homely exchanges with his wife, he ran his fingers through Pimbo's shock of red hair. "I guess I've stopped kids calling you Ginger, Maude tells me 'Pimbo' has stuck since the first day. So, you've been playing detective, eh? Going to the Kinema has given you ideas – I'll bet your friend Tom Mix couldn't have done better."

Pimbo smiled, "I miss you, Bob. I want you to get better and come home. I didn't want to cause trouble about the break-in. Miss Lucy said how a man once built a small doorway so's only small kids could enter – Dollar Smith went through a different way. I suppose that's why Miss Lucy was shocked – she didn't think children would do such a thing."

Bob smiled across to his wife and winked, "There, I'll put on my dressing-gown and show you around," he said quickly.

As they walked around Pimbo noticed that most of the inmates had thin features and hollow cheeks. Someone at Holt had explained that asthma was not like consumption – there was a good chance you would not die.

He could hear Bob joking with his wife. Pimbo

drew level with them and stopped thinking on such things. It was too fine a day, so he listened to the birds, and took in the beauty of the shrubs and trees.

# CHAPTER 7

## Pimbo's adventure

With a day off from school, Pimbo decided to spend a morning at Mr Bloy's blacksmith forge in East Road. As it was cattle-market day, this meant a steady stream of horses would be passing through for shoeing.

One or two men from Leeke Street often obtained casual employment as drovers. They would hang around until cattle were sold, then offer their services in driving them to their destination.

In the middle of a very busy stretch, Mr O'dell, a chimney sweep living in Occupation Road, rushed into the forge.

"Have you seen my donkey?" he shouted in an agitated voice. "The little blighter's gone again."

Pimbo smiled to himself. Mr O'dell's donkey seemed for ever to be running away. Rumour was that the chimney sweep did not always treat it well and was often seen whipping the poor animal. The sweep was a familiar sight in the Barnwell district, his small son Jimmy often accompanied him and people complained that Jimmy was made to climb inside the chimney piece to clean it.

Mr Bloy, the blacksmith, turned angrily, "I'm too

busy to worry about your affairs – look after your donkey, it's your living you know."

Without replying the chimney sweep rushed from the forge.

Pimbo felt more sorry for Jimmy than for his father, if the donkey wasn't found, Jimmy's dad would take it out on his son. Once the donkey went missing for five days with the brushes still strapped to its back. Mr O'dell was unable to earn money.

In the afternoon Pimbo went along to Mr O'dell's house in Occupation Road. He found Mrs O'dell in tears, the donkey was still free and the fear of losing money had been too much for her.

Reasoning that a lone search might be more successful, Pimbo decided on making a search in Kidman's Yard. The yard was a large area of building site containing huge quantities of timber and builder's nick-nacks. The site was used as a wholesale depot and the owner, Mr Kidman, was a Town Councillor.

A large wall surrounded the yard, an iron gate in its centre, heavily padlocked during closing hours, providing ample security.

By now it was five o'clock and the yard was closed. Hoping the donkey might have strayed through the gate earlier Pimbo, spotting a fence at the side of the wall found that, after a little effort, he was able to clamber on to the wall from the fence.

Pimbo felt good, he always felt good when climbing. Tom Mix would have done likewise – perhaps might have used a lariat, but Pimbo was satisfied. Pausing on the top of the wall for a moment, hoping

*Moden's shop, close by was his coal business. East Road?*

to spot the donkey, Pimbo dropped down into the yard.

Walking a short distance into the building site, Pimbo stopped suddenly. At the side of a vehicle track, apparently having been pushed aside by lorries, lay a small sack. He recognized the sack as one used mainly for carrying soot. It seemed that his hunch had paid off, the donkey might well have passed this way!

Approaching a small builder's shed, he could hear voices from the inside. Creeping up close Pimbo peeped through the cracks of the door. Inside was a group of tramps, one of whom appeared to be drunk, swaying precariously from side to side. Pimbo remembered Bob Freestone telling him about the yard being used at night by tramps and alcoholics. They would hide up during the day, then make full use of the yard at night.

He felt scared. Bob had warned him to stay away

from such people. Suddenly one of the tramps spotted him.

"It's a snoopin' kid, probably the foreman's tell-tale. Catch him, we'll teach him to mind his own business," he shouted to the other.

Pimbo raced away. He'd never run so fast in his life, his lungs seemed fit to burst. Hardly daring to look back he raced on until unable to go any further, he sank down on to a heap of shavings outside a large timber shed. But luck somehow was still with him; at the entrance to the shed, quietly nibbling at a heap of shavings was the donkey. He noticed the sweep's brushes were missing but it didn't matter, at least the donkey was safe. Pimbo taking hold of the donkey's loose reins, tied them to a post at the side of the building, then decided to search for the missing brushes.

The shed was full of timber, there seemed to be miles and miles of planks of all sizes and shapes. In the centre of the shed, fast asleep, was another tramp.

Pimbo recognised him as a man known in the Barnwell area as Old Jack. Captain Woods of the Citadel once found him a room at the *White Ribbon* but an over fondness of drink usually led to his sleeping rough. At his side was an empty meths bottle, with the cork missing. By the depth of the man's snoring, Pimbo reasoned that he was drunk.

To the right of the sleeper Pimbo spotted the missing chimney brushes, it seemed that Old Jack had stolen them, planning to sell them later for drink. As he was about to strap the brushes on to the donkey's back, a noise at the front of the entrance to the shed diverted his attention – it was the drunken tramp who had called the chase from the builder's shed. Banging the door shut, he moved menacingly toward Pimbo.

A smell of burning caused Pimbo to look down near the sleeping drunk. There was a sudden burst of flame, somehow the open meths bottle had come into contact with a cigarette end carelessly dropped by Old Jack. The threatening tramp made a sudden lurch at Pimbo, but the chase and drink proved too much for him, as he collapsed to the floor of the shed.

By now flames were spreading rapidly, the donkey began to bray and kick out. Remembering a Tom Mix film he'd seen, Pimbo moved swiftly over to the donkey, and after untying the reins, tied the straps from the brushes around the ankles of Old Jack. As the donkey moved forward into the fresh air the tramp, bumping and lurching, was dragged to safety.

Pimbo tried to entice the donkey back to the entrance of the blazing shed, but kicking and raising its head, the donkey refused to budge. The timber shed was now blazing furiously and Pimbo made a last effort to save the tramp who had fallen to the ground in a drunken stupor.

The smoke and fumes were driving him back, he felt a sudden tightness in the chest, his head was swimming round and round – still holding the reins of the donkey, Pimbo sank down – remembering no more.

When he came to Mrs Freestone was bending over him. "It's all right Pimbo," she was saying, "Dr Webb said after a few days in bed you'll be all right again."

Pimbo stared into her face. "What about the donkey, and the tramps, are they all right?"

Straightening the sheets of the bed, his foster-mother smiled down at him. "Someone spotted the smoke and called the Fire Brigade, the tramp was pulled out just in time – the donkey is back with Mr O'dell."

Going to the kitchen, Maude made a hot drink and returned with it for Pimbo. He sat up resting his back on two pillows. Sitting on the edge of the bed, Mrs Freestone leaned over to adjust them.

"Pimbo why do you do it? Must you get into everything? One day you'll be the death of me – can't you be just an ordinary little boy?"

Pimbo looked up and smiled. "Huckleberry Finn was like me, he had to go out and see what was happening. Boys can't help it. In a book I read it said that boys with problems were better for getting involved."

"But you haven't a problem," butted in Maude.

Noticing the hurt in her eyes, Pimbo hesitated. "I don't want to hurt you, I suppose my fault is in trying to fit a whole lifetime into a year . . . " Before he could finish Pimbo fell into a deep sleep.

Bobby Watson was round Pimbo's early next morning. He related to his friend how everyone was reading about the attempted robbery at the sweet-shop. "The *Cambridge Daily News* said we were proper little heroes, there was a lot in about you and the fire at Kidman's – Leeke Street is really in the news."

Pimbo asked him about Dollar Smith and the rest of his gang that were caught. Bobby said that most of them had been in trouble before – they were ordered to a Reformatory School.

Bobby stayed a while then began looking out of the window. Pimbo knew well the restless urge of his young friend. "What's on your mind Bobby?" he asked suddenly.

"Ronnie Sanders tells me that Dollar's remaining gang will be coming after us. They reckon we should have kept our noses out of it – then Dollar and the others wouldn't have been caught."

Pimbo nodded, he knew that gangs in Barnwell had a special code of behaviour. There would be a fight, usually with sticks and stones. The rival gangs would meet in a derelict piece of ground and have a pitched battle. Once the battle was over there would be peace.

He realized too that it was his fault. He'd egged Bobby on, and no doubt that played a major part in the unfortunate night's work. Somehow he felt that at the moment his health would not stand up to such a fight.

Bobby, sensing his thoughts, turned quickly. "I'm going to sort it out, arrange a day when you'll be fit enough to fight – leave it to me and don't worry."

In the afternoon Pimbo received another visitor in the person of Mr Adamson the student from St John's college. Bringing along fruit and sweets, he told Pimbo how Jennie's mother had told him about the recent adventures of his small friend.

"It's good of you to come, Sir," said a surprised Pimbo. "Why do you think about me?"

Mr Adamson's cheery face broke into a smile, he sat on the bed and peeled Pimbo a banana. "Well one day I hope to be thinking a lot about boys such as you – do you want to know why?"

Noticing the inquisitive look on Pimbo's face, he sat further on to the bed, then crossed his legs in tailor's fashion.

I'm studying sociology. That's a long word meaning people, people like you. I want to find out why boys such as you can make the best of things – others from a better environment perhaps are not so happy."

Pimbo stared, "What good would that do, isn't it just being curious? It's not kind to be curious, Jennie's father swore at me because of charity – isn't charity being curious?"

The young student nodded. "Charity can be cold, Pimbo. It's got to be mixed, that's why I want to find out for myself. One day there won't be charity, instead there'll be better houses, better jobs. You won't be living in streets like Leeke Street or Brown's Yard – you'll get a better deal."

"Mrs Freestone said we've all got to hide somewhere. If I lived in a better place than Leeke Street, where can I hide? If I don't have day dreams – shall I be happy?"

Mr Adamson touched Pimbo on the head. "Pimbo, I'm being unkind, I'm taking you beyond your years; somehow you drive me on to find out what makes you tick. I've never met a boy like you before – how old are you?"

"I'm eight next week. Everyone says the same. I don't know why I'm different. You ask me questions, then say I'm different from other boys. I like to play marbles and spin tops, but I like to know about life – can you teach me about your big word – about people?"

*The Horse and Jockey pub 1912. Fourth from the right is "Soopy" Barratt, the rat catcher.*

Mr Adamson shook his head and laughed boy-ishly. "Do you remember my idea of opening a boys' club in Occupation Road – well I have a permit. Mabel and Lucy are closing the sweet-shop, both are badly shaken by the break-in. Would you come along and bring your pals, Pimbo?"

Pimbo nodded happily, "Bobby Watson will come, so will Ronnie Sanders – he can do hand stands."

The young student peeled another banana, handing it to Pimbo, he walked to a pile of books at the side of the boy's bed. The book which Pimbo had been reading lay open on top of the pile. Mr Adam-son closed the book and read the title, *The Old Curiosity Shop*. "With your curiosity were you ever to open a shop, you'd never be short of customers," he said jokingly.

"What will the club be like?" asked Pimbo anxious to change the subject. "What kind of games will there be?"

"Oh all kinds: boxing, ping-pong, draughts, chess, and an interval during which you may buy a slab of cake and a glass of lemonade for a penny – how about that, Pimbo?"

The boy followed the student who was about to leave the room. "Jimmy O'dell, the sweep's son would come if his Dad allowed him, sometimes he is made to work late," said Pimbo suddenly.

Mr Adamson turned at the door. "By the way is it true that Jimmy is made to climb inside the chimneys?"

Remembering Jennie Smith's father, Pimbo hes-itated a moment. He didn't want Jimmy's father round causing trouble. Then again he thought, pride and means test didn't come into it after all, Jimmy was unhappy and why should a boy be unhappy?

"Jimmy told me that it frightens him, everywhere is dark and the soot makes him cough. He gets in a row at school, the teachers cane him for having dirty ears – Jimmy said it was hard to get the soot off." Somehow Pimbo felt relieved for having said the truth.

"Listen Pimbo, don't say a word to anyone, and don't think for a moment that I'm just being curious. I'm thinking about hundreds of little Jimmy O'dells. One day you'll realize that it's not always enough to get by on your own steam – you need people to fight for you – I intend to do just that."

As the young student moved away down the stairs, Pimbo wondered why he always seemed to be getting involved – then thinking again of Jimmy, he felt that he would much rather have it that way.

# CHAPTER 8

## Pimbo's Sunday-school treat

A few days later Bobby came round with exciting news. On account of his good work in the rescue of the tramps and donkey, Pimbo had been invited to the Pentecostal's Sunday-school outing.

The little wooden church on Newmarket Road, attended regularly by Bobby was holding its annual treat on the coming Thursday. Somehow Bobby had persuaded the minister to include his friend.

A Sunday-school treat was looked upon by the children of Barnwell as a major event of the year. A stamped star card showing regular attendance being the only passport required.

The local coal merchants, Gentle and Swann, usually supplied transport. Coal carts, well scrubbed and bedecked with flowers, would be waiting on East Road – a little way past Mr Bloy's blacksmith's forge. Chatting and excited children would stand in awe as the huge handsome cart-horses were led out from the yard and backed into the shafts. Flustered Sunday-school teachers supervised the loading as youngsters scrambled aboard.

Pimbo, standing next to Jennie Smith, watched her excited face as the carts trundled down New-market Road towards Teversham. Older boys started the usual singing.

"We are the Cambridge Boys,
We're the boys who make no noise.
We know our manners,
We spend our tanners.
We are respected wherever we go;
Right down Newmarket Road,
Where the children wear poor clothes —"

Then the boys would begin the verses all over again.

Passing the little sweet-shop, the boys watched as a tired looking Lucy and Mabel waved them by. Soon they were level with the gas-works and further on outside the Pentecostal church, they picked up a few late stragglers.

A grey squirrel, daringly poised on a fence sur-rounding Watts timber yard, was pointed out to an excited Jennie. Pimbo noticed that she was wear-ing the beads from the Easter parade.

On Barnwell bridge the swishing trains were in direct contrast to the steady *clip-clop* of the big hearted cart-horses. In the sunlight the brasses of the horses glinted as they mounted the breast of the hill.

Pimbo showed Jennie the little monastery at the bottom of the hill. It was known as the 'Leper Chapel' and during term students from the theo-logical colleges pledged themselves to maintain the upkeep of the stonework and grounds.

Pointing to a large expanse of water on the edge of Coldham's Common, Bobby explained how years ago, during a flood, a complete house was submerged under the water. At last the horse convoy stopped outside a grassy plateau known as Hawkins Field, it was there the children would be spending the rest of the day.

Assisting Jennie down from the cart, Pimbo noticed how pretty she looked in the new dress bought by her mother since working at the college. The field was full of exciting little dug-outs; Bobby said that years ago the field was a swamp and at

*Unidentified pub on East Road.*

the bottom of the dug-outs were many frogs. Jennie
seemed brave as Pimbo took her to the bottom of a
small dug-out – but thankfully for Jennie there
were no frogs.

Dotted about the field were see-saws improvised
from sawn down tree trunks. Creaks and groans
from the home-made contraptions echoed over the
field as happy children see-sawed up and down.

Pimbo and Bobby managed to coax Jennie into
having a ride. At first she was afraid of tearing her
dress but soon she was laughing as the boys
weighted her up and down.

Older boys exploring the damp pits, managed to
catch a few frogs, these were shown to the girls who
promptly ran screaming in all directions.

After a while Pimbo sat next to Jennie, both
resting their backs against a tree. The teachers
were setting out trestles and table tops in readi-
ness for the annual tea. The white table cloths, and
pretty plates loaned from a large manor in the
grounds, looked pretty against the background of
the spring grass.

A large tea urn was carried from the manor, and
piles of bread and butter suddenly appeared on the
tables.

Calling for Jennie in the mornings, Pimbo had
often wondered how it was that such a pretty girl
could emerge from a place like Brown's Yard. That
afternoon before the carts had moved off, Pimbo
had waited at the entrance to the yard. He had
taken in the barren brick wall, the worn cobbles
and the sunless apathy of Brown's Yard.

Then suddenly out came Jennie, new dress,
beads and all – Mr Adamson would have to learn

about such things, thought Pimbo. Maybe poor children could be happy the same as rich children. Jennie smiled as she spotted Pimbo. She was smiling now as she said, "I'm pleased with the beads, my dad likes you – and so does Mum."

Pimbo shifted his seat uneasily. He wasn't sure what it was about Jennie. Adults spoke about love and other things, Bobby said it was cissy. Pimbo always worried about Jennie, and would see no harm come to her; when he was with her it was just like reading a book, only it was for real.

Jennie spoke very little, when she did it seemed so precious. She reminded him of Coldham's Common during the holiday buttercup picking when, instead of the usual buttercups and daisies – he had found a new flower. None of the other pickers would be in on it – it was kind of 'finders-keepers'.

"Now then children, this isn't the way to spend a Sunday-school treat – my, when I was your age I was into everything. Come along now and find a place for tea." The teacher, after chiding Pimbo and Jennie, walked with them to a group of tables.

After a sumptuous tea, there was a medley of games including sack racing, egg and spoon, and one of doughnut eating, the doughnut suspended on a string, had to be eaten without the children using their hands. Bobby took a prominent part in most games.

During tea Pimbo managed to stow away a piece of currant cake. Mothers bidding their children good-bye on their way to the treat, would remind them to bring home cake as a kind of memento of the outing. Pimbo wasn't sure whether Mrs Freestone would like some or not – but to be on the safe side he tucked a piece away in his napkin. Currant cake in Leeke Street was for Sundays only.

At the finish of the games the children lined up for a bag of sweets and an orange. Then came a short prayer, followed by a mad stampede for the horse-driven carts. The journey home lacked the excitement of the 'coming' trip. Children were tired, some had overeaten – many were thinking of the year's wait until the next treat.

Pimbo, Jennie and Bobby kept together, taking in some of the scenery they had missed before. At Gentle and Swann's coal yard Jennie's mother was there to greet them, Alf Smith helping with the off loading of the children shouted to Pimbo.

"Miss Lucy wants you to call in on them, they're closing the shop at the week-end and going back North."

Pimbo looked across to Bobby who, loaded with prizes won at the games, nodded, "I'll take these home first, Pimbo, see you at the shop." Knowing that his foster-mother would still be working, Pimbo made his way to the little sweet-shop. Finally both lads walked down the awkward step into the shop. The sweetjars, cardboard containers all had gone, only the magical smells remained. Miss Lucy and Miss Mabel standing together, seemed to have aged since the Dollar Smith episode.

"We're calling it a day, boys," said Miss Lucy. "Fifty years we've put up with lads such as you," she paused awhile to study their reaction, "and we don't regret one day of them."

Miss Mabel reached under the counter producing two large boxes containing their favourite sweets and handed one to each boy.

"We close on Saturday, the day fifty years ago we opened in Cambridge. In fifty years we've never had a break-in. It made us think that perhaps we'd outstayed our welcome. Besides, we're getting old, we're going back up North from whence we came – what do you think we'll do first?" asked Mabel mischievously.

"I don't know", ventured Pimbo after a long pause.

The old ladies smiled, "We're going round all the sweet-shops that we can remember as kids – that's what you boys will do one day, just you see."

Pimbo had a feeling that the old ladies would never come across a shop such as theirs. He asked Miss Mabel to play her violin for the last time. She played 'Danny Boy' with her head slightly bowed; Pimbo knew that she was crying, as was Miss Lucy.

With a shower of thanks and clutching their carton of sweets, Pimbo and Bobby said good-bye to the little shop.

In the morning Maude Freestone was up and about earlier than usual. She took Pimbo in a cup of tea, resting it on a small table beside his bed. Sitting on the bed she said cheerfully, "Pimbo, I'm having you all to myself today. Mrs Neal doesn't want me until later in the afternoon."

Pimbo was pleased, it was not often that he enjoyed the company of his foster-mother for long periods. Since her husband's illness it had been a hard slog for Maude.

"You've got something up your sleeve, Mum," it was the first time he had called her Mum. For a long time Pimbo had wrestled with the word on the tip of his tongue – now it was out. He wondered why it had taken him so long.

Mrs Freestone hugged him tightly. "Oh Pimbo, I've longed for you to call me Mum, wait until I tell Bob – or should I say Dad?"

At that moment came a rap on the front door. Whilst Maude moved away to answer, Pimbo peeped between the curtains into the street below. It proved to be Mr Cooper's second-hand furniture van. Mr Cooper, with a shop in Newmarket Road, was well known in Barnwell, having started business with a horse and cart by selling hardware and brushes to outlying villages. Mr Cooper and his assistant carried two armchairs and a sofa into the front room, and were quickly back with a sideboard and four chairs. A bright red carpet square completed the delivery.

Maude beamed happily as the furniture dealer drove away. "I've saved up a deposit, Pimbo, the money from Mrs Neal comes in handy. I can manage two shillings a week – I want Bob to come home to something, he frets at Papworth; thinks he's no man at all because he hasn't been able to do much about his home."

Pimbo felt as happy as Maude, first it was the kitchen – now all this; number ten Leeke Street was something to be proud of. At times, with Bob away, the home had seemed little more than a base; a base from which Maude left for work – or a base he had used for school or play.

Maude ruffled his hair. "I know you love going out, living out your day-dreams as you call it. I wondered if the home were better – you might be tempted to stay in more?" She laughed as though the thought was unthinkable.

"I don't suppose I'll change," said Pimbo, "now I

have the best of both worlds, a lovely home and adventure just around the corner."

The boy set-to helping his mother straighten up the new furniture. Maude moved things over and over again, until settling for a pleasing lay-out. "I suppose you thought it funny my being home today – well, I wanted to surprise you. Mrs Neal gave me the rest of the day off – now what about a nice pot of tea?" she said, bustling into the kitchen.

Mrs Bruce from next door came round on the pretence of borrowing a cup of sugar. "Very nice, I don't know how some people can do it. I suppose the boy brought in a bit of cash from his bravery lark. You wouldn't have thought he had it in him, still waters run deep – never a truer word spoken."

Pimbo remembered Mrs Bruce from the first moment he stepped into number ten. He had a vague suspicion that it might have been she who reported his foster-mother for allowing him out too often.

"Be able to stop in a bit more now you're ship-shape," Mrs Bruce went on, as she sized up the new furniture. "Roaming the streets won't do him a fat lot of good, eh Maude?"

"If I stopped in, I wouldn't get a chance for bravery; some boys stop in, some go out a lot. I don't cause trouble and I don't gossip," Pimbo found the words coming out unchecked.

Picking up her cup of sugar Mrs Bruce turned angrily on Maude. "Cheeky as well as brave, eh? I hope you don't put him up to this; maybe the Welfare people don't know about your little job at St Barnabas Road – on the side, eh? He'd better hold his tongue." Mrs Bruce stormed out slamming the door behind her.

Pimbo looked crestfallen. "I'm sorry Mum, I didn't mean to be rude – but somehow it just had to come out."

Maude poured two cups of tea, pushing one across to Pimbo, she seemed more serious than usual. "Do you remember your first day with us? Mrs Bruce followed me into the kitchen, she said something about 'not being able to beat a mother's love'. Next day I warned you about the danger on Newmarket Road as it was race day."

Pimbo nodded, he had remembered every moment of it.

"Well then Pimbo, I've something to tell you, I think you should know on account of your remarks about Mrs Bruce." Maude watched the surprised expression on Pimbo's face. "Mrs Bruce lost her only son, killed on race day at the top of the road. I'm afraid you remind her of her son. That's why she seems so concerned at your going out. Perhaps it was she who split on us to the Welfare – who knows? Perhaps she does it out of jealousy, because nothing ever happens to you – or because of a fear that one day it might."

Pimbo walked across to her and sat on her lap.

"I'm glad you told me, I want to know about things like that. Mr Adamson told me he's studying something about life – do you still like Mrs Bruce?"

Maude smiled, "Of course I do Pimbo, because I understand her – we must try and understand each other."

"But how can poor people understand – they can't do any good? When Mr Adamson understands, it's different – he can afford to do something about it. What can we do?" asked Pimbo.

"Just make things a little easier for each other,
that doesn't cost anything – now does it?" Maude
hugged Pimbo tightly and kissed him.

## A Cambridge Boyhood – revisited

### Coldham's Common

Undulating green mounds catch the eye,
Narrow winding paths afford quick "cuts",
In the background stand the Rifle Butts,
Where young territorials practise shoot-or-die.
In contrast, kiddies kneel to pick,
Their daisy chains – presents for the sick!

Coldham's Laundry hooter begins to holler,
A message to its dithering staff,
That wearily, take the well-worn path,
Back, to steam press, cuffs and collar.
The lazy stream trickles past the ridge,
On its surface, hover thunder flies and midge!

In a hollow, stagnates the swimming pool.
Young lads revel in the nude,
Innocence debunks all thoughts of rude,
As they swim in water, fresh and cool.
Across the way, sound of frenzied cries,
As Abbey United prepare for coming-Ties.

Courting couples, shyly pass,
Their shadows to slide,
From side to side,
Along the nettley grass.
But, now, their shadows gone,
Remain, just hallowed ground they fell upon!

Arnold's cows laze and munch away,
Blue tits cling to wayside trees,
United's flag wavers in the breeze;
As picknickers sound a round-de-lay.
Dear Common, with heart so stout,
Remain with us, till time runs out!

Fred Unwin

*Coldham's Common, scene of many boyhood adventures.*

*Elfleda House (Newmarket Road).*

# CHAPTER 9

## Pimbo fights the gang

River Lane school had broken up for the summer holidays; Pimbo finished top of his class, glowing with pride as he showed his foster-mother the end of term report.

"Tries hard in all subjects. I would like to see Jackie play a more active part in sport," the report read.

Maude smiled. "Sport must be about the only thing you don't play an active part in – what about it Pimbo, next term, eh?"

The chance came sooner than expected, Bobby Watson bringing round the news in the afternoon. Maude was out at Mrs Neal's.

"Dollar Smith's gang want a show down. Dollar's been away a month – and now you're better, they're screaming for revenge." Bobby's voice sounded less confident than usual. The rumour being that Dollar's gang had recruited boys from the near-by Romsey Town – a tough neighbourhood.

Pimbo nodded, he wasn't afraid. Many times his cowboy heroes, Tom Mix and Buck Jones, had been in similar situations. Thinking hard he tried to remember some of the ruses adopted by the cowboys. Somehow it wouldn't click.

Bobby went along with Pimbo to Mr Mansfield the stall-holder and carpenter. Pooling their money, and with a little goodwill thrown in by the friendly toy-maker, they managed to buy a number of wooden swords.

Wooden swords were a must for any gang worth its salt. There seemed a vast difference between an ordinary stick and a wooden sword. It was the same with badges. Milk bottle tops had no place in the equipment of a good gang – badges had to be something special.

Names too, had altered. 'Black-hand gang' or 'The hooded Terrors' had long since been thrown over. Bobby's 'Barnwell area gang' kept good standards. 'Barnwell area gang' sounded good, but not too violent. Many smaller gangs fought shy of challenging Bobby.

The fight was scheduled to take place at three o'clock. Bobby sent Ronnie Sanders to ferret out information. The battleground was a clearing in Gas Lane. A low brick wall running parallel from Petworth Street into Gas Lane shielded most of the waste ground from view.

Bobby's gang was running into difficulties. The end of term was an awkward time. Some of the gang had planned to spend part of their holiday in the country with relatives. The usual arrangement being that a relative, working on a farm, would give the town children a cheap holiday by allowing them to assist with the harvest.

Parents were only too pleased to get their youngsters away as soon as possible. Bobby was hit badly through many of his gang making an early exit to the harvest fields. Tich Coulson, Dollar's deputy –

must have been shrewd, thought Bobby. It was funny the fight being called for at a time when the Barnwell gang was so depleted. To worsen matters, Ronnie Sanders returned with the news that Tich had gathered together a formidable force and would indeed take a lot of beating.

Pimbo suddenly decided it about time his own considerable imagination were put to use as Bobby marshalled as many of the gang he could muster, and began a cautious march to the battlefield; Pimbo thought deeply as to how he could turn a likely looking defeat into a brilliant victory.

On the way to the battle Pimbo began thinking about Mr Adamson. Carrying a sword on the way to a fight was about the last thing the young student expected of Pimbo. He had told Pimbo that gang warfare amongst kids, resembled lion cubs at play with each other. It was a method of learning how to take hard knocks; poor kids had to do more of it than rich kids – because they had more problems. It was a kind of frustration, he said, like knowing that other people are better off than you – you just had to get it off your chest.

At last they were at the end of the brick wall in Petworth Street, the wall which ran alongside a narrow passage, carried on down to Gas Lane. On the other side of the wall was the battle area, peeping over Pimbo could see Tich Coulson and his gang also carrying wooden swords. The gang was practising lunges and parries and seemed in confident fettle.

Pimbo called Bobby over to discuss the plan he'd thought out on the way to Petworth Street, the boys huddled together as Pimbo's idea unfolded.

After a short time they dispersed under cover of the wall to the top end of Petworth Street.

Bobby at once started putting the plan into action. Jumping on the wall facing the Coulson gang, he bawled between cupped hands, "You've still time to call it off, Tich. I've got more men than you have – what about it?"

Tich Coulson seemed annoyed at Bobby's challenge and after a few moments deliberation with his gang, shouted back.

"You're bluffing, Watson, half your mob's on holiday – you're yellow – anyhow let's see them!"

From the cover of the wall Pimbo gave the signal for his plan to be put into operation. Suddenly the Barnwell area boys let go a terrible whoop – as though a horde of Indians were let loose. Boys with their wooden swords held two feet above the wall, began rushing from one end of the wall to the other. Reaching the end of the wall which led into Gas Lane, they suddenly lowered swords from view then crouching below the wall doubled back to the Petworth Street end – only to begin the mad onslaught again.

The loud screams of Barnwell's war chant, plus the seemingly endless supply of warriors, held Tich Coulson's gang rooted to the spot.

From his side of the wall Tich saw wave after wave of flashing swords, it seemed that Barnwell gang had hundreds of boys at their disposal. With only the top of the swords visible, Tich reasoned that things might be even worse – perhaps Watson was keeping his stone throwers as a final ace?

Without waiting further discussion the majority of the Coulson gang turned and fled.

Pimbo, although out of breath, felt strong and flushed with pride at the success of his plan. Walking across to Tich Coulson, he stood side by side with the dejected leader.

"It wasn't fair, you cheated us. We had more men after all," Tich stormed, catching sight of Bobby's depleted gang as they for the first time entered the battle zone.

"You called the fight, because you thought we'd be outnumbered – so now it's all square," broke in Bobby.

Pimbo looked at Tich, no doubt Mr Adamson would have said 'Brain over brawn', but somehow Pimbo didn't feel that way.

"We're starting a club on Monday, Tich. You can come if you want, there's boxing, ping-pong, and tea and cake for a penny. We're going to Hunstanton soon, if you join you'll be able to come, too," said Pimbo.

Looking round at the Barnwell gang, Tich felt that he could have won easily. Surely a skinny little runt like Pimbo hadn't enough brains to think up such a clever trick. Then he'd heard lots about Pimbo. Didn't he have a go at the sweet-shop? He was brave enough about the tramps and the donkey. They said he was a day-dreaming weakling, well then he wasn't doing too badly.

"I'll join, Pimbo. I reckon anything you tackle's bound to come right in the end. I'm glad I wasn't with Dollar that night, Mum said it's all right being in a gang – but Dollar wrote and told me to have the fight – now I'm glad it's all over."

On the way home Pimbo smiled to himself. The plan had worked out just as in the film, at the last moment he'd remembered Douglas Fairbanks doing it in the *Three Musketeers*. He knew the boys would have to be quick in running back to fool Tich into thinking they were a new batch of swordsmen. He reckoned Tich had at least thirty boys to Barnwell's dozen – something just had to be done.

The club was started off by Mr Adamson on the following Monday in premises which were once an old primary school long since finished. The building stood in Occupation Road almost opposite Mr O'dell the chimney sweep.

Pimbo called at the sweep's home to ask his son Jimmy to come along to the club. Mr O'dell seemed in good spirits, for once the donkey had been behaving well, and Pimbo was called into the house.

"Thanks for what you did about the donkey, boy, I haven't seen you since, they told me you were ill," the sweep said kindly. "By the way, the chap who runs your club had a chat with me the other day – it was about Jimmy cleaning inside the chimneys. I was wrong to use the boy, now Frostie the other sweep in this area is retiring, I shan't have the competition, Jimmy won't be doing it again." Mr O'dell's long speech caused him to cough and reach on the table for a large mug of tea.

The club started with a swing. The young leader told all the boys to call him Skipper, Pimbo thought it seemed much better than plain Mr Adamson. With Skipper were two undergraduates named Blackie and Silver. Blackie was a fair haired slim young Norwegian, who was studying sociology. Silver was a theological student from Africa studying for the Church.

Silver boxed for the University, his job was to teach the boys the basic skills of boxing. Pimbo had read about Jack Johnson the coloured world champion. Silver was a huge man and being coloured, Pimbo reckoned him hard to beat. He also reasoned that boxing must be a good thing to do, especially as Silver was going in to the Church.

Tich Coulson with several of his beaten gang turned up early in the evening. Tich, a small wiry boy showed an immediate interest in Silver and boxing. After a few rounds of shadow boxing with his instructor, Pimbo was soon out of breath and was content to watch other boys play ping-pong.

Skipper came along and sat next to Pimbo, offering him a sweet and chewing gum.

"Thanks for what you did for Jimmy O'dell," said Pimbo. "I'm glad that I can call you Skipper – it sounds nicer."

Skipper smiled. "Jimmy's dad took my chat well, I think he'll be treating the donkey better from now on – I had a word with him about that."

Pimbo noticed Bobby Watson was finding Tich Coulson quite a handful during the two boys' sparring session.

"The sweet-shop's closed, the old ladies had gone up North – I miss them," said Pimbo.

"The club will make up for the sweet-shop – I want all the boys to attend regularly," answered Skipper.

Pimbo looked up. "Are you running the club to find out about the boys around here – is it to do with what you learn at College?"

"Partly, but mainly for your pleasure. Now look at Tich Coulson, he's trying to belt the daylights

*S.A. Rolfe's famous shop. Nearby, can be seen Tiplady's dress shop.*

out of Bobby Watson and yet they're both smiling. You boys teach me – I just have to think about it."

A little later Silver walked over to Pimbo and sat down beside him.

"Want to ask me a question, Pimbo? They tell me you're a rare one for questions – I want to fix a special time as soon as the club gets going – 'Question Time' we'll call it, eh?"

Pimbo wasted no time. "You're going in to the Church, Mr Silver. Why are mothers with babies, called sinners? At the Citadel, Captain Woods calls them sinners."

Silver's broad genial features broke into a smile. "I guess I stuck my neck out for that one, Pimbo. But here goes. Jesus wanted every baby to have a real mother and father – it was a kind of unwritten law. It's not a good thing to start a kid off with something missing. There are two partners, one cares for the baby, the other provides food and clothes," whilst he spoke several boys ceased playing to form a group and listen. "I reckon some mothers don't stop to find a partner to provide food and clothes. Then trouble begins, sometimes the baby is put into a home – or the mother struggles on her own."

"But why do they go to the Citadel – why are they sinners?" broke in Pimbo.

"They realize that something is wrong, they know that Jesus forgives. They start all over again – then the baby receives a new kind of love. People at the Citadel do their best to help one another – does that satisfy you Pimbo?"

The boy nodded, he was glad to have asked the question. From the first day at the Citadel the problem had worried him.

Silver was now preparing tea and cakes, the boys had returned to their respective games. Bobby, who had been listening to Silver seemed deep in thought, Pimbo reckoned he was thinking up a way to beat Tich Coulson.

With the tea and cake interval activities stopped.

The boys formed a large circle with Skipper and his two colleagues sitting in the centre facing the boys.

The cake purchased from Pearks stores was liberally dotted with currants, at a halfpenny a large slice, most boys ate greedily.

"Well, what do you think of the club – so far?" asked Skipper.

Ronnie Sanders, small son of the escapologist, between a mouthful of cake managed to blurt out, "My mum thinks it's a catch – she says something's bound to happen."

"Such as?" smiled Skipper.

"You'll want money for this, money for that. She said she can't afford fancy things. If we play cricket – we'll have to play in ordinary togs," answered Ronnie.

"My dad reckons it's a catch," said a lad from Dollar's gang, "he said the authorities will be sending him notes, why haven't I got good shoes, why is my shirt patched? – he reckons it's to do with the school."

"What do others think – do you all think it a catch?" asked Blackie, who had been listening thoughtfully.

Tich Coulson spoke up, "I think it's good, I can learn to box, it's better than fighting. I reckon we can have a good club – we can challenge another club from the other side of the town."

"Why don't you give us the cake, instead of making us pay?" asked Jimmy O'dell.

Silver smiled across to Skipper, who had braced himself for the reply. "You'll enjoy things better when you pay for them. It's a lesson that we all must learn. I want the club to help you in more ways than sport. It's your club, you must make the rules, and I would like to see good rules. Next week bring along any rules which you consider should be adopted – that way your dads should know there's no catch – eh boys?"

Bobby Watson voiced his approval, saying that his dad was willing to put money into the club to give it a start; to everyone's surprise he produced five pounds.

"My dad said it's really because of Pimbo. He reckons I've been a better boy since meeting Pimbo he said that if Pimbo were a racehorse he'd back him every time."

Pimbo shyly lowered his head. Bobby had said nothing about the money to him, it was a complete surprise. As for his helping Bobby to become a better boy – he felt that Bobby had done much in making him feel stronger and ready to face anything.

"The club's for all of us. Skipper's started it to help us do things we can't do at school. I reckon Miss Lucy and Miss Mabel would be pleased the way we're going," replied Pimbo.

Skipper received the five pounds from Bobby. "Tell your dad the club will be firmly launched. The money will help pay train fares to Hunstanton – the whole club appreciate his gift."

Silver closed the club session with a short prayer. Pimbo peeping between his fingers – felt ashamed. Bobby's eyes were firmly shut – and hands clasped. Bobby usually didn't go much on this sort of thing.

# CHAPTER 10

## Pimbo's birthday parade

Bob Freestone was discharged from Papworth hospital on Pimbo's eighth birthday. The Citadel at Tenison Road put on a special tea for both. Bob looked much fitter, his cheeks had filled out and the suntan gained from the extra open air life had given him a more robust appearance.

In the morning the Salvation Army began their annual parade around the neighbourhood of all who were unable to attend the Citadel. The band and songsters met outside their building mustering a grand display of brass, bonnets and blue.

As the band moved off Pimbo, who marched at the rear with the songsters, felt proud as the column turned from Mill Road into East Road. The first call was at a small house at the bottom end of Bradmore Street. Mr Reeves, the occupant, living alone, was unable to do anything for himself; he was known as the Golden Dustman.

Bob and Maude Freestone, in the long winter evenings often told Pimbo stories about the people who lived in the East Road area.

Mr Reeves in his younger days, whilst working as a dustman, showed a warm spot for the extra poor and needy. Cast-off clothing of any value found in the bins from the better-off areas, would be deposited on the doorsteps of deserving cases.

One morning Mr Reeves was found badly injured in his little home. It was believed that thieves, hearing a rumour that the dustman had found a bag of golden sovereigns, attacked him in order to steal the money. After the incident he was known always at the Golden Dustman. But most people defined the word 'Golden' in memory of the kind acts done for his beneficiaries.

Opposite the Golden Dustman lived Nellie – no one knew her by any other name. For years Nellie had nursed her sick mother. One day whilst running an errand, Nellie was knocked over by a coal lorry – losing both legs.

Bob Freestone told Pimbo that after knocking at the door of her home, one would be kept waiting ages before receiving a reply. There would be a peculiar sound coming from the interior of the house and leading to the front door. It gave an impression of something being dragged along. The noise turned out to be Nellie, pulling her body along on a small trolley. As soon as money became available the Welfare people promised better things for Nellie; she was ever cheerful, looking foward to the band and songsters.

The Salvation Army next moved into South Street, a small street with a mass of terraced houses from end to end. In the centre of the street lived Granny Moden, aged ninety and almost blind.

Whilst away at war Granny's son had the misfortune to lose his wife. Granny Moden was left to look after her only grandchild Susan. Later her son was killed at Mons, leaving her the sole guardian of her son's child. Kindly neighbours helped sufficiently to allow Granny, despite her near-blindness, to keep her granddaughter at home.

One day Susan, then sixteen, was late coming in. She was talking to a group of soldiers at the corner of South Street. The girl, attractive and pretty, was good company for the young soldiers.

Granny, through scrimping and making do managed to dress her granddaughter very well – but Granny wore the poorest of clothes. Going into the street to fetch back the young girl, the old lady groping her way along suddenly came across the group of soldiers talking to Susan.

"Is that you Susan?" she cried out, half sensing her granddaughter's presence.

The soldiers began baiting the old lady, "Go away you old crow," they shouted. Then turning to Susan asked whether she knew the dirty old woman.

Susan denied all knowledge of her grandmother, who stumbling past was eventually taken home by a kindly neighbour.

Granny never seemed the same again, some people said that she knew what Susan had done. The old lady sat mumbling to herself, now and again seeming to be saying, "She denied me – she denied me."

Enjoying the band and songsters as much as the onlookers, Pimbo decided that one day he would join the songsters, at eight years of age he was feeling really grown-up.

Going round with the collecting bag, Pimbo sometimes drew back when a poor person wished to put in a coin. Then remembering the talk at the club he realized that they would feel better paying a little – even a halfpenny added up.

On East Road, next to Barbrooke's grocery store was a group of tiny houses with their front doors opening on to the public pavement. Pimbo smiled as the band approached. Bobby Watson some weeks previous had pointed out a curious building quirk.

When retiring to bed the resident of the centre house would be obliged to walk out on to the pavement in full view of the public. Next to his front door was a door leading up to a bedroom. On a windy evening the candle held by the frustrated resident became difficult to keep alight – causing much amusement to passers-by.

Bob Freestone was taking the marching well, despite his recent lay-off his stride seemed firmer than before.

During a pause for the giving of individual testimonies, Pimbo noticed an opening leading into a small yard. He remembered Bobby Watson telling him it was known as Whippet's Yard. Breaking from the column Pimbo ventured through into the yard.

In the yard centre stood an old standpipe. Around the square were old houses, most in a dilapidated condition – the standpipe appeared to be the only means of water supply. At night the yard was in complete darkness – only its inhabitants dared venture out. Sitting in the shadows, was a figure Pimbo thought he recognized. Moving closer in, to his surprise it was Old Jack the tramp he had rescued from the fire at Kidman's yard.

"Hullo," said Pimbo drawing closer to the tramp, "how are you? I'm surprised to see you here."

"You're a regular one for nosin' around – aren't you? Still you done me a good turn, I shouldn't complain. With the Sally Army, aren't you?" the tramp's voice seemed friendly enough.

Pimbo, pleased that the tramp was not angry with him, nodded.

"I used to be in the Sally, had a room in the *White Ribbon*, got kicked out for drinking. Reckon it was too much pressure from me so-called mates – they wanted to see me back in the gutter with them," Old Jack went on.

"Why are you telling me all this? You said I was a rare one for nosing around – yet you're making me want to ask questions," said Pimbo.

"Kids are easy to talk to. Helps to get it off my chest. You don't blame me, grown-ups do; they say 'you've made your bed – now lie on it.' They make me build a wall around myself to keep them out. You're different, you're inside that wall. People after the fire told me all about you Pimbo, that's your name isn't it?"

Pimbo shook his head. "I wish I could help you, I don't know why people talk about me – a boy my age wants to know about things – I can't help that can I?"

"All boys are nosey, Pimbo. I guess instead of being accident prone, you're sort of extra-nosey-prone. Something seems to lead you into situations beyond your years. Instead of my treating you like a kid, I feel that I mustn't let you down. You're driving my engine on a journey I want to go on – and yet as a passenger I feel it's a two way trip."

"What do you mean – a two way trip?" broke in Pimbo.

"I want to get back into the Sally Army, but deep down I'm afraid that I might not make it. If I could get my room back at the *White Ribbon* – I'd have another go at a job. That's one way Pimbo – the other way is back here in Whippet's Yard. That's what I call a two way trip.

From outside the yard Pimbo could hear the band striking up a well-known hymn.

"What if I speak to Captain Woods and tell him you'd like another chance – would you mind?" asked Pimbo.

Old Jack smiled at the boy, "I've nothing to lose, Pimbo – do that, you'll know where to find me – I'll not likely move away."

"Why do they call you Old Jack?" queried Pimbo.

"Old Jack, don't seem much of a name, I reckon that goes for the lot of us – just a symbol of all drunks," replied the tramp.

Pimbo stared at the group of derelict houses. At that moment the band was playing stronger than ever. He thought how strange it was the band visited places that seemed bereft of hope. Bob Freestone once told him that it was because poor people needed reminding that hope was for them, as well as rich folk who went to Church.

"Do you need hope?" Pimbo asked suddenly.

Old Jack smiled, "I keep up hope Pimbo. When you dragged me from the fire I said to myself if a kid bothers about me – well then I ought to have another go. I tried again, but drink got the better of me. Now I've seen you I'll have another bash, but kid, you get back to the band – you've seen enough

squalor for one day. I swear this time I'll fight
harder – tell Captain Woods, won't you Pimbo?"

On his return to the Citadel Pimbo told the
Captain of his meeting with Old Jack. The leader
seemed pleased at Pimbo's effort and promised to
see the tramp next morning.

During the birthday tea Pimbo met Mrs Neal
from St Barnabas Road who invited them all to her
home for a pleasant evening. Bob and Maude accepted with thanks, and Pimbo looked forward to
the welcome change.

The Neals' home was a large Victorian dwelling,
one of many in an exclusive residential area. Mr
Neal owned a tailor's shop in Trinity Street, situated in the centre of Cambridge. He was a friendly
little man, who immediately invited Bob and
Maude into his garden where his cultured roses
were the main attraction.

"The boy can stay with me," said Mrs Neal, who
seemed keen to make the most of Pimbo's first visit
to the house.

As he sat in the drawing-room Pimbo took in the
wonderful oil paintings that hung on the walls.
Heavy carpets, porcelain and china, brasswork of
all descriptions, were in direct contrast to the scene
he had left in Whippet's Yard.

Mrs Neal peeped through the window at her
visitors, then turned to Pimbo. "Your foster-
mother has told me all about you. Are you getting
better now? You know that you'll need plenty of
good food, fresh air, and warm clothing."

Pimbo nodded, "I know Ma'am. My mother does
what she can, I may not have to go back to the
Sanatorium. I'm very happy with her."

The tailor's wife frowned slightly. "These are hard times, my boy. A recent war, unemployment, strikes, means tests; how do you think you'll get on when you leave school – what sort of job will you be able to get?"

Bob Freestone would often search the *Cambridge Daily News* for job vacancies. Pimbo sometimes pretended that he too was searching for work. The vacancy list for school-leavers read usually: 'Errand boy wanted. Carrier bike, 5/- weekly'.

"I don't know really, I suppose something will turn up", answered Pimbo.

"Not much chance for such as you these days, wouldn't you welcome a better chance?" Mrs Neal's voice changed into a more urgent tone. Mrs Bruce and the losing of her son, came suddenly to Pimbo's mind – somehow there seemed to be a kind of connection.

"Have you lost a son?" he asked.

Mrs Neal stared at him for a moment. "Why do you ask? Your foster-mother has told me of your strange questions. I was going to ask whether you would like to make your home with me. I could give you a better chance, your foster-mother could see you every day – no I never had a son, no children at all."

Pimbo somehow felt sorry for her. "Mrs Freestone said that no one would take me away from Leeke Street. I want to stay with her, she'll be cross at what you have asked."

"I've been a fool, Pimbo. I ought to be ashamed of myself. I think only a woman would understand. You could never give me what I expect from a child – you've seen too much Pimbo. Now I realize that

you are where God meant you to be, captivating the
hearts of your own kind – you keep on doing just
that Pimbo."

"I'll not say anything about this to Mum," said
Pimbo. "Like Mrs Bruce, you mean well."

He suddenly thought of Skipper, Silver and Blackie,
and all the boys at the club in Occupation Road.

"Our club needs money. Bobby Watson's father
gave five pounds."

Pimbo's dimpled cheeks, the saucy smile,
brought light hearted relief for Mrs Neal.

"If that isn't bribery – what is?" she replied
laughingly. "Pimbo you're everything and more
that people say about you. I'll see that Mr Adamson
receives five pounds, now how about a nice piece of
cake. You're welcome at my home any time you
care to come."

With her husband's and visitors' return from the
garden, the remainder of the evening was spent
talking about Bob's sojourn at Papworth hospital.

At Leeke Street later in the evening Pimbo told
his foster-parents about Old Jack. Bob shrugged,
"It might work, remember what you did for Alf
Smith, he looks after his family a lot better now –
Alf and Old Jack might go back a few years, see
themselves in you; with a kid they can start from
scratch, that's why they don't want to let you down
– they'll be letting themselves down."

Bob paused for breath, then went on, "Here my
boy, you've done enough for one day, Mrs Neal gave
me five pounds to give Skipper towards your club
funds – you been up to your tricks again?"

Pimbo felt a little guilt, sometimes it seemed
that he didn't have to try, things just happened.

*A large fence surrounded the works. Squirrels could often be seen racing along the top of the fence in full view of passers-by. An adjacent clay pit supplied clay for children at the Open Air School.*

# CHAPTER 11

## Pimbo's day at the sea

During the next club meeting, Skipper told the boys that a trip to Hunstanton had been laid on. The news was received with loud cheering and clapping from the excited lads.

On the day of the outing the club met outside its premises in Occupation Road. Skipper carried a set of cricket gear, Blackie and Silver each had a large pack strapped on their back.

The boys walked the short distance to Cambridge station. Many were chatting and laughing, asking questions of those lucky ones who had travelled by train to the seaside before. Bobby Watson, one of the lucky ones, said the train would be reversed at King's Lynn, allowing another engine to be connected before making the last phase of the journey to Hunstanton.

Pimbo kept in company with Ronnie Sanders and Jimmy O'dell, both boys being so excited they seemed in danger of becoming lost. At Cambridge station the hustle and bustle of the cheery porters, the shrill whistling of the guards and the rush of passengers for the London trains kept the boys wide-eyed with excitement.

Tich Coulson with a few members of Dollar Smith's old gang was in the party. Pimbo noticed how friendly he seemed. He wondered whether Dollar would have tried to rob the sweet-shop had he been a member of the club . He reckoned belonging to a club made boys more loyal to each other.

"Now Pimbo, no day-dreaming. Here, carry this bag – they're potato crisps, you'll be hungry before we reach Hunstanton." As he spoke, Skipper began hustling his charges into the train. The boys excitedly craned their necks out of the carriage windows, arguing whether the train was moving or not. Skipper promptly made each boy withdraw his head. At last with jerks and pants, the train moved slowly out of the station. As it worked up a fine pace, Bobby Watson pointed out the approaching Barnwell bridge, then the magnificent sight of Ely Cathedral came into view.

Pimbo had been told at school how amidst poverty and unemployment the great cathedral was built. Many villages at the time considered it a waste of money. Now the cathedral had become world famous, bringing trade to the small fenland town of Ely.

Next King's Lynn appeared. The boys watched entranced as, true to Bobby's information, the engine was changed over to complete the remaining twenty miles of the journey.

Cries of, "I can see the sea" echoed through the corridors as the train chugged past fields of poppies, carnations, and many other flowers. Sandringham Castle flashed by but boys were too busy pointing out ships outlined on the vast horizon to listen to Skipper's guide-like monotony on the merits of Sandringham Castle.

Hunstanton with its red bricked buildings, friendly station, large green hills overlooking the sea, the wide expansive beach (so suitable for children) was now a stark reality.

Skipper, Blackie and Silver, could no longer hold back the excited lads. With a loud whoop, reminiscent of the Gas Lane battle, the entire club rushed on to the yellow inviting sands.

Taking the edge off the lads' excitement Skipper at once set up a two-sided game of cricket. As scorer, Pimbo was able to rest his back against a break-water, giving him an opportunity between overs to gaze out to sea.

He remembered a painting at the River Lane school showing a boy with wistful eyes watching an old sailor point out to sea. Often he'd wondered where the finger pointed. Now he could see the sea, so big he reckoned by the time one reached the other side, there would be very little to explore further.

Blackie drew his attention to the state of the cricket match, but like Pimbo other boys felt the call of the sea too strong – the match having to be abandoned.

Most of the boys had brought with them cotton bathing costumes. Mr Brown the rag man, to save his foster-parents extra expense, managed to look out one for Pimbo. The club leaders split the boys into three groups. "You must stay close together in the sea," warned Skipper. Pimbo's group leader was Silver, who, holding Jimmy O'dell by one hand and Pimbo by the other, jokingly thrust his big toe into the sea pretending to be afraid. As his feet entered the water for the first time, Pimbo felt a cold chill all over his body. Silver laughed as he cajoled the two boys to enter further watching with obvious delight the different expressions on their faces. With the sea lapping just below the knees, Silver called a halt.

Jimmy displaying an unexpected bravery, suddenly dipped his cupped hands into the sea – and splashed Pimbo. Not to be outdone, his pal returned the compliment. Soon Silver and the two boys, were merrily splashing each other. Boys from other groups joined in creating a huge spray of silver sea, cascading over white-skinned bodies.

"Right," shouted Skipper after a while. "Towelling and hot drinks – my lads. Last one out of the sea's a cissy."

Pimbo and Jimmy, between laughs and splashes, were the last to touch down.

"You two dish out the tea – that's the forfeit," laughed Blackie who already had made a dixie of hot tea.

Sitting cross-legged on the warm sand, the boys drank hot sweetened tea. From nowhere Skipper produced slaps of rich currant cake, smiling at Jimmy O'dell he laughed, "This is on the club, help yourself."

After the welcome snack a few boys began exploring the rocks. The sun now at its height was beaming down. Pimbo sitting alone took off his shirt. Before leaving home Bob Freestone had advised him to allow the sun to penetrate his body. "The sea air will do you good, boy. People won't believe that you've been to the seaside unless you're brown.

Pimbo reckoned he'd get nice and brown to show Jennie – she would be pleased. Suddenly he felt a cooling substance being rubbed gently into his back. Turning round he saw it was Silver who, with a huge grin, was producing the liquid from a bottle marked sun-lotion.

"You'll most likely blister, Pimbo. You see fair skinned people blister more easily."

Pimbo noticed Silver's dark torso as he too prepared for basking in the sun. "Why don't you need lotion, Mr Silver?" he asked.

Silver smiled. "I come from a hot country. My body is ready for the sun otherwise I too would blister."

Pimbo reckoned there was no such thing as a coloured person – it was just a matter of where they lived. Silver seemed to read his thoughts. "Should you visit my country your skin would gradually take on a darker hue, it's a kind of protection against the sun. Now you know, eh Pimbo?"

The boy started reckoning again. Silver was a coloured man, coming miles from across the sea to help out with a boys' club. He'd heard people grumble about such people coming into the country. Yet what was Mr Silver getting out of it. True he could no doubt afford it – but why?

"Why do you bother about us, Mr Silver, you seem so kind and think of even little things?" Pimbo asked suddenly.

"I reckon you're spoiling for another sermon, Pimbo. You do as much in your way – you help people. People that know about Jesus have to do things that Jesus did. He doesn't make you, it's a kind of loyalty – like the club's. Well,

THE BIRD IN HAND INN.

*An old picture of the "Bird in Hand" pub on Newmarket Road.*

say you join a cricket club – you play cricket. When you become a Christian – well then you do Christ's work."

Pimbo nodded. The Salvation Army was a good thing, he reckoned. Perhaps if he stuck at it he might be able to do things like Mr Silver.

"Hey Pimbo. That's enough. We're at the seaside remember. Come on, back in the sea, then we're going round the shops; you'll be wanting to take home a present for your parents – won't you?" shouted Skipper.

Silver helped Pimbo get ready for another bathe in the sea.

After a swim the leaders collected their groups and made plans to visit the shopping areas of Hunstanton. The streets were narrow and everywhere was colour. Bright coloured dresses, painted buckets, gaudy hats and pretty girls. Silver, pretending to be a grabbing money lender, handed each boy of his group a shining half-crown. Stopping outside a quaint little shop its window crammed with ornaments and sea shells made up into various shapes, the boys stood, trying to decide what they might take home as presents. Pimbo at last settled for a pretty little windmill. Painted near the bottom were the words, 'A present for Mum and Dad from Hun-stanton'. For Jennie Smith he purchased a small trinket box. He handed over the money to the shop owner, it came to exactly half-a-crown.

At length the shopping spree was over. Outside the shop Silver called out the names of the group. After a time it seemed that Jimmy O'dell, the sweep's son, was missing. With a worried look the leader returned into the shop. But Jimmy was nowhere to be found.

Pimbo suddenly remembered that on the way to the shops, the group had passed a small sandy field in which there appeared to be a kind of carnival in progress, a group of donkeys was being used to entertain the children. Knowing his friend's love for the small animals, Pimbo wondered whether Jimmy had made a quick trip to see the donkeys.

After listening to Pimbo's theory, Silver hurried the group down to the carnival. Elbowing their way through the crowded enclosure they at length reached the donkey stand. At the side of the fore-most donkey stood a small figure – to the relief of the group it was Jimmy.

"I'm sorry Mr Silver, I wanted to see the donkeys," said a disconsolate-looking Jimmy.

Silver smiled. "Thank goodness we've found you – well what do you think of the donkeys now you've seen them, my lad?"

Jimmy shrugged. "They're fatter than my Sooty, he's skinny. The neighbours make fun and say it's because my dad doesn't feed him – they're always saying something nasty."

"Don't worry what they say Jimmy, it's because Sooty moves about more. He'll probably live longer than the fat ones – it's not always good to be fat. Now come along all of you – else we'll miss the train," Silver patted Jimmy's head.

On the train bound for home, Pimbo adjusted his new cap, bought specially for the occasion by his foster-mother. The money had made a hole in the weekly budget and Mrs Freestone had warned Pimbo to take care and not lose it. But as he leaned out of the window to catch a last distant view of Hunstanton, a sudden gust of wind blew the cap billowing yards down the receding line.

Pimbo panicked. The words on a brass plate above his head caught his attention. 'To stop train pull cord'. He read no further. Standing on a seat he reached up and pulled down the cord.

The reaction was startling. Everyone stared in disbelief. The train begun slowly to grind to a halt. Excited murmuring swept through each corridor of the train, heads were poked out of the windows and arms were waving to and fro indicating from whence the cord had been pulled.

A fat little guard came panting down the line shouting, "Who pulled the cord? Who pulled the cord?" Reaching Pimbo's carriage he stared up at a sea of faces. In the centre was the red-haired dimpled face of a startled Pimbo.

"It was me, Sir. I've lost my cap, it cost one and six. I'm sorry but my mother will be cross," said Pimbo.

The guard almost exploded. "One and six is nothing against five pounds my boy. Can't you read? Wait until the station master hears of this."

Silver stepped out on to the line beside him. Bending over to the guard he whispered in the little man's ear – something inaudible above the hubbub of the excited children. From further down the line Pimbo could see another guard walking toward them carrying the coveted cap.

The little guard to whom Skipper had been talking, snatched the cap and handed it to Pimbo. "I don't suppose you'll ever pull another cord for the rest of your life, let that be a lesson."

Skipper climbed back into the train. With flags waving, and whistling, the train slowly pulled away. Pimbo started to cry, it was something he hadn't done for a long time. Things that happened, happy things, sad things, came easily to him. But somehow stopping the train was different. He had let Skipper down, perhaps the whole club as well. Most of the boys were staring at him, not knowing whether it was a good thing to do or bad.

Skipper smiled. "I suppose you could say it's a lesson about reading the small print of life, Pimbo saw only the words 'to stop train – pull cord'. In years to come you lads will remember this day – a day when you saw a communication cord pulled. Come to that I'd never seen a train stopped before."

Pimbo felt better, looking across at Jimmy O'dell he realized that now they both had something in common – first the donkeys, then the train. Jimmy too, was smiling.

Blackie and Silver, anxious not to lose dignity with the boys, eyed each other with misgivings. Suddenly Skipper let go a laugh which acted as a spur to set the whole carriage rocking with laughter.

The rest of the journey was spent in singing camp songs from a chorus book brought along by Blackie. Pimbo enjoyed the singing and quickly forgot the incident of the train. By the time Cambridge was reached the boys were feeling tired. Blackie piggy-backed Jimmy from the station to his home in Occupation Road.

Arriving home Pimbo told his foster-parents the exciting happenings of the day. Suddenly a sun-burned lad proudly brought out the ornamental windmill. Bob Freestone eyed the lettering 'To Mum and Dad', catching sight of the slightly dewy eye of his wife, before he too hastily wiped away a potential tear.

After a while Pimbo decided to take the trinket box round to Jennie.

When he arrived she was preparing for bed. Her mother appeared worried. Sensing Pimbo's enquiring look, she exclaimd, "Jennie doesn't seem to be well, I must get her the doctor – you may stay a little while but . . ."

Pimbo carefully unwrapped the trinket box handing it to Jennie. The girl's eyes sparkled as she took the box and fondled it.

"What's it for, Pimbo?" she asked gently.

Pimbo paused. Boys didn't know much about such things as trinket boxes. Funny thing he hadn't given it a thought, girls liked fancy things – then he remembered.

"You can put rings in it, fancy things, you can put your beads in when you go to bed," answered Pimbo.

"I put my beads under the pillow every night, don't I Mum?"

Mrs Smith smiled, happy to see her daughter looking brighter. "Well then you can put them in the box first, then under the pillow," she offered kindly.

Pimbo realized how much Jennie thought of the beads he'd bought at Easter. He supposed Mrs Neal would have real beads, real silver trinket boxes. But then she couldn't be any more happy than Jennie looked at that moment.

Jennie's mother gave Pimbo a look which seemed to mean that Jennie should be getting to bed. Catching a side glance Pimbo noticed how pale and drawn Jennie looked.

"Good-night Jennie. I'll call for you in the morning – if you don't go to school I'll be able to see you," said Pimbo. Somehow he felt that Jennie was going to be away from school a very long time.

# CHAPTER 12

## Pimbo visits Jennie

Next day Pimbo called to see how Jennie was getting on. Mrs Smith looking very worried, told him that he could stay a short while as Jennie had been asking for him.

"The doctor will be calling at eleven o'clock, you'll have to go as soon as he comes," her voice trailed off into a sob.

Jennie was sitting up in bed, her face flushed, she complained of a sore throat. "I'm starting cookery classes next term – the school is in East Road," she said softly.

Pimbo remembered Dobbler's Hole where Chatty Collins' barber shop stood. The cookery school was a large black hut further down from the shop. He remembered seeing girls in long pinafores going in and out during an exchange of classes.

"Miss Mason said learning to cook might help me when I grow up – do you think it will Pimbo?" asked Jennie.

Pimbo smiled, he thought of a story in *Chips* about a girl who, despite being poor, learned to be a good cook. Her ability soon spread around and she married a well-to-do gentleman who was always happy because not only did he love the girl, but was also fond of her cooking. He told Jennie the story, and of how it ended in pointing out that sometimes rich girls, who are bad cooks, drive husbands away – and therefore are no better off through being rich.

"You'd better rest your voice, now," warned Pimbo. "I've brought you some comics – would you like to read them?"

Jennie picked up a copy of *Tiger Tim*, it was coloured and easy to read.

Just at that moment Jennie's father entered the room with a special drink for his daughter – he handed Pimbo a cup of tea.

"Haven't seen much of you lately Pimbo, how are you?" Alf asked good-naturedly. "I've started a job at the Maltings in Ditton Walk – it's hard work shovelling dusty barley, but I'm going to give it a try boy." Pimbo nodded. Nowadays people were talking well of Alf. They said he drank less, and with his wife bringing in more money from her college job, Alf was steadily building a better home. Alf went on. "They tell me you've been putting in a word for Old Jack. Captain Woods has put him back in the *White Ribbon*. He's found him a job on the ferry at *The Plough*."

*The Plough* was a public house in Fen Ditton which college students patronized during the 'bumps' rowing season. The ferry transported townspeople and students alike, from the Chesterton side of the river to the Ditton side in which *The Plough* stood. Pimbo presumed that Captain Woods must have decided in putting Old Jack to a real test, as *The Plough* was a favourite drinking haunt.

By now Jennie had finished reading *Tiger Tim* and was finishing her drink. Pimbo heard a rap at the front door, then the voice of the doctor as he mounted the stairs.

"I'll see you again Jennie," said Pimbo.

Outside the entrance to Brown's Yard, he waited until at last the front door opened to reveal a worried looking Mrs Smith and the doctor.

"Don't worry Mrs Smith, the isolation hospital will take care of your little girl – it shouldn't be too long before she's back with you again." The doctor turned to Jennie's father. "Ring for the ambulance right away, I must go on ahead with my notes," he ordered, as he hurried away.

After the doctor had gone, Rose Smith beckoned Pimbo to the door.

"Jennie's got diphtheria, she's going to the fever hospital in Mill Road. I've heard awful reports about the place – but Dr Webb says she must go – because it's infectious," she began to cry. Before Pimbo could console her, the sound of the ambulance sent her scurrying upstairs to prepare Jennie for the short journey to Mill Road.

After Pimbo had related the bad news, Maude Freestone warned him of a possible danger to himself. "The report from Dr Phillips on your last X-ray showed an improvement. More consistent reports might mean putting you on long term – which is a good sign of recovery. I hope you've picked up nothing from Jennie – diphtheria's a killer Pimbo, remember you're far from out of the wood yourself. You'd better stay away from the Smiths until things clear."

Realizing that his foster-mother's worry must not go unheeded, as the days passed by Pimbo felt an uncontrollable urge to find out how Jennie was getting along. He decided on catching Alf Smith at his work place, the Maltings. On the second attempt Pimbo was lucky. Alf was about to mount his cycle outside the Malting gates, he looked worried as he spotted the boy.

"It's bad news Pimbo. Jennie's got paralysis, she can't move her legs. It's on account of the poisons from her diphtheria, the doctor says it might affect her breathing." Jennie's father stared at Pimbo. "She insists on us putting your present from Hunstanton under her pillow. I wish you could see her Pimbo – it would cheer her up. We told the doctors about you, but they know about the Sanatorium and wouldn't hear of your coming to the hospital."

That evening Pimbo called on Bobby Watson who had an aunt living close to the hospital. Bobby listened intensely as his pal told the story of Jennie's misfortune.

"What's the hospital really like?" asked Pimbo suddenly.

Bobby paused for a second, staring at his friend. "I've heard that you have a soft spot for Jennie, I can't say that I blame you – you're that sort. I'm different, 'me dad and mum are always arguing' I told Silver at the club, he said 'that's why you're so keen on fighting'. I reckon your dad and Mum don't argue, they go to the Sally Army, so you look out for gentle things – Jennie's gentle, ain't she Pimbo?"

"But what's that to do with it?" said Pimbo.

Bobby shrugged. "I've heard me aunt talking, she used to work at the hospital where Jennie is.

She reckons they do all they can, but they put kids on their own in little rooms. Sometimes they die because no one's allowed to see them, she reckons there's no love from their parents – just nurses. It ain't the hospital's fault, it's because they call it infectious." Bobby watched Pimbo's intense look as he went on. "I can tell you something awful – shall I?"

Pimbo gave a look meaning him to go on.

"Auntie told me about a kid with diphtheria. One night an attendant was left alone with the kid in a side room. The kid had been breathing so badly that the doctor inserted a silver tube in her throat. The kid was found dead in the morning. They reckoned that the attendant was a heavy drinker, she stole the silver tube, and sold it to buy drink."

Pimbo stared unbelievingly. "But the hospital, they weren't to blame."

Bobby shook his head. "Me aunt reckoned if the kid's parents had been better off, a proper nurse would have been in charge."

Pimbo wondered why it was that small boys had to find out such things of life.

"Still they don't all die," said Bobby, noticing Pimbo's worried frown. "Me aunt said that some parents demand to take their children home, Jennie's parents love her – p'raps they may do the same?"

Arriving home Pimbo found that his foster-parents had heard about Jennie's paralysis. "I spoke to Mrs Neal about Jennie, she hopes that she'll soon be better. Once the crisis is over, she said, it'll be just a matter of time before Jennie will be up and about again." Maude placed her arm around Pimbo's neck and kissed him. "Besides, Captain Woods mentioned Jennie in the prayer circle – what about that, eh?"

Two days later Pimbo met Alf Smith at the top of Brown's Yard. "I haven't been to work for a week, Pimbo. I'm worried sick, Jennie doesn't seem to want to live." As he spoke Alf turned, pointing to the yard. "What's she to come home to, a brick wall and cobbles. Another thing Pimbo, this worry is giving me an urge to go drinking again – for Jennie's sake I'm fighting hard, but I just don't know how it will end."

Pimbo thought of Mrs Neal's beautiful garden, and her husband's cultured roses. He visualised Jennie sitting in the garden amongst the roses. Bob Freestone once told him that he thought Mr Neal had more concern for his garden, than his wife and home. Pimbo wondered whether Mrs Neal's approach to him about living at St Barnabas Road, had something to do with this theory. Somehow, thought Pimbo, Jennie had to get better; also if Alf went back to drinking the little family would sink to nothing.

The following day Pimbo called on Mrs Neal. He told everything he knew about Jennie, the hospital and her father.

Mrs Neal smiled kindly. "I understand Pimbo, I too have heard stories about the Mill Road fever hospital. Some are true, many are not. Mothers whose children had been spared speak kindly of the hospital, others not so fortunate become bitter and look for somewhere to lay the blame. Diphtheria is a terrible thing, I agree that Jennie at her home in Brown's Yard might not do as well in

*Abbey United. First Team 1926-27 Season. Now Cambridge United.*
*Back Row: C. Morley, Bill Walker, Joe Livermore, Fred "Erstie" Clements, Harvey Cornwell, Harold "Darley" Watson. Front Row: Dick Harris, Edward Fuller, George Alsop (Captain), C. Clements, Freddie Stevens. Photograph by Scott and Wilkinson.*

convalescence as . . ." She paused and glanced across at Pimbo who seemed surprised at her sudden change of mood. "You're at it again Pimbo. But remember, there's no place like home, however poor. Home is home. Your foster-mother has told me about the beads and trinket box. I think Jennie will get better, especially when she can see you again. When Jennie's crisis is over I'll contact the hospital, Jennie may stay with us until she's well again – now does that make you happy?"

Before he could reply, Mrs Neal handed him a chocolate from a large ribboned box, then walking into a small box room at the side of the hall, returned carrying a new steel bowling hoop. Fixed to the hoop was a steel loop and leather handle with which to trundle it.

"Pimbo, I want you to promise that whenever you feel unhappy you'll use this hoop. You see, I don't want you to grow up too quickly. Now you may go and tell Jennie's parents all I have said."

She handed over the hoop to a smiling Pimbo. No boy in Leeke Street owned anything to match this new shining hoop, most were made of a cheap wood and broke easily.

Outside Mrs Neal's home he started bowling the hoop. It clanged merrily along the pavement, bounced over kerbs, and righted itself with a skilful twist of his wrist. It seemed that nothing else mattered, bowling a hoop was grand thought Pimbo, shops, houses, whole streets and people flashed past, mere incidentals in a new found world of childhood, displaying Pimbo no longer an old head on young shoulders, but a boy, bowling his hoop, a bouncing clanging circle of metal taking him away from illness, stealing, fighting, into a scurrying whirligig of childhood.

Past Gwydir Street, home of his beloved Kinema, into Milford Street, through to Occupation Road, and finally on to Newmarket Road. Pimbo felt the colour rising to his cheeks, his legs felt stronger than ever before. Skipper said that one day he would be strong enough to do all the things that boys like Bobby could do. Somehow Mrs Neal must have known what a hoop could do for a boy – she was very kind.

Leaving the hoop outside Brown's Yard, he went

inside to tell the Smiths the goods news from Mrs Neal. Jennie's parents were delighted with the proposal.

A week later Jennie reached the critical stage of her illness, meantime Mrs Neal had convinced the hospital authorities of her willingness to allow Jennie to convalesce at St Barnabas Road. As soon as the crisis had passed, Jennie was sent directly to Mrs Neal's splendid home.

On Pimbo's first visit, Jennie was sitting out in the garden. It was a beautiful day with the roses looking their best. Mrs Neal had produced a pretty bed-jacket in pink, which Jennie was wearing. Against the girl's wan complexion it enhanced the delicate paleness of her skin.

"Hullo, Pimbo, I'm so glad to see you, I asked for you at the hospital – but they wouldn't let you come," said Jennie gently.

Pimbo looked at his little friend, they were alone in a pretty garden. "I'm glad to see you too, Jennie. Mrs Neal said that you may stay here until you're better. Skipper said you can come with the club to Hunstanton when next we go."

Jennie smiled, "What's it like at the seaside, Pimbo? I've never been."

"It's lovely, the sea's so big, and the sand so soft. You can enjoy yourself, and yet it doesn't cost a penny. It's just like God saying, 'This is yours – have it on me'. The time goes so quickly Jennie, you don't want to come away – that's why everyone wants to go again – to make up for lost time.

Mrs Neal came into the garden, giving them each a glass of lemonade. "Try not to talk too much, Jennie," she said kindly.

"Jennie must rest as much as possible – why not read one of the books to her, Pimbo?"

From a pile of books at Jennie's side, he picked up a small brown volume. The title read, *What Katy did at School*.

Pimbo read softly and slowly. The warmth of the afternoon sun gradually permeated into the frail body of the young girl. He watched as the mounting colour of her cheeks contrasted with the brilliance of the roses. Sleep at last overtook her, as the story of Katy unfolded into her world of Brown's Yard, the isolation hospital, and now the lovely garden of the Neals'.

Pimbo stayed on as Jennie's sleep grew deeper and deeper. Then as he moved away from the sleeping figure, Mrs Neal beckoned him into the kitchen, offering a piece of cake.

"The more Jennie sleeps, the stronger she will become. Thank you for coming Pimbo – you are like a medicine. I told the doctor about you, he said it was good for Jennie to have someone her own age around."

Pimbo smiled at the compliment. "How is my foster-father getting on at Mr Neal's shop? He told me about your husband giving him a part-time job, but he doesn't have much time to tell me about it."

"Pimbo, I would think it difficult to nail you down for five minutes during any part of the day. Bob's doing well, Mr Neal is thinking of offering him a full time job, as soon as he's strong enough to do the extra hours."

"When I leave school, Mr Neal might find me a job – do you think so, Mrs Neal?" asked Pimbo.

The tailor's wife smiled, "I see you've brought your hoop, now cut along home. I suggest you find time to talk to your foster-father – tell him about Jennie. But please Pimbo, think about yourself a little – it's good for you."

Alf and Rose Smith were delighted when Pimbo called and told them of Jennie's progress. They each planned to visit her on the morrow. Alf looked across at Pimbo, who sat at the table. "At first, I wouldn't agree with Jennie going to the Neals, I thought people would talk and say that we weren't capable. Then I realized that Jennie came before pride. Thanks for all you've done Pimbo – with you around Jennie will soon be well."

Pimbo smiled back at the happy couple, he compared the quality of their home to that of the Neals'. He remembered Mrs Neal saying, "Home is home, however poor" it was the same for him, he thought. The Freestones were so kind, they allowed his wandering as a stray cat – but they knew he loved them, and would always respect number ten Leeke Street.

Looking once again at the Smiths' smiling faces, Pimbo reckoned that the world ought to stay that way – for everybody.

# CHAPTER 13

## Pimbo visits Nelson Street Mission

On a wet Sunday evening whilst at a loose end, Pimbo decided to call in at the little Mission hut in Nelson Street. Often while making a call on Bill Westley the ragman, Pimbo would pass the tiny place of worship. He had often been tempted to find out exactly what the services had to offer.

Mr Twinn, a wizened little man with a high pitched voice was its leader. At the bottom of the hall was a kind of balustrade similar to that used in Pimbo's favourite films of cowboys. Mr Twinn would stand in its centre delivering a passionate plea for all to repent. At a certain point in his delivery the leader would actually cry real tears; with arms waving emotionally, he would beckon youngsters to the front of the balustrade where in a prominent position was placed a wooden form, this was known as the repentant form. Usually a fair number of adults were present and of these Mr Twinn would attract a good percentage who would obey his call.

Shaking hands with Pimbo the leader led him to a front row which was mostly taken up by boys. Recognising a few boys from East Road school

Pimbo accepted the dog-earned hymn book which was passed from hand to hand. The boys began lustily to sing the opening hymn "Onward, Christian Soldiers". Undoubtedly Mr Twinn had chosen a good number, the boys, as though fighting against the very conditions of their lives, stamped out every line swinging sideways to the marching lilt.

After a few local forthcoming attractions had been read out Mr Twinn standing dead centre of the balustrade began his address. "We have new faces here tonight, my friends. Boys who are hungry to know about Jesus. I too was as these lads, roaming the streets, getting into trouble. In those days there was no Nelson Mission, oh no my friends. Plenty of pubs, plenty of gin, but no place for a child to drag himself out of his misery." Pausing for his words to register he went on, "but all the time Jesus was beckoning me, calling me to do this work. I found a place like this, yes, it was raining as it is now. I looked in for comfort and found a Comforter. Years later I opened this Mission hoping that I would find other boys in need such as I was. Boys came and brought their parents. Jesus doesn't do things by halves. The Mission grew and today I stand here and ask you to Come. Come boys, leave misery behind and find a new joy in the Lord. You may be poor in kind but you'll be rich in spirit. Jesus will make you happy as a King. In old boots, in old clothes you can be dressed in the robes of the Lamb."

Now the tears were streaming down the Leader's face. Real tears running on to his chin and in glistening droplets hanging precariously until finally dropping into nothingness.

"You Come, you Come, Mums and Dads, sons and daughters – you Come and taste His blood."

Bill Westley was in Pimbo's thoughts. He remembered how mentioning the Mission had wrung a little kindness from the old man. I can hear the singing Bill had said and the boy wondered how many kindnesses had been lullabied from the rag-man over the singing years.

Several people were moving from their seats, some clutching children walked starry-eyed toward the wiry little man who, beckoning, ever beckoning, bending low over the railings, chanting, crying, singing choruses, edged them on and on towards the mercy seat.

"Leave it all behind" he was saying "you Come and sample the Blood of Jesus Christ."

Pimbo watching entranced as the group reached the wooden form. Kneeling down they placed their heads sideways on the form. Mr Twinn came down from his lofty dais, touched them each on the head "Jesus, Jesus" he breathed over them. A soft cushion of words, gentle amd forgiving, they sighed in ectasy as though their burdens had been lifted.

Then the remainder of the congregation sang "Just as I am without one plea". Somehow for that moment poverty was forgotten. Careworn mothers were smiling at beaming youngsters, a rainbow of hope had lit the little hall as Mr Twinn, turning tears into smiles sang gently and comfortingly to the congregation.

From his position on the flank of his row Pimbo had a good view of the spectacle. A door at the side of the building suddenly attracted his attention. It was being slowly opened revealing the unkempt

figures of three boys. Pimbo recognised them immediately. Moving silently from his position he
tiptoed across to the door. The boys whose hands
were holding half bricks dodged quickly back. As
the singing continued Pimbo, noticing a key in the
inside of the lock, grabbed it and slipping through
the half-open door to the outside inserted the key
into the lock and turned it.

This action caused him to come face to face with
the young ruffians in a small passageway. "Proper
little hero ain't you Pimbo" remarked the tallest of
the three boys "spoiling our fun eh? A nice brick
dropping on to the organ might have given us a
laugh – how about us dropping one on you
instead?"

As he spoke the boy beckoned the others to move
forward, a move which caused Pimbo to be trapped
with his back to the passage wall. "I don't spoil fun,
I like fun. Throwing bricks isn't fun, Mr Twinn
does his best for us – why interfere with a good
man?" said Pimbo quietly.

"My Dad reckons he ain't that good. Talk's cheap
– what happens to the collection every week. Besides it don't get people jobs, it don't bring extra
food into the house – it'll still be rainin' when they
go home."

"Throwing bricks will do more harm than Mr
Twinn. Your Dad's never been, it's only hearsay.
Bricks will turn to dust, it says so in the Bible. But
Jesus's word will last for ever – the crowd stoned
him, but Jesus is alive today – Mr Twinn said so"
answered Pimbo.

"You won't do good against bricks" mocked the
boy, who Pimbo remembered was known as Bob

Mountford. He was well known for vicious behaviour and at one stage had been before the
Probation Officer.

Looking sideways down the alley Pimbo reckoned that the passage led out about halfway into
Nelson Street. The singing from the hall, to his
relief, had reached a crescendo. A shaft of light
suddenly forked out from the back way of one of the
houses. Turning his head in the direction of the
light Pimbo luckily evaded one of the half bricks
thrown by the smallest member of the trio. Crash-
ing against the wall close to his head it dropped at
his feet unbroken.

Stooping quickly Pimbo snatched it up and faced
his tormentors. "One of you will get it, if it was good
enough for David against Goliath – it'll do me" said
Pimbo defiantly. He remembered Mr Twinn saying
"the Devil doesn't have all the tunes."

In the ensuing silence Pimbo watched as in the
direction of the light the closing of a back door
could be heard. The shaft of light must have been
caused through a door opening thought Pimbo – if
only the occupant were coming out into the street
he would have to enter the bottom of the passageway. To his relief the slow tread of a man could be
heard moving away from the house. Suddenly a
white figure from the gloom of the passageway
trotted into their presence – it was the dog belonging to Bill Westley.

"Here boy, here boy" shouted Pimbo excitedly
"come and get 'em, bite 'em boy, bite 'em."

Dropping the bricks as though they were hot, the
three boys rushed past Pimbo into the street. Bill
Westley's slow moving figure followed behind that

of his dog, whose age would allow no more than a slow wavering gait. Pimbo's call had made no impression at all.

The bobbing white eyeshield of the ragman showing up in the passage gloom was coming closer. "Having me constitutional boy, I like to come by when they're singing – what's the commotion?" Bill asked as he drew level with Pimbo.

"Some louts throwing bricks. Trying to break-up the meeting, it's a good job you came along – they were three-to-one" said Pimbo noticing the cessation of the singing and the sudden emergence of Mr Twinn.

"You must come into the Hall for a cup of tea" said a thankful Leader. "You both have played a part against those young ruffians I'm sure!"

In the warmth of a little side room Pimbo and the ragman sat drinking hot chocolate, a sudden change by Mr Twinn on the promised tea. "Do you more good on a wet night. I'll leave you awhile, I've some writing to do, see you later" smiled the Leader.

Bill's dog, to Pimbo's surprise, was lapping up a saucer of the welcome beverage which his master had artfully supplied on the exit of Mr Twinn. Looking down at the unlikely pair Pimbo was thinking how it was that God seemed to utilise every conceivable force. Mrs Todd appeared as a shining Angel amongst the Smart's Row residents, Billy Sparkes from such unreliable influence as his father still managed to trot out enough principle to help a school chum. And now Bill Westley and his dog had emerged as knights in shining armour.

"I know what you're thinking, boy" said Bill suddenly. "Why don't I come along to the Mission. I couldn't leave me dog for one thing, and for another I reckon I'm too old for an apprentice. I found out all about religion years ago, I like to hear the singing – but there's nothing new in it for me. When they sing 'Give me an old time Religion' that about sums it up for me."

"But how can you put what you've learnt to a good purpose?" asked a perplexed Pimbo.

"I'm doing it every day, boy. Take my trip into Barrow Road and such like. Proper toffs those ladies. They throw out good clobber. But they don't appreciate the good things. I reckon they come too easy. Take those boots for Billy Sparkes, his old man would have flogged 'em for a pint. I reckon God has to have a kind of middle man, someone to fetch and carry. That's why I don't waste time at the Mission, I kind of get on with it, a bit of singing, I love me dog, and I think about God when I'm on me own.

Mr Twinn was back. He was beaming as he entered the room. "Any more chocolate, ah, a saucer eh? Seems your dog is well trained Mr Westley – he doesn't leave a drop. I must thank you over again. I'm sure the Lord has smiled on us all tonight." Glancing down at Pimbo the evangelist smiled "I hope we shall be seeing you again – each week I hope. Pimbo they tell me, that's what they call you isn't it?"

Nodding, Pimbo got to his feet. "I go to the Sally Army as well. But I'll come again, Mr Twinn, I feel good when I hear you preach, my parents reckon that going somewhere is good for you. Mum says it stays with you all your life no matter how poor one is. Some boys come in just because it's raining but I reckon God knows and doesn't mind. Boots take water and boys catch cold, your Mission hall is warm, and you don't mind – do you Mr Twinn?"

"The three boys who were molesting you outside, I would welcome them in, anytime they like to call. You tell them Pimbo, do you know them?"

"Only one, Bob Mountford" replied Pimbo "the other two just follow him around, I reckon they're not bad really, it's just that no one seems to be able to help them."

Bill Westley was moving to the door with his dog in close pursuit. He had been taking in the conversation. "I know Mountford's father – went to school with him. Like father, like son they say. Not far wrong neither. He was a tear-away, wouldn't listen. Got killed in the war he did. They say that he was real brave, threw himself over a mortar shell to save his pals. His son's got a bit of it in him, must have excitement. I reckon he'd do the same in a war, just like his father. How do you explain what God thinks about that, him saving his pals – I reckon it takes a bit of doing, I mean – him saving his pals."

Mr Twinn, stroking his chin looked across to the ragman. "You're so very right, Mr Westley. It takes all kinds to make a world. We must allow for God knowing a little more than we. This Mission hall is for everyone, as I said Bob and his friends are ever welcome. And Pimbo, I would like you to speak to them. Boys have their own way of putting things over – I'll leave it to you."

"What can I say that might improve on you – I'm not a preacher man, Bob's tough, he might laugh" said Pimbo.

Walking with Pimbo to the door Mr Twinn ruffled his fingers through the boy's carroty hair.

"No such thing, my lad. When I preach I watch carefully. Some accept what I say as a kindness to them, they see in my words an offer from Christ, it gives them a chance to choose. They know that they'll never be rich, but they also accept that their lives may be made easier. It will be a means of making life tolerable. But maybe Bob Mountford accepts it differently. To him it's a condemnation, it makes him feel guilty, then he gets mad and fights against it in the only way he knows – bad behaviour." Pimbo frowned as he stared up at the Leader. "Do you get disappointed when people don't get out of their seat. When you say 'Come', and they don't come? There were only a few tonight, what about the others?"

"I never went down to a mercy seat, I did it myself when alone. It's all the same, there's nothing magic in it. It's what you do afterwards, how you feel. When you do it properly it lasts a lifetime, and you know that you were right. People can laugh, they make fun, but usually you outgrow them. As you grow older, you get desperate, you want to have time to tell more people – that's why I asked you to see Bob, he won't expect you to preach to him – that's where a boy might well catch a boy."

Thinking of the 'I will make you fishers of men' phrase, Pimbo, on the way home gave it much thought. He reckoned that the Mission hut was a good place to go. In the nearby streets he knew that behind the windows sat many an old grannie clutching a Bible. It was they who were instrumental in getting grandchildren off to Sunday school. Some mothers had given up the struggle, but Granny would have none of it. Hadn't it seen her through the lean years. Now with plenty of time to sit at the window and think – well at least she would hand over the Torch to her new generation. Pimbo reckoned that Sunday schools were all over the world in some form or other. People who didn't go to Church or anything might still be used in helping. Bill Westley was one, Emma Todd another.

Walking along East Road he passed a few people on their way home from the Mission. They were discussing him as he passed. "Bit young for Bible punching – must be a bit crackers if you ask me" one person was saying. "Got to start some-time I suppose. His parents are Sally Army, real staunchers, I suppose they force him to go."

A small figure standing at the top of Moden's hill greeted him – it was Billy Sparkes. "Where've you been. I called for you, I was going fishing, they say that mud gudgeons bite better when it's raining."

Looking down at Billy's new sturdy boots, the jam jar, cane and string with bent pin, Pimbo laughed outright. He thought of Mr Twinn's hint of fishing for men, Bill Westley's kindly services and Billy's remark that fish bite better when it's raining – and he thought again about the crowd of lads that pop into the Mission hall when it rained.

*The Nelson Street Mission Hall conducted it's first service in 1905. Mr Alfred Mansfield, a Bible Study pioneer, used the hall until the members, outgrowing the premises, then moved on to Lower York Street mission building.*

## Staffordshire Street – on Saturday Night

From East Road end, comes drifting down,
smell of Taylor's fresh-baked roll.
Haynes' bubbling peas, Spiv's chocolate brown –
far better than the dole.

Old Bowie's dogs, sound watchful bark,
Tom King's ponies show their stride;
the street's alive from dawn to dark,
no child is kept inside.

Hop-scotch screams pollute the air,
boots, clear chalk-marked zone.
Come blaring tunes from summer fair,
but children stay at home.

Bedders return from College chores
with baskets weighted down,
luck has opened larder doors,
and hid their hungry frown.

In Tom King's Yard, deep in mud,
men show bright orbs of steel:
their quoits, tossed skilfully into slud,
may win an extra meal.

Terraced homes, packed so tight,
house families fraught with strife
Heaven for them – is Saturday night –
and dreams of a better life.

Fred Unwin

*Staffordshire Street, a scene of Pimbo's boyhood –
now a neat array of new homes.*

# CHAPTER 14

## Pimbo goes down to the river

A few days later Bobby Watson called for Pimbo earlier than usual, it was the day of the New-market races. Cars and all types of vehicles would be teeming past the top of Leeke Street overlooking Newmarket Road. Whilst awaiting the arrival of the first batch of racegoers the two lads popped into the bootmaker's shop owned by Mr Cash.

The old bootmaker made riding boots and all kinds of equipment appertaining to the horse rac-ing industry. He was a kindly old fellow, bent in stature, but lively in wit.

Owing to the nature of his vocation Bobby's father would often call in the little shops, making it easier for his son when bringing in a friend.

Mr Cash pointed out a beautiful pair of shining riding boots, that were proudly prominent in the centre of a small window facing the street. "There you are my boys, the first pair of riding boots worn by Fred Archer," he said proudly.

Pimbo was allowed to fondle them and feel the quality of the lovely brown leather, he compared them with those handed out at the police station. Mr Cash smiled, pointing out into the street. "From this shop I've watched kings, theatre folk and celebrities pass on their way to Newmarket. I've seen fashions in both dress and cars change unbelievably."

"Is that why they call it the Sport of Kings?" Pimbo asked.

The old leather worker put down his awl, "I wouldn't say that boy, for many years poor people have lined up on both sides of this part of Barnwell just to see rich people go by in cars, buses, even taxis. In so doing they took part in something that otherwise they were denied – they watched people doing things which they couldn't afford to do."

Mr Cash paused as he studied Pimbo's attentive face. "But remember, they were always on a winner. It's a big word for you, young Pimbo, but we call it vicarious. As the open cars flashed past on their return from the races they watched the faces of both losers and winners alike, you see without using money they were able to share in the laughter and tears. Well now Pimbo, any more questions? Then I think you'd better run along, it looks like being a fine day – too fine for young boys to be cooped up in here."

Outside the shop Pimbo asked Bobby a question, "How does your dad manage to live if people win their bets?"

Bobby smiled. "Dad always says that two people can't get a living at the same thing. That's why they call it the Sport of Kings; poor people only have poor bets, like threepence each way, any to come, threepence each way some other horse, you see they get the same excitement as the rich, or better – but can win only a small amount – Dad handles more losers than winners, that's how he gets a living. Well, anyway," said Bobby, "let's go to the Bumps today, it'll make a change – Jesus College is head of the river."

Pimbo agreed, Bob Freestone had explained to him all about the Bumps. The rowing races were an annual event on the river Cam in which crews from the colleges took part. 'Bumps week' was a kind of holiday too, for many Cambridge residents who shared with students' families the picnics beside the river, and the excitement, as frantic rowers struggled to avoid being bumped by a rival boat.

On their way to the village of Fen Ditton, where the finish of the races could be watched, the lads saw much of the gaiety of the occasion. Cars passed them laden with straw-boatered gentry, accompanied by young ladies wearing frilly, coloured dresses and carrying bright parasols.

Walking along Ditton Lane they saw the green foliage at the river's bank. The river would now and again appear like a giant snake wending a silvery way into the heart of Fen Ditton, adding spice to a scene that both lads found in direct contrast to that of Leeke Street's dull routine.

At Grassy corner the boys decided to stay. It was a popular site for many sightseers, affording an excellent view of the final run-in, when the crews had their last chance of securing or avoiding a 'bump'. Beyond the bend of the river a few hundred yards along was *The Plough*, which not only signified the end of the race – but also a welcome place for refreshments.

In the distance Pimbo could see a familiar figure working the ferry attached to *The Plough*, he re-

membered Alf Smith telling him that Old Jack had
been given a chance to work at the ferry. Leaving
Bobby engrossed in the activities of the rowers,
Pimbo walked along the river bank toward the old
ferry-boat.

The ferry had been in existence for many years.
It was manipulated by a large wheel and chain,
thus adding a picturesque touch to an already
colourful scene. Old Jack, looking brown as a berry,
was turning the wheel transporting a load of cheering students across to *The Plough* inn where no
doubt they would replenish a thirst brought about
by incessant cheering.

During a lull in proceedings Jack turned to
Pimbo. "Thanks to you Pimbo, I've got another
chance. The boss reckons he might find me a room
at the pub, and I can stay on during the winter,
helping out at the restaurant."

"What's in the bottle?" laughed Pimbo, as Jack
picking up a large brown unlabelled bottle, pro-
ceeded to have a drink.

Old Jack smiled back, "Never fret my boy, nowadays it's strictly lemonade only. They make it up
for me at the *White Ribbon*, this is a thirsty job –
but I've learnt my lesson."

Noticing a little water at the bottom of the ferry-
boat, Pimbo pointed it out to Jack.

"Nothing to worry about, Pimbo. It's an old boat
but provided I don't allow too many on at a time –
it's safe enough," Jack replied.

When Pimbo rejoined Bobby, both lads watched
intently as Clare college, who now had taken the
lead over the favourites Jesus, were about to se-
cure a 'bump' over their rival Pembroke.

Clare, straining every muscle were drawing slowly on their coveted 'bump', advice which, coming from the bank through precariously held megaphones clutched by cycling students, was shouted over the noise of screaming, squealing excited young ladies, who clapped and jumped up and down as Clare with a thumping smack broadsided into the enemy crew.

Sagging backs, and trailing oars told its own sorry tale – as Clare shamefacedly paddled out of sight.

Suddenly, came more shrieks from the ladies as Jesus college crew, straight backed and pulling on oars for all they were worth, gradually pulled away from Trinity.

From further down the river there came shrieks and cries of a different nature – all at once everyone had fear of an impending disaster.

Pimbo, scarcely able to believe his eyes, watched in horror as the ferry-boat managed by Old Jack appeared to be sinking slowly into the water. The boat, stuck fast in the deepest portion of the river, loaded with screaming occupants, had changed from a pleasure trip into a veritable death trap. A dangling broken chain lay helpless against the side of the sinking boat, making it impossible for Jack to move safely to the other side of the river.

Rowing crews whose races were over plunged into the Cam and began pulling out those unable to swim. Bending over the side of the ferry Old Jack was doing his best in pulling younger children back into the boat, hoping by some miracle that the ferry might stop sinking. Frantic screaming women were making it difficult to hear authoritative direction likely to help the situation.

Pimbo and Bobby, spotted a motor launch moored alongside the river bank, its occupant, a swarthy looking river type, had his back to the disaster.

"Quick," shouted Pimbo, pointing to the ferry-boat, "can you turn round – we might pick someone up from the water?"

The launch owner, looking round realized the situation. With a healthy throb the launch started up, moving swiftly to the scene. Rowing crews already in the water helped to push non-swimmers into the motor launch. Pimbo and Bobby having jumped into the launch, helped by handing out blankets taken from the inner compartment of the cabin. 'Many other small craft appeared on the river each picking up survivors from the ferry which by now had disappeared from sight – Old Jack, the last to leave climbed into the launch occupied by the boys.

"I'll lose my job", said Jack, "they'll blame me for this – they'll say I allowed too many on the ferry."

From the opposite side of the bank where *The Plough* stood, Pimbo saw the ferry owner and publican of the popular inn, shaking his fist at Jack.

"I saw you from my window, you were drinking from a bottle – I might have known you'd never alter. The police will hear more about this – now get out," he shouted.

Suddenly all was quiet. Rescue boats had drawn into the side of the river to allow kindly occupants from near-by cottages to take in bedraggled soaking victims, and offer hot drinks and change of clothing.

The publican of *The Plough*, Mr Driver, was opening up the bar before scheduled hours in order to dole out hot toddies to the drenched unfortunates.

Old Jack, wet through made his way dismally to a small outhouse in *The Plough*'s gardens to collect his belongings. "This will finish me – Captain Woods won't give me another chance – not even if you were to ask him," he told Pimbo.

Pimbo stared gloomily into the water, he decided suddenly that Old Jack would go down fighting. The river churned up by the swirling river craft was tossing flotsam and jetsam from one side to the other. A brown object suddenly caught his eye – it was a bottle. As it splashed into the side of the bank, Pimbo bent over and retrieved it. Pulling out the cork he sniffed inside the bottle – the smell was unmistakable, it was Old Jack's empty lemonade bottle.

Pimbo found Mr Driver happily dishing out medicinal drinks. The publican looked up as the boy entered the bar. "What do you want boy, can't you see I'm busy? You're not wet, you've no place in the bar at you age – you'd better go lad."

Feeling nervous at the sea of faces watching him, Pimbo was almost too afraid to go on. Someone catching sight of the bottle clutched firmly in his young hands, taunted, "Want a refill boy? Starting early aren't you?"

Others caught on, remarks such as, "Give it him, it won't hurt." "You've got to start sometime," echoed throughout the bar.

Pimbo caught sight of Jack passing out of sight carrying his belongings and he thought of him bending over to pull youngsters to safety. Pimbo stared at the publican and thrust forward the bottle.

"That's all Old Jack was drinking – you smell it."

Suddenly there was stillness. Everyone stood staring at the thin spindle-legged boy. There was something about his defiance – truthful and innocent. Someone from the back shouted. "It's Pimbo, goes to the Sally Army he does – give him a chance."

Mr Driver anxious not to offend his patrons, turned to Pimbo. "Can you prove it – that could be anyone's bottle?"

Thinking quickly, Pimbo said, "Ring up the *White Ribbon*, East Road, ask them what kind of drink and container they make up for Old Jack – Mr Dryden sees to that, ask for Mr Dryden the cornet player."

The publican walked to a small side room where the phone was kept. After a while he returned to the bar.

"The kid's right," he told the waiting customers, "it's the same bottle – I guess I owe Old Jack an apology." Turning to Pimbo he touched the boy on the shoulder. "I'm sorry boy, I thought Jack had been drinking, it's a case of give a dog a bad name. In the heat of the moment I lost my temper – there's no one been drowned – tell him the job's still open."

Rushing from the bar, Pimbo tore down the gravelled drive he knew Jack would be taking on his journey back to the *White Ribbon*. He caught him just as he was turning into the road.

"It's all right, it's all right. Jack. You can go back, Mr Driver knows it wasn't your fault."

Staring in amazement, Jack turned facing Pimbo. "I reckon you've done it again boy. Now you can really say that you've been through fire and water for my old bones. I'll go back and explain about the broken chain – I suppose you can't blame him for thinking the worst."

Back at *The Plough*, Pimbo watched Jack make things up with the publican. By then the police had arrived to make enquiries concerning the disaster. Mr Driver seemed on good terms with Old Jack, and as Pimbo left, the two men were shaking hands and helping the police as best they could.

When Pimbo arrived back at the river Bobby sat moodily looking into the churned up water. "Wish I'd brought my fishing tackle, Pimbo. I reckon the water's murky enough to bring a few pike to the surface."

"Do you reckon they'll get a new ferry-boat?" Pimbo asked. Bobby nodded, "People were saying it's time something was done, there was an accident here thirty years ago – twenty people were drowned – they reckon Old Jack worked hard at getting some kids out of the water ..."

On the way home through Green End the two boys stopped at a small field at the end of the High Street. Students left their cars, tightly packed in this field before leaving for the river bank. By guiding the cars through the small spaces Pimbo and Bobby were able to earn three shillings each.

Despite the ferry-boat calamity, straw boaters were still very much in evidence – as were pretty girls and frilly dresses. Some had decided to stay and picnic along the river bank.

Reaching the end of Ditton Lane which led into Newmarket Road, the boys saw the many cars returning from the Newmarket races. The day was still warm and sunny, the returning Bumps parties mingled with the racegoers and set up a truly colourful scene.

The day had been a grand experience, thought Pimbo. He felt good in many ways. Bobby turned suddenly and faced his pal. A scene from a recent film at the Kinema had crossed his mind. With both hands on his hips, Bobby said laughingly, "And another fine mess you've gotten me in ..."

Pimbo guessed at once – it was *Laurel and Hardy*, and joined in the laughter with his friend.

# CHAPTER 15

# Pimbo and Jennie at the May Ball

When Jennie had fully recovered from her illness, Skipper invited her and Pimbo along to the Trinity college May Ball. Although termed as such, the festivities really began in early June.

Jennie was delighted to receive a present from the Misses Hart, and Bragg, of the Children's Welfare. The present was a beautiful new dress to fit the occasion.

Skipper had chosen a secluded spot in the corner of G court, overlooking the river. On arrival the two youngsters were met with almost dignified ceremony by Blackie and Silver, who together with Skipper, walked the children down to their spot. The position afforded an excellent view of a giant marquee which towered above the shrubbery and floral niceties of the college gardens.

Jennie was growing stronger each day and due to the many sunny hours spent in the Neals' garden, the colour was returning to her cheeks.

Pimbo, sitting next to Jennie, looked across to Skipper. "Jennie's mother said that students, if they didn't work hard, would get sent down – is that right?"

Laughingly, Skipper replied. "Not a bit, we must let off steam sometime, that's why we celebrate May Ball, Remembrance Day, and Rag Day, in fact the townspeople think we play around too much."

Walking across to a gaily coloured ice-cream stall, set in the grounds, Skipper, purchasing two cones filled with vanilla, handed them over to a delighted Jennie and Pimbo. "By the way, Pimbo, before I forget," Skipper said suddenly, "I'm getting Mr Sanders, the escapologist to come along to our future club meetings – we'll give you chest expanding exercises. I've heard that Dr Phillips is quite pleased with your last visit."

At that moment the sound of music floated out from the vicinity of the river. Looking across the lawns, Jennie and Pimbo spotted a large punt laden with gaily dressed students and instruments, balanced delicately in the swaying punt, were played by the happy students with rare abandon – blaring out rollicking tunes into a warm June evening. Pimbo watched Jennie's excited reaction as she absorbed the musical scene.

Remembering the huge volume-filled library they had passed on the way to G court, Pimbo looked searchingly at Skipper. "Jennie and me are in a different world – aren't we Skipper? Here it's all book learning – what chance do we get?"

Skipper seemed taken aback at Pimbo's out-of-the-blue question. "It's not like that at all. Jennie and you are both very important people. My work at the college is to find out why you think things like that. Your actions and remarks help me discover the end result of poverty and illness. Instead of showing resentment through means of crime and unsocial behaviour, I want young people to be like you – talk it all out in questions and answers. One day I hope to see it taught in all schools – is that asking too much. Pimbo?"

"You mean poor kids can learn about psychology as well as students in college? It seems like a dream, Skipper", Pimbo replied.

"Here we go again Pimbo, spoiling the May Ball with this kind of talk – it's not fair to Jennie. I'm taking you youngsters into the marquee for a feast – now come along the pair of you."

Jennie and Pimbo stared unbelievingly as they passed through the awnings of the festival tent. Running through its centre was a long continuous table, made up of table tops and hundreds of wooden trestles. Each table top presented a separate item of food turkey, chicken, great legs of pork, meats of all description were on view.

"Who pays for all this?" whispered an overawed Jennie.

Laughingly, Skipper picked up the small girl, hoisting her well above the heads of the mingling students he pointed out a table at the rear of the marquee, where sat a company of distinguished looking gentlemen.

"The gentlemen you see at the special table are the committe, made up of Masters and Dons. They contribute a fair proportion, and with students, too, who help a little, some of the expenses are met in one way or another – but of course the college has most of the burden in finding large sums."

Lowering Jennie gently to the ground Skipper turned to Pimbo. "I know what you're thinking, Pimbo, about your friends in Leeke Street, sometimes they go hungry – eh, my boy? Well, I'll surprise you, seeing all this good food helps in a way. It goads many of us into thinking about the likes of Jennie and yourself."

Skipper pointed to a table on the opposite side of the tent which was stacked with bottles of expensive wines and liqueurs. "You see Pimbo, if I work hard at my research, I may get a research scholarship. The college then pays me to expand my thoughts further, which means I'm able to do more for your friends in Leeke Street. The world is like that Pimbo, one half may not realize it – but it unwittingly helps the other."

Jennie suddenly spotted her mother who, wearing a pretty apron, darted through an opening in the marquee which led into an improvised kitchen. She remembered her mother saying that she would be late home because the May Ball went on through the small hours of the morning.

Bed-makers helped out at large functions, some were able to take home left over food from the banquets.

Jennie and Pimbo sat next to Blackie and Silver. The students laughed at the children, whose smallness was emphasized against the huge food laden tables. Rose Smith appeared with the first course placing it proudly before her daughter. "I'm not really a waitress," she whispered to Jennie, "but Mr Adamson asked me to do your table – he said it might put you at ease."

The huge tent was beginning to fill, young gentlemen in evening dress, escorted pretty flowing-gowned young ladies to their table. Jewellery of all tastes gave sparkle to the splendid occasion. A jazz band mounted on an improvised dais played tuneful music.

Stealing a glance at Jennie, between mouthfuls of the succulent fare, Pimbo noticed how she was taking in all the happenings with her usual quiet excitement.

"When are you leaving the Neals?" asked Pimbo suddenly.

"Another two weeks, the doctor thinks a little longer will do me good. He said that I must go to the dinner centre like you Pimbo," Jennie replied.

Pimbo nodded happily, next term he would be starting a new school in Young Street. It would be an all boys school and he would miss Jennie. Now with Jennie going to school dinners in Eden Street, he would see her every day.

Jennie was a little backward at school, perhaps it was why she would be staying longer at River Lane primary. At the club Silver had said that sometimes a kid's home life affected work at school. Skipper was studying this and told Pimbo that making friends with Jennie was a good thing for them both. He liked Jennie, and wanted to be with her whenever he could. Boys came first of course, Bobby Watson said that a boy had to be a boy, if he wasn't, then something was wrong. Pimbo reckoned that kids play all kinds of games, most were an imitation of whatever grown-ups do. Being with Jennie was like playing at being a grown-up – just as the students were doing with their ladies.

He felt a touch on the shoulder, it was Skipper. "Now, Pimbo, you're day-dreaming again, finish your meal and I have a surprise for you."

After the meal, Skipper with Blackie and Silver took Jennie and Pimbo along to a large quadrangle overlooking the river. There they were joined by a score or so youngsters, the children of Masters and Dons.

Laughing and chatting excitedly the young people quickly made friends. Blackie soon had a game of Ring o'roses under way. Jennie enjoyed the 'Atishoo, atishoo, all fall down' aspect of the game, but Silver keeping a watchful eye made sure she took little part in the more strenuous games.

When the games finished the children went down to the river's edge. Scores of punts loaded with Madrigal singers were idling on the river. Soon the singing began, the children's voices joined those of the Madrigals. Pimbo recognized a few tunes often played by Miss Lucy at the old sweet-shop.

As the evening wore on couples danced on the lawns to the strains of the river boat music. The swirling of the pretty gowns as they brushed the grass, the steady lap lap of the backwash of the many punts and other river craft brought new sounds to the youthful ears of Jennie and Pimbo.

After a while two children, Peter and Mary, whose father was Dean of Trinity College, invited Jennnie and Pimbo for a walk around the college grounds. Skipper arranged to meet them afterwards in the marquee.

Crossing a great stone bridge, the Dean's children pointed out the intricacies of the ancient stonework. The bridge was a hundred years old having been donated by an old master of the college. From the bridge weeping willows hung

loosely into the water's edge, young ducklings
played hide and seek amidst the green foliage on
each side of a pathway leading into a small courtyard were beautiful flowers of every variety. In
the centre of the courtyard stood the Dean's house,
an ivy covered porch hid the entrance to the splendid home. Peter and Mary invited their newly-
found friends inside.

Jennie and Pimbo stood aghast at the magnificent edifice. In a corner of the oak-panelled hall
stood a massive suit of armour. Hoping it to be a
figure of his favourite knight Sir Lancelot, Pimbo
was disappointed when Peter explained that it had
no specific origin. Not to be outdone Mary showed
Jennie a beautiful tapestry of Christ.

Presently they were in the library, massive vol-
umes, tightly packed wall to wall, brought a gleam
into Pimbo's eyes.

'Whoever finds time to read all these books?"

Mary smiled, "Daddy calls them his collection
over the years. He reads only the reviews, then
ticks them off in the library inventory. If we're
naughty, he threatens to lock us in and make us
read the entire stock – as punishment."

The four children suddenly burst out laughing.
Peter, who was a tall boy for the age of nine, looked
across at Pimbo. "I'm sure we're all thinking the
same, it's jolly stuffy all this, let's go in the garden
and play – it's still a ripping evening."

Jennie fell instantly in love with a large rocking
horse that stood in the corner of the garden. Pimbo
gave her ride after ride, sending her squealing with
delight as she soared up and down.

Trying his hand at croquet, Pimbo found the

mallets more than a trifle heavy giving Peter and Mary plenty to laugh at, as he made wild attempts to send the ball through the gateway of the large staple-like contraption.

Peter and Mary invited them into their music room. A large horned gramophone supplied Peter with the means of getting through a plentiful supply of records. To Pimbo's surprise Peter's selection of records was similar to that of his own. Tunes such as, 'Tipperary', 'Long, long trail', 'Keep the home fires buring' and 'Colonel Bogey' were among those played.

"I lost a favourite uncle during the war," said Peter, a little wistfully. "When I play these tunes it makes me think of him – he bought me a pedal car for my birthday."

Pimbo got to reckoning again. It was funny how the war tunes bound them together. Pimbo's dad was killed in the war – it gave Peter and he something in common to think about. However rich Peter's parents were, it made no difference when it came to getting killed in the war. A dead man was a dead man – in any language.

Then too, he noticed how after using the tricycle and scooters, Peter and his sister placed them all tidily away. In the back gardens of Leeke Street, Pimbo often spotted rusting toys which had been left outside during inclement weather. He supposed Skipper would find in his research a good reason why poor people sometimes wasted things. Psychology has something to offer poor people – rich kids weren't too bad, after all – he liked Peter and Mary.

"Do you play football?" Pimbo asked Peter.

"Well, no not much. We're taught rugger at St Faiths, can't say I'm good at it though, my coach thinks I'll make a good hooker."

Pimbo shrugged at Peter's reply. No one at River Lane played rugby. Rugger was probably a stronger game than soccer. You had to push and shove; boys from River Lane weren't strong enough, only Bobby – you had to eat plenty of good food.

"Boys are selfish, always on about sport, girls don't get a look in, do they Jennie?" chipped in Mary. Jennie smiled in confirmation, and the four youngsters returned to the marquee to find Skipper. They found the club leader with Blackie and Silver, talking with Jennie's mother, who had ready a small supper for the children. Peter and Mary were invited to sit in with Jennie and Pimbo. Mary sat next to Jennie, whom Pimbo noticed was talking more readily than ever before. It seemed that Mary had a knack of drawing out inhibitions.

"Do you like school, Mary?" Jennie was asking.

"I don't really, I think that you start learning about life when you leave school – at school you're just told what to do," said Mary.

Mary glanced at her brother and smiled. "Peter does, he says he's going to be a lecturer like Daddy. I want to be like Mummy, she does social work – I think I would like that."

Staring at Jennie, Pimbo noticed her new dress and beads, and the delicate way that she handled the cutlery. As she sat at the table in a tent overflowing with finely dressed people, talking with the Dean's children, he wondered whether Jennie at that particular moment needed social help. She

seemed a real Cinderella at the May Ball, very soon
Jennie would be taking off her dress and thinking
of Brown's Yard and school dinner centres.

It seemed good, thought Pimbo, that sometimes
you could think your way out of poverty – he
supposed that was the reason why the author
wrote *Cinderella*. He realized how clever Skipper,
Blackie and Silver were, allowing them to go off
with Peter and Mary on their own – he hoped that
Peter and Mary both got something out of it, too.

Pimbo suddenly remembered the incident on the
Hunstanton train, where he had pulled the communication cord. He had never asked Skipper
exactly what had been said to the angry guard.

"I thought by now you might have forgotten,'
replied Skipper at the boy's question. "I told him
that he must allow a child to make a few mistakes –
he seemed to have taken the point."

Jennie's mother then asked Silver the time. On
looking at his watch, Silver nodded to Skipper who
immediately rose from his chair. "It's ten o'clock
Pimbo, you must be getting along home. The Ball is
really only just beginning – but I'm sure you've had
a good share of the fun."

From a small bag she was carrying Mary pulled
out a set of perfumed handkerchiefs and handed
them to Jennie.

Accepting them nervously, Jennie said, 'I'll
see you again I hope, I'll find a present for you
then."

Pimbo stared at Peter and thought that had
Bobby Watson been present he would have said,
"Cissy". He shook Peter's hand promising an eve-
ning at the club where Silver would teach Peter to

box. In return Peter promised to teach Pimbo how to play rugby.

Bob and Maude Freestone were waiting up for Pimbo. They listened attentively as their foster-son related the happenings of the exciting day. Maude told Pimbo how Mrs Neal had missed Jennie in the few hours she was away.

"I reckon you're bringing out Jennie real well," said Bob.

Pulling from his pocket a crumpled table napkin, Pimbo presented each with a sizeable portion of chicken. "To the best Mum and Dad in the world – a present from the May Ball", he said, before running up the stairs to bed.

*A popular dance band in the early thirties, playing at a college ball.*

# CHAPTER 16

## Pimbo and Jennie go to the Fair

It was Midsummer Fair. The week previous to the long awaited visit of the fairpeople had been one of glorious weather. Most townspeople wondered if the weather might hold good. Usually the opening day was heralded by a shower of new pennies tossed to the clutching hands of a mob of excited youngsters by an anxious-to-please Mayor.

Jennie had called for Pimbo well in time for the opening ceremony. "You can catch your own pennies. I'm hard up this week, you'll have to wait until Friday for your pocket money" Jennie's mother had told her and from that moment the young girl decided that Pimbo must go all out in an effort to provide them both with spending money.

Moving into the surging crowd of youngsters Pimbo first of all gauged the length of the stocky little Mayor's arms. Noticing that the Mayor was hemmed in from both sides by austere looking dignitaries he then concluded that the Mayor would throw a short distance into the centre – with this strategy in mind, Pimbo, although small in stature, waited confidently for the first splatter of new pennies.

To Jennie's delight Pimbo had judged correctly. The Mayor seemed to throw straight at Pimbo who, pulling his jersey out apronwise caught a good supply of yellow shining passports to fun.

By now the music was blaring away the usual well known tunes of the annual Fair. The two happy youngsters moved quickly away from the crowd and found their way to the edge of the sideshows which were always an attraction to most children.

Sharing out the money with Jennie, Pimbo found that he had managed to catch three shillingsworth of pennies. Both bought a toffee apple and sucking this enjoyably, wended their way among the "Bearded Lady", "The Thinnest Man in the World", "The Human Cannon-ball" and suchlike wonders.

"How're you doing at school, Pimbo?" asked Jennie between sucks at her toffee apple, "your Mum told Dad that you'd been in trouble – is that right?"

"I suppose so, but none of it was my fault. I reckon that everybody gets into trouble at some time – through other people, that is. How about you, you been into trouble Jennie?"

Shaking her fair tousled hair, Jennie smiled. "I still can't get my sums right. But my cooking's good. Miss said I was the best in the class. Reckon I'll make you a good wife Pimbo, and you with your penny catching would be a good provider!"

Pimbo reckoned that Jennie was always listening to grown-up talk. That's how it went, no one seemed to get married for love. It was for cooking or providing. He hoped that things might be different by the time he was old enough to get married –

anyway he wouldn't always be able to catch pennies.

Arriving at a small sideshow the two youngsters were accosted by a large fair dweller wearing a cowboy type hat and a large silver watch chain suspended across his velvet waistcoat.

"You look a likely pair" he bellowed "want to earn some money minding my stall. You look like brother and sister, that should pull 'em in. You've got to have gimmicks you know – what about it? Half-a-crown a night, each, that is!"

Looking at the stall Pimbo could see at once that the possibilities were good. It was a toss-the-ball-in-the-bucket stall. There were six buckets, each tipped at a certain angle making it very difficult to win. But most people accepted the challenge of throwing the ball sideways hoping it would gradually spin around the outside to finally peter out into the bottom of the bucket. Throws cost three a penny and the prizes seemed very acceptable.

"But I don't want no pinching. You'll get no pay if I think you've been pinching. I'll search you before you go – but I reckon you two are made for the game." The big man lifted the two youngsters over the wooden partition at the front of the stall, plonked Pimbo at one end and Jennie the other. Taking a handful of coppers from a cloth bag he handed them each a two shilling float. "That's for change. You'll hand the float in first before I count your takings – now get cracking. I'll pop in now and again to see how you're doing."

Staring across to Jennie, Pimbo recalled the Laurel and Hardy statement which was used at the end of most of their escapades. "And another fine mess you've gotten me in." Somehow it seemed incredible that a moment ago they were enjoying the fun of the fair – and now they had become part of it. Before they could speak Jennie received her first customer. A young college student arrayed in bright blazer with boater to match proffered sixpence for half a dozen throws.

"Roll up-roll up" cried Pimbo in an effort to capture the spirit of the occasion. He had watched many times the ways of the fairpeople and to his surprise was not at all nervous.

The young student foolishly threw each ball straight into the centre of the galvanised bucket only to have them bounce springingly back to him. His failure attracted his friends who, some with young lady partners, seemed anxious to show off. Soon the two youngsters were doing a roaring trade, Jennie's fragile appearance and complete innocence served as the showman had implied – a profitable gimmick.

The money gradually piled up and both youngsters were growing in confidence. After a while the big stall boss came along taking away most of the silver in a cloth bag. "Well done kids, I thought you'd turn up trumps. Keep it up, I'll be round again later."

Gazing at a large backcloth at the back of the stall Pimbo could see that the man's name was Bill Parker. The name Parker was well known among the fair folk. Stalls, round-abouts, sideshows, and amusements all bore the magical name, and Pimbo felt proud that he was working for such a well known celebrity.

To Pimbo's surprise from among the crowd to

step forward was a familiar figure – it was Miss Perry, a teacher from East Road School. "Oh it's you eh?" she said brightly "helping out at the fair. I must say that you lads never give up. What'll be next my boy – fire eating?" Before the startled Pimbo could reply Miss Perry collected her ration of wooden balls and methodically placed each one gently at the side of the bucket, watching confidently as the ball trickled quietly into the bottom of the bucket for a prize.

On receiving her prizes, looking across to Jennie, she held out three of the pretty dolls she had chosen. "For you, I suppose you have a sister, if not keep them in remembrance of this year's fair." Turning again to Pimbo she said smilingly. "I like your little friend. I'm glad that you keep good company when you're not at school – see you again soon".

Watching her figure recede into the conglomeration of musical whirligigs Pimbo was pleased that Miss Perry had not humiliated him in front of Jennie. Perhaps Mr Baldry might well have said something of a sarcastic nature. Pimbo reckoned that women teachers were good for boys – it seemed that they understood a boy's feelings.

As darkness grew the appeal of the little stall waned. The burly figure of Mr Parker suddenly loomed upon them. "Well you two, you can pack up now. Let's see how much you've taken since I was here last. Then I'll search your pockets before I pay you."

Running his hands over Pimbo's pockets he felt the bulge of the new pennies which the boy had caught from the Mayor. "Hullo, hullo, what's this,

pilfering eh? Now I warned you about this my lad.
Let's have 'em, they belong to me." As he turned,
the three dolls given by Miss Perry caught his eye,
"little innocent at it too eh? Stealing prizes from
the stall eh?" Leaning over he snatched the dolls
away from a frightened Jennie.

Pimbo made an effort to struggle away from the
showman, "I'm not a thief. The money was mine, I
got it fairly from the Mayor. The dolls were given to
Jennie, I can easily prove it to you – Miss Perry, a
teacher will explain."

"A likely story, how come you take the job if you
had money. Most kids want to spend what they've
got. You'll get no pay from me, I'm keeping the
coins – you're lucky I don't call the police. Now
push off before I lose my temper."

Catching sight of Jennie's crestfallen appearance Pimbo began to cry. She too was sobbing
bitterly and to worsen matters the only people
around seemed to be a rough looking mob of gipsy
lads.

Mr Parker made Pimbo empty his pockets and
also searched Jennie. The gipsy boys hanging
around began catcalling and shouting obscenities.
For the second time that day Pimbo was surprised
by the emergence from the shadows of a familiar
figure – it was Miss Perry.

Standing at her side was a policeman, who
walked directly up to the surprised stall owner.

Up to your old tricks again Mr Parker. Working
on the principle that you can always get a couple of
kids every night to make you a pound or two? You'd
better give back the new pennies and the dolls,
Miss Perry has told me all about it!"

"Yes, Guv, I'll do that. But you know what kids are nowadays. I really thought they were pulling a fast one" the beaten showman hastily gave back the coins and the dolls.

"Now you can pay them for their evening's work. I've been watching, they both have worked hard" said Miss Perry in her school-marm voice.

Paying out the children's dues Mr Parker stumped away. "He's lucky that you didn't prefer a charge, Miss" said the friendly copper "how on earth did you cotton on to what was going on?"

Miss Perry smiled at the two youngsters. "It's taught in our Teachers' curriculum. It's an old trick practised mostly up North. But sometimes as was the case tonight they try it anywhere they might get away with it."

After the policeman and Miss Perry had gone Pimbo suggested they should now enjoy themselves. Jennie agreed and in no time the youngsters were in the thick of the amusements centre. The penny mat was ever a great favourite with Pimbo and breathlessly he carried both his own and Jennie's mat to the top of the giant spiral staircase.

From the top both children paused to admire the scenery. Twinkling lights sprinkled out from the darkness like giant glow worms. The spinning wheels of the round-abouts jostled for priority against the slow heaving sombre lighting of the Cake walk. Chair-o'-planes swung gracefully through space, splitting the rays of light into cascades of tiny stars as though a mammoth welding torch were biting into the night's illuminations.

Music and singing blended into a whirligig of fun and splendour. Little streets could be identified by solitary gas lamps placed at routine intervals. Against the carefree expanse of the generated electricity Pimbo thought of the many candlelit homes present in the quiet streets, around his home.

Jennie shook him from his reverie. "Come on Pimbo, give me my mat, they're all waiting behind." With Pimbo leading, she sat perched solemnly on a mat, which for one fleeting moment had turned into a magic carpet. Down past the mysterious Eastern cities, swinging gaily past the Taj Mahal, the young friends open mouthed and wide eyed, tore on and on, in a madly exciting pennyworth of adventure. The small space between landing mat and ground was their last wild thrill. Pimbo first catching his breath at the sudden jerk into space, Jennie following with a delighted little squeal as she bumped into Pimbo who had lain almost drunkenly on the large mat, which acted as a buffer to the sudden plopping figures.

Next the youngsters ambled curiously around the china stalls. Jennie loved the porcelain figures, the funny little Toby jugs, the pure crystal glass candelabra. The chatter of the salesman as they held full tea sets at arms length, imploring fairgoers to purchase the amazing bargains on offer. Pimbo listened to the remarks from the crowd. "They're seconds" "Ah, they show you the best – but you don't get them" "The pattern comes off when you wash them" "They don't come back next year – so you can't change them."

Suddenly the smell of hot peas attracted them. Mr Haynes from Staffordshire Street was busy as usual. "Got yer girl friend with you eh Pimbo? Does your mother know you're out?" His friendly banter cheered the young couple as with a large bowl in hand they sat in a quiet corner of the huge "Hot Peas" tent. Jennie moved close to Pimbo and through the awning they watched fair-goers pass by on their way to varied pursuits.

"I wish we could do this every day" said Jennie "no school, no exams – what do you think, Pimbo?"

"Mr Baldry said you've got to earn your pleasures, else you don't enjoy them. It wouldn't be any good every day. Miss Perry said you've got to save for a rainy day, she reckons poor people sometimes don't think of tomorrow" replied Pimbo.

"But all the money is used every day. My Dad says live for today and let tomorrow take care of itself – what about that?" Jennie retorted.

Finishing his peas Pimbo shrugged as he collected Jennie's empty bowl. "Kids have got to think for themselves. Things change, if what we've done in the past don't work out – well then we must do something different."

Mr Haynes accepting the empty bowls smiled at the young couple as they prepared to leave his tent.

Jennie was feeling tired, and as Pimbo had had a full day they made their way slowly back home.

"What are you going to be when you leave school?" asked Jennie, as they reached the iron railings leading into Newmarket Road. "I sometimes don't know what to make of it. When I'm happy I feel that everything will come right. I think about the people in our street; all they seem to do is slog hard and are just able to live. But me, I'm, going to be different. The world is changing and I'm going to be in on it. Then again when I'm down, I think how can things be different? Bob and Maude

Freestone tell me I can get a job easily, they seem to
think that to get a job is enough. They've been
brought up on unemployment, I could be an errand
boy – but what then . . . ?" Helping Jennie across the
road into Fair Street, Pimbo held her hand firmly
and continued, "maybe if a boy gets a girl he doesn't
mind what he does. Just being with each other is
enough; that way you can be happy, just as happy
as rich people."

Nodding her head Jennie looked up at her young
friend. "Girls don't have to worry like boys. Mum
says a woman's place is in the home. I'm going to be
a good wife Pimbo. I can cook and sew and do
anything."

On their way back to Brown's Yard the couple
passed into Wellington Street. On the corner was
Biggs Dairy. The street was cobbled and on each
side were tightly packed terraced houses. At the
bottom of the street Pimbo was fascinated by the
position of the doorways of the last few houses.
They were much lower than the level of the pavement and the occupants of the homes when standing at the door had only the top halves of their body
visible.

"The houses are very damp" Jennie told Pimbo,
"they only charge one and sixpence a week. One up
and one down, that's what they call it. Dad said he
wonders how people can bring up a family under
such conditions. The voting men say things will be
different – we've got to vote for it."

Then it was through Wellington Passage, a tiny
throughway just wide enough to take a pram.
Houses faced each other an arm's length away.
There was no sun and Jennie said that at the back

a few neighbours kept cockerels. When walking through the passage on a summer day the crowing of the cockerels seemed the only living thing. She said it didn't seem real, just brick walls then suddenly the cockerel's crow. It was as though the people meant to get something out of their existence, "Perhaps that's why God made cockerels – they could crow even if they weren't on a farm!" said Jennie.

A sudden screaming and shouting came from the back of a house in the passage. A man's voice could be heard telling someone to "Get out, and stay out you dirty slut."

Pimbo clutched at Jennie's arm. Don't worry, they always make it up in the end. Mum says they'll be at the Salvation Army on Sunday – bold as brass. Dad reckons it's why they do it."

A sound of something being thrown against the wall broke the conversation of the youngsters. A child's cry followed and then a woman's shrill voice could be heard. "You've woken the kid, now I suppose you're satisfied – go back to the pub with your mates – that's all you're fit for."

In the distance the fairground music wafted over the night air. Pimbo reckoned it was funny how things changed. One moment everyone enjoying the fun of the fair – then back into the little side street listening to other way of living!

"Did you like the fair?" asked Pimbo.

Jennie smiled. "I look forward to it all year. It's funny but it's not like spending real money. I suppose it's because we all seem the same – we all have the same chance to laugh. The college boys can miss hitting a coconut the same as Dad. I love to watch them have lots of goes; I don't envy their extra cash because somehow the fair is different. Mr Rumbelow the coalman can make the bell ring every time with the heavy mallet – I reckon once in a year he's the king of his own particular castle."

"You're talking differently Jennie. You never used to say much, now you can say big words – and sensible too!"

"Teacher says I'm doing better, more confidence. She says that's because Dad's doing better. She reckons when Dads are in work their children do better. But I don't show off with other kids – one day Dad might be out of work again. But you help me Pimbo, because you take interest in everything – I try to be like you."

"I'm starting a job on Saturday, Jennie. It's at Mr Neal's the tailor in Trinity Street. I can ride a bike and Mr Neal said that I can do errands for the shop – I'll get 2/- for the day."

"Then you won't be able to come with me to the Fair?" asked Jennie a trifle hurt.

"I finish at 6 o'clock, we can go then. I shall have a shilling to spend, I'll give half to Mum to help out with the housekeeping."

Outside Jennie's home Pimbo kissed her and promised to meet her on the morrow and take her to the Fair again.

# CHAPTER 17

## Errand boy Pimbo

Pimbo was all excitement and wide eyed curiosity as he approached Mr Neal's tailor shop in Trinity Street. Having obtained his Saturday job as errand boy for a day, Pimbo wondered what was in store for him. The long winding street contained lodging houses, three Colleges, a Church, and the additional tailors shops of Pratt Manning, Roper, and Adamsons. A wine store, grocers shop, booksellers and the Blue Boar hotel made up the bustling little street. Coming from the tailor's shop of Pratt Manning, Pimbo caught sight of a man carrying a black cloth draped over one arm.

He remembered Bob Freestone telling how after a suit was cut out it would be sent out to a trouser hand, a coat hand, or waistcoat hand. The articles were wrapped carefully in the black cloth and would help supply a living for the many self-employed tailors and seamstresses in the town. Pimbo found Mr Neal awaiting him in the shop.

"You'll find the bike at the back. Keep it well oiled, and the tyres free from stones. Plenty of air in the tubes my lad and no reckless riding. Bring

the pump into the shop when you've finished –
there're plenty of thieves about."

His first delivery was that of a pair of trousers to
a Mr Dungate of Oxford Road. The trouser hand
was a little man wearing an old pair of patched
spectacles.

"Hullo" he said brightly to Pimbo, "another new
lad eh? I didn't think the other boy would last long
– too cheeky by half."

He invited Pimbo up a set of crotchety stairs into
a small room. At a kind of bend at the back of the
room, Pimbo saw a flat iron nestling firmly on a
metal stand. A huge pair of scissors, peculiar
shaped chalks and reels of assorted threads
adorned the remaining space on the bench.

Brown paper patterns hung on the walls as did
various clothing in diverse states of completion.

"Meet my wife" said the master tailor pointing at
a fat lady busily pulling out long stitches from a
waistcoat.

She smiled warmly at the boy "I'm what you call
basting. You'll soon get to know the jargon, are you
going to be a good boy and bring us plenty of work?"

Not knowing how this might be achieved Pimbo
smiled back "I hope so, I'll do my best."

Mr Dungate took a bowler hat from a large
mould at the rear of the bench. Fondling it lovingly
he peered at the name on the band inside the hat.
"Lord Wormald", that's his bowler. I've just
blocked and pressed it." He look at Pimbo and
laughed, a deep belly laugh. "Lord Wormald does it
every time he comes down for the Term, says the
hat is too small and wants it altered. Mr Neal kids
along with him, I never touch it, just block and

press. The Lord puts it on his head in front of the mirror taps it, and unfailingly says "Splendid, my man, splendid – a perfect fit."

Noticing Pimbo's quizzical look the tailor tapped the boy lightly on his shock of red hair. "Tricks of the trade my boy. We must make up for the vacation, not much about then. We've had a Wormald on the books for years. They'll keep coming until they run out – I'll be gone by then, and so will Trudy."

Laughing at her husband's joke, Mrs Dungate offered Pimbo a sweet. "I'd like a boy your age, never could have children. I'd be sewing up holes in his trousers, patching his knees – reckon your Mum ought to think how lucky she is!"

Her husband wrapped up two pairs of completed trousers then placed the bowler hat in a strong looking hat box and handed it to Pimbo. "Don't drop it, and tell Mr Neal I'll have the waistcoat done by Monday – I'll bring it down myself."

Holding the articles firmly, Pimbo managed the stairs without mishap. Outside he placed them securely into the large basket entrapped inside the iron frame of the carrier cycle. Whistling a popular tune he pedalled steadily down Oxford Road into Huntingdon Road then to the top of Castle Hill.

From the hill Pimbo could see the large chimney stack just visible in the distance of the Norman Cement Works. Bob Freestone in a reminiscent mood would tell him of the days as a Territorial Army range finder when he would use the tall chimney as an aiming point – 2,000 yards exactly Bob said.

Remembering Mr Neal's warning of reckless riding Pimbo freewheeled down the steep descent of

Castle Hill. At the bottom of the hill leading into Magdalene Street Pimbo waited until the road was clear before venturing forth into the final stage of his journey back to the shop.

The clanging of a bell attracted his attention. It was the Muffin man. Carrying a large wooden tray balanced precariously on his head, buffered only by a green baize cloth, the tall seller made his way along the narrow street towards the Magdalene College entrance. "Hot muffins for lunch, hot muffins for lunch – only a few more left," he cried, stopping to supply his wares to a student who had run from his room in eagerness to purchase the delicious goodies.

Pimbo recognised the Muffin man as Mr Hempstead who lived in the East Road area. On Good Fridays he would change his fare to that of hot cross buns. Starting as early as five a.m., Mr Hempstead would cover many miles of the Town selling to all classes and finishing at dusk. His bell was his trade mark and the man had become almost a legendary figure. The Muffin man's small son was at school with Pimbo. The boys would tease "Hocker" as he was known, by singing an old London cry "Do you know the Muffin man who lives down Drury Lane?"

Recognising Pimbo, Mr Hempstead rested his tray on the parapet of Magdalene bridge. "Care for a muffin Pimbo. Young Hocker tells me that you're a rare one at school – sort of teacher's pet, ain't you?"

Knowing that muffins required lashings of butter before (to a small boy) they could become edible, Pimbo declined the offer and decided also not to take up the teacher's pet allegation. Before he could reply however, somehow the tray shifted from its perch on the smooth parapet of the bridge and slide baize cloth and all into the river below. The bell too was knocked from his grasp as he excitedly made a grab at the disappearing tray.

Staring at Pimbo in utter dismay, Mr Hempstead swore in the manner that only a man in his position could swear. Pimbo resting his errand boy's bike against the bridge ran quickly down a flight of stairs at the back of a small antique shop which luckily he had spotted. Arriving at the river's edge Pimbo was just able to lean over and retrieve the tray which was floating upside down close to the bank.

Placing the tray and cloth safely aside, Pimbo concentrated on the bell. The wooden handle of the bell and the amazing way it had landed in the water smack in the centre of drifting weeds, with its hollow cup uppermost, reminded Pimbo of the theory behind the large steamship – wood and iron keep afloat!

But suddenly Pimbo found himself in the river; he had reached out once too often. Still clasping the bell and thrashing madly with both arms he floundered about wondering what might happen next. From behind his coat collar he suddenly felt a steel like contraption bite into the sodden cloth. Frightened to move or even to look about him Pimbo felt himself being pulled into the bank. A large jovial looking man who had been using a large boat hook in order to land his catch – hooked Pimbo ashore.

"You're a bit small boy, good job I'm not fishing, according to regulations I'd have to throw you back."

Mr Hempstead and students from the College were seething around the boy. "He can have a bath at the boathouse" remarked a student whom Pimbo recognised as the one who had purchased the muffins, "maybe I can fit him out with a few togs – might be a trifle large, but they'll be better than wet gear."

Suddenly Pimbo remembered his carrier bike, the bowler hat, and trousers. He pointed to the top of the bridge where the handlebars of the bike were just discernible. "I shall get the sack, it's my first day. Don't let anyone pinch them – Mr Neal has been good to me."

"Don't worry boy" replied the young student. "I get my stuff from Neal's. Know him well, he'll never get another order from me should there be any trouble for you. I'll phone him up, then we'll get you a bath and a hot drink. They're bringing your bike down to the boathouse, everything is still in the basket – now stop whittling my lad."

Noticing the calm of the river Cam, the languid passing of the punts with their blazer clad occupants Pimbo thought how nice it must be to be able to learn and also enjoy such harmony. "I'm Roger Fleming" said the student, breaking the boy's day dreaming. "It seems that you know our friend the Muffin man, I'm afraid that his muffins have gone for a Burton – what sort of a chap is he?"

Watching the muffins floating up-side-down Pimbo looked across to Mr Hempstead whose face was a line ridden map of despair. "He's a good man, works hard for his family. He'll have to pay for his stock – it'll put him back a shilling or two."

Smilingly Roger picked a few coins from his

trouser pocket handing them to Pimbo. "You give it to him with my best wishes – now what about the boathouse, a hot bath, and tea and cakes?"

The boathouse stood well back from the river with a wide expanse of gravel covering its frontage. Muscular young men were carrying a rowing skiff into a side building at the edge of the boat house. Thinking of the boys at East Road school Pimbo realized that none of his friends was likely to ever attain such development. Their fathers too were in the same category. Bob Freestone used to say kids born in the bad years would be lighter and shorter than kids born under better circumstances – but Pimbo reckoned that jockeys were small, yet managed to control high spirited horses.

After a bath Roger managed to kit Pimbo out with fresh dry clothing. Looking down at the crest of the college emblazoned on his makeshift blazer Pimbo felt proud at being in such company.

The table at which they sat eating doughnuts and sampling tea overlooked a good portion of Jesus Green. In the distance Pimbo could see lithe brown limbed figures smacking a white fluffy ball backwards and fowards to each other. The entire green seemed alive with sporting activities. Roger Fleming eyed Pimbo closely, as the young boy remained absorbed in the scenery.

"A penny for your thoughts, Pimbo. I'm sure that I heard the muffin man call you such. I reckon that one day you're hoping to be able to do similar things like playing tennis, maybe not sculls – but who knows?"

"Our club leader, Skipper Adamson, reckoned that if I pass my exams I might get to Grammar School.

You have to wear whites at cricket, at my school it doesn't matter – but I think it's nice to have everyone wearing the same, the game seems better."

Roger nodded. "And why not, my father was an ordinary postman, studied when off duty – brought me up to do the same – that is, be interested in studying to get somewhere – where do you want to get, Pimbo?"

"I read as much as I can. Some boys at school only read comics. In the books it says everyone must try and make something of themselves. I reckon reading can be work, just like woodwork only you can't see anything being built. But I build up hopes that one day I might be able to help people, people like where I live – in my street everyone seems a product of by-gone years. I want to be different – think of the future."

"You must show me your friends. One day I'll come with you, I too think of the future. But perhaps we must think of your return to Mr. Neal." Roger looked across at Pimbo's clothing which was flapping on the balustrade of the boathouse stairway. "Put your address on this piece of paper, I'll bring your clothes, all pressed, back to you."

Mr Neal smiled at Pimbo's return to the shop. "Mr Fleming rang me. I know all about it. A fine start to a day's work. But you did well boy. Hats renovated, muffin bells recovered, why indeed, muffins soaked in the Cam give special flavour – there's no end to the capabilities of Neal's errand boys."

Not realizing that the tailor was capable of such humour, Pimbo at first seemed nervous at what he thought was sarcasm. But a closer scrutiny of Mr Neal's face, quickly dispensed with such thoughts.

"I'm sorry Sir, But I didn't mean to be late back, but I just had to help. Mr Dungate said that he would finish the waistcoat by Monday, and bring it along himself."

Suddenly realizing that he was dressed still in Roger Fleming's makeshift clothing, Pimbo blushed as he caught Mr Neal eyeing him up and down. The master tailor walked over to a small cupboard, beckoning Pimbo over to see its contents.

Pulling from a rail at the rear of the cupboard, he produced a kind of page boy outfit. It was made of uniform cloth, beautifully cut, and the front of the tunic was studded with bright buttons. The trousers were of special cut tapering down to an elegant finish as that of the smartest military man.

"I had it made some years ago. The boy was one of my best lads. Came from somewhere around the Gas Lane area. Always turned up with shiny boots, but his clothing was appalling. One day, whilst in the shop a student came in and openly laughed at the boy's appearance. He happened also to be one of my bad debtors. I vowed there and then, that this boy would be dressed impeccably – he would be a credit not only to my shop, but to himself."

Mr Neal smiled as he watched Pimbo's intense expression.

"The boy was with me until he joined the Army in 1914. He never came back – and somehow the suit has stayed in the cupboard. I never thought a boy would turn up with a similar motivation for me to feel the same way as I then did. When I saw you in the borrowed clothing, it all came back – go and try it on boy!"

Looking into the mirror inside the fitting cubicle Pimbo thought at once of Lord Wormald. The suit was a perfect fit and he ran his fingers along the array of shining buttons. Turning around he could view himself from all angles. For a moment he became a new being. "Splendid my man – splendid, a perfect fit." Tapping his head as though pressing down the freshly blocked bowler, he studied himself carefully. He felt as good as anyone, for that matter looked as good as anyone. He thought too of Mr Neal's remarks about the scoffing student customer – one of my worst payers, he'd called him. That made Pimbo as good as he, he reckoned that he'd always try and pay his way. Bob Freestone had things on tick at Mahoney's. Paid at the end of the week. Maude would worry like hell if she couldn't pay. Pimbo reckoned that character was at the finger tips of any one that tried to pay his way.

Mr Neal suddenly walked into the fitting room. "A good fit my lad. Keep that shock of ginger hair under control and you'll be able to fetch and carry to the students' college rooms. I have a customer who sends in his riding breeches weekly for cleaning – they tell me that he often leaves two-and-sixpence in the pocket."

Walking into the shop Pimbo felt proud of his new attire. He reckoned that anyone dressed smartly all the week was a toff indeed. Best was best to Pimbo. He supposed it was the reason why rich people got on better. He felt better on Sundays, when dressed in his best suit – going to school next day was sometimes a let down.

His next duty was taking the post. The parcels were not too bulky and to his delight he was able to walk. Turning into Rose Crescent on his way to the General, at the corner of Petty Cury, he almost bumped into a cluster of laughing graduates. They eyed him with a kind of patronising respect – no doubt half in admiration at his smart appearance. The Post Office bustle was petering away to its week-end rest. A portly veteran was serving behind the grille. "Hullo, hullo, a new uniform eh? I've been here a few years – you're new to me boy, where're you from?"

Without waiting for an answer he turned over a parcel to scan the address. "Neal's the tailor. Nice bloke, he'll look after you, goes to the Sally Army. Going to learn the trade boy?"

Pressing on the appropriate stampage, Pimbo looked up. "I'm only working Saturdays. I don't know about learning the trade – is it hard?"

The veteran smiled. "They pay well for a good cutter. He gives them style. But I reckon you might be too late boy. There's a rumour that Burton's the thirty-bob-a-suit people will be opening at the bottom end of the Cury. I suppose it will mean off the peg suits in the coming years."

On the way back Pimbo reckoned that there would be enough Lord Wormalds to keep Mr Neal busy for a few years. He supposed that at twenty one he might be able to look smart in a Burton suit. By the time he reached the tailor's, Roger had returned his dry clothing. Hanging the smart little uniform back into the cupboard Pimbo felt somewhat like Cinderella on her return from the ball. He could however, have been her "Buttons". He had enjoyed the day. Pocketing the five shillings Mr Neal gave him he thought of Jennie and the fair.

# CHAPTER 18

# Pimbo and the magic cycle

Pimbo was having another day out with Mr Brown the rag and bone man. The morning was sunny, and the rag man was in a cheerful mood. Arriving at the village of Cottenham, some eight miles out from Cambridge, they both prepared for a busy time.

Pimbo's first call was at a small cottage which was situated on the edge of the village green. The white-haired old lady who answered his knock seemed pleasant enough. "Rags, haven't had anyone round for ages, bit young aren't you? Come round the back to the shed, we'll have a look boy."

The path leading to the shed showed signs of little usage, moss in dark and light shades clung to its edge. An old well displayed a rusting chain and bucket that bore down into green stagnant water. The old lady's ruddy cheeks reddened deeper as she bent to pick up a bundle of clothes that lay in a corner of the shed.

"There you are my boy," she said, handing the bundle to Pimbo. "I've held on to these for a long time, belonged to my granddaughter. My son had a bit of a row in the village, emigrated to Canada, the whole family – I've heard nothing of them since."

At the rear of the shed, Pimbo spotted a girl's cycle, it had been vaselined over against the rusting damp. The old lady who had been watching Pimbo, looked up. "You can take the bike, too. Before he died my husband's last job was to vaseline the frame. He said that if ever she came back it would be good as new. Perhaps you can make something of it?"

With difficulty Pimbo managed to retrieve the cycle from its awkward position. Placing the bundle of clothes close to the cycle, as though to clinch the deal, he said:

"Thank you Ma'am, how much would you have me pay you?"

The old lady smiled. "Take them for nothing, my granddaughter was about your age when she was taken out of the country. Somehow you both have something about you – I would never have parted with them otherwise."

Pimbo carried the bundle and cycle back to the motor cycle and side-car. Looking back at the cottage, he could see the old lady waving as she closed her door.

Mr Brown appeared from a near-by house carrying a well-filled sack of woollens. Pimbo noticed how contented he seemed, at least he was his own boss, perhaps the wooden leg could be more of a blessing than one thought.

"Nice cycle, boy – how much?" asked the rag man.

Pimbo smiled. "Nothing, the lady gave it, and the clothes – I was wondering . . ."

Mr Brown broke in quickly, "Don't tell me, let me guess. You want it for Jennie, eh boy? The missus tells me everything, I know about you and Jennie. You can have it boy – lucky though, I've got no kids Jennie's age."

Pimbo's next call was at a white-painted detached house, standing well back from the village high street. The lady who came to the door was wearing going out clothes, with a girl about Pimbo's age standing quietly beside her.

"I thought you were the taxi-man, I was expecting him," the lady said sharply, "what do you want, anyway?"

For the first time that morning Pimbo was stuck for words. He had felt that he was becoming a first class rag man, he had picked up many wrinkles from Mr Brown, things such as dirty milk bottles meaning poor management of the home, patched and darned clothing on the clothes line meant little business, tiny garments gave hints of perhaps a broken pram or fairy cycle . . .

The lady broke his thoughts. "Well, what do you want, you seem to be day-dreaing?"

Pimbo lost his nervousness. "Oh, I'm calling for Mr Brown, Ma'am, have you any rags, woollens, metals, or anything to sell? I'm sorry to have come when you're expecting someone."

Pimbo's utter innocence brought a faint smile to her features. "I was about to take my daughter along to her doctor, I'm afraid she's going through a bad spell – aren't you dear?" The mother placed her arm around the girl's shoulder.

The girl remained expressionless, there seemed something strange about her – as though she wasn't really present. To Pimbo's surprise the girl clasped him suddenly by the hand. The mother watched unbelievingly. "It's the first time for weeks that Sarah has shown the slightest interest in anything – normally she just sits and stares."

Pimbo took in the girl's nice looks, her neat clothes, he thought of the old lady's granddaughter in Canada. Somehow to Pimbo the world didn't seem right.

The lady laughed again at Pimbo's day-dreaming. "I'm Mrs Seymour I'm afraid I've nothing to sell, but would you like a cup of tea?" The mother's voice was now warm and friendly.

Pimbo watched Sarah closely, her eyes met his – she seemed to be saying, "Do say yes, please!"

Accepting the invitation, he followed mother and daughter into the neat modern kitchen, and sat with Sarah at a table next to a window, looking out into the street. As Mrs Seymour was about to make tea, the phone from the hall rang. "It was the taxi-man," she explained on her return to the kitchen. "He's been delayed, Sarah will have to wait a little longer."

Over a cup of tea Mrs Seymour spoke about her daughter. "I'm afraid we've been to blame, thoroughly spoiling her. We sent her to a private school, promised her everything if she showed promise. Now she's turned out to be an ordinary little girl. The children in the village are not friendly to her, they think she's a snob."

She smiled across at her daughter. "Then Sarah seemed to lose confidence in herself. As I said she would sit for hours staring into space, after a time I had to call in her doctor. He sees her once a week in a special clinic, they use a large hall with other children, but most are much older than Sarah – somehow she doesn't fit in."

Sarah who seemed to have been listening, suddenly smiled across to Pimbo, and pointed through the window at Mr Brown's motor bike and side-car. Pimbo smiled back, he felt Mrs Seymour's elbow dig into his side, suddenly he realized Sarah's wish – it was to walk to the rag man's transport.

On reaching the motor cycle and side-car, to Pimbo's surprise Sarah pulled out the cycle given him by the old lady. Although the tyres were worn, it was still rideable. Smiling at him, Sarah stood astride the cycle. "Do you fail exams, too?" she asked softly.

He smiled back at the girl. "I don't do any, I might one day though – Skipper helps me study life and people. I get by."

Sarah was suddenly away like the wind, pedalling the cycle for all she was worth hair blown back, cheeks ruddy with effort, down the high street she rode. Pimbo tried to remember a poem he was learning at school. It was something about the thoughts of youth are long, long, thoughts, and the child's will is the wind's will, but he couldn't remember the exact words. But he knew how Sarah was feeling, just as he felt when bowling the hoop. Free as the wind, no lessons, no promises to fulfil – he thought again of the old lady's granddaughter in Canada. perhaps the cycle was a magic cycle, Jennie would be having it soon, he wondered what it might do for her.

Returning to the motor bike and side-car, Sarah was resting against the side-car, still astride the cycle. "I'm glad I met you, somehow you are what I want to be, just free and happy," this time there was laughter in her voice, her inhibitions seemed swept away by the wind.

At that moment the taxi-man arrived sent down by Sarah's mother. Sarah jumped from the cycle, running to the open window of the taxi. "I'm not coming any more, tell them I won't go," she said in a firm strong voice. The taxi-driver drove slowly away.

Sarah turned to Pimbo. "I've been a prisoner, Mummy and Daddy mean well, but it's been, 'You must do this – you must do that.' As soon as I started private school, my friends left me – they said I was getting too big-headed."

Noticing how much happier Sarah looked, Pimbo smiled, "I know how you must have felt, it happened to me. At the Sanatorium I was regarded as a boy who belonged to every one but himself. I wasn't allowed to grow up, since then I've been lucky; a little home, a little of school, and this, meeting people like you helps a lot."

Sarah went on. "I seemed to lose interest in everything, I gave up and went into a shell. When you came to the door, you did something for me – you and the cycle were like a key to the freedom I was yearning for . . ."

"Do you think that we're too old for our age? Some people say I am, do you think you are?" Pimbo said suddenly.

Sarah smiled. "Just because we're children people think we should just play games and learn tables. I'm really like you, I want to do more . . ."

In the distance she spotted her mother walking towards them. Radiant and smiling Mrs Seymour raced to her daughter, kissing her on both cheeks she turned to Pimbo. "I've been watching from the window. We promised Sarah a cycle were she to pass the exam, foolishly we did nothing about it when she failed. Now we shall see that Sarah gets her cycle – win or lose, it has taught me a lesson."

From a handbag the mother took out a pound note giving it to Pimbo. "That's for you my boy, I'm sure that you had something to do with it, you've accomplished more than the doctors – I suppose that you being of the same age, gave Sarah something to go for."

Waving good-bye to Pimbo, Sarah walked arm in arm with her mother back to the house.

Arriving at the side-car Mr Brown deposited a sack of rags into its interior. He spotted the note in Pimbo's hand. "A pound note, eh boy, not bad – what kind of magic have you been up to?"

"It must be a magic cycle, I've done nothing. Here you take ten shillings Mr Brown, I've been wasting some of your time – it's only fair," said Pimbo earnestly.

Smiling at the boy's sincerity, the rag man took the proffered note, handing back ten shillings. "I reckon you're right boy, fair's fair, now we're off to collect a load of horseshoes from Gingell's farm. Mr Bloy from the forge at East Road has sent a note saying they were ready to be collected."

Mr Gingell, a Cottenham farmer used Bloy's forge regularly as a shoeing service. Discarded shoes as soon as the pile had grown large enough, would be collected by Mr Brown and sold as old iron to Mr Wheatley.

The route to Gingell's farm, being well away from the main road – was enjoyed by Pimbo. They passed orchards and smallholdings, pigs and cows were a common sight, and often a mare could be seen suckling its small foal.

The pile of rusting horse shoes was in a field some way from the actual farm buildings. Mr Brown made Pimbo put on an old pair of gloves before attempting to load them into the side-car. "I reckon a lot of steel was used in the recent war, boy, these tips are worth fetching. I suppose they melt them down and make something new out of them," said the rag man as Pimbo and he busily loaded the shoes into the side-car."Why are they kept so far from the farm?" Pimbo asked.

"Never did fathom it out, I reckon it's because old Gingell doesn't want too many vehicles in and out of his farmyard. In wet weather it cuts up the ground – that's all I can think of."

Pimbo remembered that Barley Newman, his giggling school pal from River Lane, would often spend a summer holiday at the farm, put up by a relative who worked for Mr Gingell.

At last the loading was finished, Mr Brown tied up the horseshoes safely with a tarpaulin, and the transport was chugging away towards Cambridge.

On the way home Pimbo was thinking about Sarah and the cycle. Skipper once told him that there was no such thing as mental illness. It was the way people accepted things, he supposed it was the same with Sarah, she wasn't really ill – but just couldn't think of a way out of her problem.

Reaching Cambridge, the load of shoes was dropped off at Mr Wheatley's in South Street. Mr Brown seemed well pleased with the cash he received and took Pimbo for a meal at the White Ribbon on East Road.

Mr Dryden the cornet player was serving meals. "Hullo Pimbo," he said brightly, "I hear you got Old Jack out of a scrape, he's doing well now. They're getting a new ferry, the police praised Jack for his part in the rescue and he's got a room of his own at *The Plough*."

The hungry pair were served eggs and bacon, followed by a pot of welcome tea. On the way back to Leeke Street Pimbo was thinking about handing over the cycle to Jennie, and how long it might take her to learn to ride.

At the bottom of Leeke Street he was surprised to see the burly figures of two policemen standing outside Mr Brown's home. He recognized Banger Day and the young constable who had questioned him about the sweet shop robbery.

"I want a word with you Mr Brown," said Banger Day, as the dealer dismounted carefully from his motor cycle, "you've been to the Gingell farm today – you'd better tell the truth, or it'll go hard against you."

Mr Brown nodded in a surprised manner.

Yes, I have, why what's up – I've done nothing wrong?"

Banger sighed disbelievingly. "What's up you say, a quantity of expensive harnesses has been stolen from the farm – that's what's up – you may as well own up."

Mrs Brown came running from her home, she was crying as she raced up to her husband. "What are they trying to do, put you away? You've served your country and try to get an honest living," turning to the two policemen she shouted hysterically, "that's what you get for losing a leg – but you won't get far, my husband wouldn't touch a thing that didn't belong to him."

Looking nervously around the little street, Pimbo could see curtains being drawn back from the tiny windows. More brazen folk were standing openly at their doors, obviously enjoying the discomfort of the unfortunate man and wife. Pimbo thought of the occasions where Mrs Brown had sold clothes cheaply to these very same people, often allowing them to pay at a later date.

"Very well, if it's going to be like this, I'm taking you to the police station. Put your machine away, you'll sign a statement when you get there – perhaps we shall then get to the bottom of this," Banger said authoritatively.

Spotting Pimbo, he turned to the young constable. "Better take the kid home, he's too young. Tell his parents we'll be coming round later – to see if the two statements tally."

Pimbo wondered what might be in store for Mr Brown – one thing for sure, the dealer had stolen nothing.

# CHAPTER 19

# Pimbo and Bobby turn detective

A day or so later, Pimbo was visited by the two constables. He told them everything that had happened including Sarah and the cycle. After signing a document, Pimbo was told that he probably would be hearing more about the case in a week or so. Mr Brown had been allowed home on bail, but would be going to court on a charge of theft.

Pimbo immediately got in touch with Bobby Watson, telling him everything about the happenings. Bobby liked Mr Brown, sometimes the old dealer would ask him out for a day and he, like Pimbo, had found him honest and straightforward.

"Dad said old Brown couldn't have stolen anything, the side-car had been loaded with horseshoes, there was no room for stolen harness. Mr Brown told him that the police should have checked up with Mr Wheatley – he was the only one who saw the loaded side-car," said Bobby anxiously.

Pimbo was in deep thought. Suddenly he looked up. "Why steal harness? What good would they be unless you had horses, then if you had horses you could afford to buy harness, so why steal?" he asked Bobby.

Bobby nodded. "Mr Cash makes harness. He told me once, that harness is very expensive – it's real leather. Sometimes he buys second-hand harness, burnishes it up to sell again."

Both boys suddenly stared at each other. What if Mr Cash had purchased harness of late? It might work out – the stolen harness could perhaps turn up unexpectedly.

For several days Pimbo and Bobby kept an eye on the little leather worker's shop. They knew the old man was honest, but Pimbo had read in the paper, that sometimes honest people got involved in shady deals quite innocently.

One morning Pimbo spotted Barley Newman, his school friend, entering Mr Cash's shop carrying a heavy object which was well wrapped up. It suddenly dawned on Pimbo that Barley had been helping with the harvest at Gingell's farm. But how on earth could there be any connection with the theft he thought?

Waiting for Barley to reappear, the boys were at last rewarded. Newman, busily counting a handful of silver, was coming down the steps leading from the shop.

"Hullo Barley," said Pimbo brightly, "been doing a bit of business, eh?"

Barley's usually happy face clouded a little. "Why yes, I'm helping Mr Goldsmith the dealer in Fen Ditton. I often go with him on rounds, like you do with Mr Brown – you seem a bit nosey – what's up?"

"Poor old Brown's in trouble, they say he pinched some harness at Gingell's farm. I was with him that day – I know it's a lie," replied Pimbo, a little hurt.

Barley frowned. "That's funny, I'd been working in the fields, my uncle sent me back to the shed at the farm to fetch a grease gun because a wheel of the tractor seized up. Old Goldsmith asked me where the harness room was, he said he'd purchased some from Gingell – I showed him where to go, I thought it funny that he was alone."

Pimbo looked across to Bobby. "It looks very much as though Goldsmith pinched the harness – but how can we prove it? What did Mr Cash buy from you Barley?"

"A stirrup iron and bridle, Goldsmith told me to say that there was more to come, that he'd brought it from a farm which was selling up – I've been a fool to get mixed up in this," finished Barley.

"We must say nothing to Mr Cash," said Bobby, "or he'll think we're mixed up in this. I know where Goldsmith's caravan is, he's a didicoy, kind of half-gipsy – what say we go to his place, find out where he's keeping the rest of the harness – then tell the police?"

Barley seemed scared. "I'm keeping out of it from now on. I didn't know Goldie was a crook, although a boy once told me that he'd been in prison for stealing hens, but I didn't believe it."

"Just go back and give him the money Mr Cash gave you – leave the rest to us," said Pimbo bravely, "how much was it?"

"Three pounds," answered Barley. "Goldie said he would give me two shillings, if I made three pounds."

The gipsy dealer lived in a yard which housed a dozen caravans at the bottom of Ditton Lane, a few yards from the Maltings where Alf Smith worked.

The two boys waited a while to allow Barley to deliver the money. On the way, Bobby filled in a few gaps concerning the life of the gipsy.

Bobby's father had told him that Goldie was a frequent visitor to Newmarket races. At times he was suspected of being a pick-pocket, was known to be violent, and always seemed flushed with money.

At last Barley was seen coming from the entrance to the caravan yard, he waved back to the two boys, and made off quickly in another direction.

"I can't make out why Barley hobnobbed with Goldie, it doesn't seem like him to do anything dishonest," said Bobby suddenly.

Pimbo nodded. "I reckon it was to earn money. Barley was a poor reader, slow at school, usually bottom of the class. He would sometimes show off by letting us see how much money he had. But I don't believe he meant to be dishonest – that was the only way he could be somebody."

The two lads moved slowly into the yard. Several ponies were grazing together on a small patch of grass at the bottom of the compound. Gipsy women with small toddlers around their swirling skirts were hanging out washing on lines strung between caravans. Large bony dogs, tied to stakes, with just enough room to patrol their own little patch, lay drooling in the sun.

Pimbo and Bobby suddenly realized that things weren't going to be too easy. Furtive glances were bandied backwards and forwards between the women as they watched the two boys walk further into their province. So far the boys had not set eyes on a man. Pimbo reckoned at least it gave them a

chance, sometimes women just thought boys were
a nuisance – but men had other ideas.

Suddenly Pimbo stopped, opposite to where he
stood, was a caravan with the name, 'Levi Goldsmith, general dealer' written on the side, in gold
painted letters. Suddenly the half door of the caravan swung open. A large swarthy face was staring
down at them.

"What are you up to, snoopin' about eh? What do
you want round here? You'd better have a good
answer – or I'll set the dog on you both." The gipsy
walked menacingly down the steps towards them.

To Pimbo's surprise Bobby looked scared, it
seemed he was too scared even to run away. Pimbo
thought of all the stories he'd read, but couldn't
think of any situation quite like this.

"We're doing an essay, we've got to write about
how gipsies live – teacher said it would be nice if we
were allowed in a camp," stammered Pimbo he'd
remembered suddenly a story in *Magnet* where
Harry Wharton had done a similar trick.

The gipsy scowled. "More than likely you've been
talking to that Barley Newman boy – been opening
his mouth has he? I followed him down to the Cash
shop just to see, you don't think I'm a fool do you?
So teacher wants you to look round, eh? Right you
can stay with us for a while. I saw you two hanging
around waiting for Barley – now get a move on
before I set the dogs on you."

Pimbo and Bobby hurried up the steps into the
caravan, looking round for a moment the big gipsy
then slammed the door shut.

In a corner of the caravan Pimbo could see a pile
of harness, saddles, bridles, girth braces and a

quantity of stirrup irons were amongst the loot. At
the other end of the room was a wooden bunk
displaying untidy dirty bedding thrown over a
filthy-looking mattress. A table with unwashed
crockery completed the picture.

"If you boys don't keep your mouths shut, I can
make things look pretty bad for you. I shall say
that you helped Mr Brown steal the harness, Barley will be too scared to deny helping you. We
gipsies stick together." Goldie's voice was hard and
demanding.

The boys stared at each other. Somehow Goldie's
threat seemed convincing enough. The police
might want to know why in the first place they had
visited the gipsy site. Barley to save his skin might
even tell lies. If things got too deep for the gipsy, he
no doubt would swear that Mr Brown had sold him
the stolen equipment.

Goldsmith suddenly began picking up the harness, and accoutrements, placing them in a pony
and trap, brought alongside the caravan by a similar looking rogue to himself. The gipsy turned to
the boys and laughed. "Gettin' rid of the evidence,
they call this. You two can stay here to cool off, by
the time I get back, you'd better decide to know
nothing about this affair."

Closing and locking the caravan door, the two
gipsies drove off.

Pimbo and Bobby pressed hard against the door,
but it wouldn't budge. The windows were very tiny
affording no chance of escape.

Searching around Pimbo noticed a small sink at
the corner of the caravan. The waste pipe from the
sink, led down into the underneath part of the

caravan. A bucket to receive the waste could be discerned through a cut away portion of the floorboard of the caravan. Easing it away with his fingers, Pimbo found that with extra force, this portion of the floorboard could be lifted away.

Bobby and he pulled away as hard as they could. To the boys' delight , with a tearing sound, the whole portion was pulled away. There was just enough room left in the gaping hole to allow the boys to scrambled through. Pushing the waste bucket gently aside, the two lads found themselves free.

From the under part of the caravan, Pimbo and Bobby waited for an opportunity to slip away. The women had finished their washing chore and were probably inside making a meal. Both boys crawled quietly clear of the caravan, and stood at the rear waiting for a chance to run for it.

Sniffing around the caravan next to the boys was a large black mongrel dog. They wondered whether they would be able to make a dash for it without disturbing the remainder of the gipsy camp.

"We must take a chance on the dog," Pimbo said suddenly, "the longer we hang about the sooner Goldie and the other gipsy will be back."

Bobby agreed, "I'll count to three, then we'll go. You first, I'll hang behind in case you get in trouble – right, one-two-three."

Both boys dashed forward on 'Three', passing the dog, Pimbo to his relief found it was attached to a long chain hidden from view behind the caravan. With lungs fit to burst he ran on, past one caravan and another.

A gipsy woman screamed out as they neared the opening into Ditton Lane. "Stop them, stop them, they're thieves," her voice trailed off into a wail as they turned into Ditton Lane.

Running madly Pimbo and Bobby waited until they were safely on Newmarket Road before stopping to gain their breath.

"You did well Pimbo", said Bobby, "I could only just keep up with you, you're getting stronger – it's since starting the club."

Leaning over Barnwell bridge, and looking down on the trains Pimbo got to thinking about the next move in helping Mr Brown. Bobby thought it best to tell the police about what they'd seen, but after a time Pimbo, to avoid getting Mr Cash into trouble, persuaded him that telling Mr Cash, who could then inform the police, might be a better plan.

"I hope Mr Cash doesn't get into trouble, some people get sent to prison through handling stolen property," said Pimbo, as they approached the leather-worker's shop.

Reaching the shop the boys were surprised to see several official looking cars outside, amongst them a police car. Barley Newman could be seen in the centre of a group of policemen, it seemed that he'd been crying. An officious looking man in Inspector's uniform was taking notes on what Barley said.

Spotting his friends, Barley brightened considerably. "They can prove it, Sir," he said excitedly, pointing to Pimbo and Bobby, "they know all about it – I didn't steal anything, Sir."

Banger Day, with hands on hips and legs akimbo, greeted the entrance of the two boys. "Well, if it isn't Sexton Blake and his assistant Tinker. First it's the sweet-shop mystery, now

you're solving the harness afffair," patting them on
the head in turn, he remarked to the other policeman, "these kids are tops, treat 'em well – they
deserve it."

Pimbo and Bobby related all they knew to a
smiling Inspector. To their surprise he showed
little concern when told of the gipsies taking away
the harness from the caravan.

"Thanks to Mr Cash we were informed well in
time. Your young friend Barley told us where to go.
We were waiting for them outside the yard – but we
didn't know you had been trapped in the caravan –
it might have turned out sticky for you both," said
the Inspector to the relieved lads.

"Mr Brown won't have to go to court now, will
he?" Pimbo asked.

The Inspector stroked his chin. "The charge will
have to be made – but it will be dismissed immediately. Mr Brown will leave the court without a
stain on his character – does that satisfy you,
young man?"

Pimbo turned to Bobby, "But the neighbours will
still talk, they'll gossip about it, Mr Brown will be
the loser."

Banger Day who had been listening, broke in.
"Don't worry about the gossip, Pimbo. Who knows
what they said about you lads in the sweet-shop
ɒreak-in? That's life, you two lads get through
what it takes some a lifetime to achieve."

After the police had gone Pimbo and Bobby were
left wondering how the old leather worker had
managed to see through the gipsy's tricks.

Over a cup of tea and a chocolate biscuit the lads'
queries were answered. "As soon as a robbery takes

place a list of stolen property is circulated to shops concerned. When Barley Newman brought in the bridle and stirrup iron I noticed at once it was stolen stuff – I rang the police, the rest you know."

"But why did Goldie take such a chance? Why couldn't he wait a little longer?" Pimbo asked.

"The only way crooks get caught is by making mistakes. I suppose the gipsy wanted money quickly – your guess is as good as mine." The little shoe-maker finishing his tea, walked to the door.

"Now boys, you'll finish up old men before you're young ones – run along and play, it's too nice a day to be inside."

When Pimbo arrived home Bob and Maude had been given the news about the gipsy's arrest. Bob greeted Pimbo with a half smile. "One day my boy you'll land in deep trouble, you should have told us first. Mr Watson came round blaming you for enticing his boy away."

Pimbo smiled to himself, grown-ups were like that, people in Leeke Street had been ready to talk about Mr Brown – but not too ready to help. But anyway, kids can take chances that grown ups can't . . .

"Banger Day said that we'd done well," Pimbo answered defiantly, "but I'm sorry to have worried you, Dad, we both got carried away – but I'll never let you down again."

A knock at the door brought in an excited Mrs Brown, who hugged Pimbo until he was almost breathless. She was followed by a more than grateful husband who handed Pimbo a large bag of sweets. Next came Mr Watson and an excited Bobby.

"Well, what do you think of our two heroes? They do Leeke Street proud," said the bookmaker as he looked around at the shining faces. Producing from the inside of his coat a bottle of sherry he smiled at Mrs Freestone. "Drinks all round on me to Mr Brown and his acquittal – the boys will have to settle for ginger pop."

The boys stared as the adults drank the proposed toast, their faces glum – Mr Watson had forgotten to bring along the ginger pop.

Silently Pimbo handed his friend a sweet.

# CHAPTER 20

## Pimbo finds his feet

The next club meeting found Skipper in serious mood. Mr Sanders the escapologist, had been invited along to help Pimbo develop more chest muscles. In a small room next to the improvised gym, Skipper was having a word with Pimbo. "My sociology studies allow me access to your medical reports," said the club leader. "Dr Phillips is very pleased with your X-rays, he reckons that so far there is no active source to worry about – with regular exercise, and good breathing, you should throw this off for keeps."

Pimbo looked pleased. "Why doesn't my foster-mother know about this – why didn't she tell me?"

Skipper smiled. "Tuberculosis is something every one is afraid of, no one likes to mention it. Mrs Freestone least of all. You're a boy that needs telling, you've done your bit to fight the disease – you deserve a break, now just be yourself and have fun."

Mr Sanders with his son Ronnie as model, quickly got down to work. Pimbo being put through the unusual gymnastics of a professional escapologist, began to feel proud, as gradually he was able to master a few of the movements.

The deep breathing required to enable many of the tricks to be expounded, gave Pimbo a grand feeling of well being. He realized how it was that Mr Sanders was able to keep going for so many years. After an hour or so, Pimbo was given a breather.

"How did you first begin your unusual trade?" asked Skipper between the breaks.

"I started as a tumbler in a circus," replied Mr Sanders, "in those days I was single and full of adventure. The life was good, and I enjoyed travelling from one county to another. After a few years as understudy to the resident escapologist, I took over when he died. However, getting married gradually put paid to my circus career, my wife was unhappy, and wanted to settle down – along came Ronnie, well, here I am."

The next session was spent in twisting and turning, with Ronnie supplying most of the opposition. Pimbo was surprised at the amount of work he was able to get through without feeling too tired. It seemed to him that he was about to begin a new lease of life. Skipper, he thought, had been a real friend, he noticed too, that the leader made sure that other boys had a turn as well as he.

Jimmy O'dell wanted to join in, as did Tich Coulson, Bobby Watson was able to master many of the tricks, and found in Tich Coulson, a good foil. Skipper noticing Pimbo looking a little tired, called him over for another chat.

"I see young Jennie is back home again from Mrs Neal's," said Skipper, "learning to ride a bike too. Her mother tells me you gave it to her."

Pimbo smile. "I call it the magic cycle, I hope Jennie learns quickly – if I had a cycle we could ride together."

Skipper nodded appreciatively. "You remember Peter and Mary, at the college May Ball, they're coming tonight. Peter's bringing an old cycle along for you."

Pimbo stared. "How did Peter know about the cycle?" Skipper smiled back. "Kids stick together, they often ask how Jennie's getting along. When I told them about the cycle, Peter seemed to think that you ought to have one, too."

A little later Peter and Mary walked in. The cycle turned out to be quite a good one, Pimbo remembered riding it in the Dean's garden. Mary seemed disappointed at not seeing Jennie, but Pimbo promised to take her along to Jennie's home a little later in the evening.

Silver began putting Peter through his paces with the boxing gloves. Peter was quick to learn, and very soon was exchanging a flurry of blows with the varsity boxer.

Tich Coulson, who stood watching, suddenly threw out a challenge to Peter. "I'll give you a round or two, you're taller than me, but I reckon I can beat you."

Silver stopped, a little surprised at the aggressive tone of the ex-deputy gang leader. "All in good fun, remember Tich, Peter hasn't done too much of this, not as much as you Tich." Turning to Peter, he said, "You sure you want to accept the challenge, it's up to you, if you think . . .?"

Peter nodded. 'I'll have a go, it's only sporting – three rounds, eh?"

Silver adjusted both boys' gloves. With a few coats and chairs an improvised ring was set up. Silver acting as referee, set the two boys in motion.

Tich rushing forward, swung a vicious blow at Peter before the Dean's son had a chance to parry. The blow caught Peter flush in the face. A spurt of blood shot forward, splashing on to the white vest Tich was wearing. Peter, blinded by the blow, could only stagger around; Tich Coulson, with a leering grin, was about to deliver another blow when Silver moving quickly forward, grabbed his arm.

"I think that's enough Coulson. I think you've taken advantage enough – not quite the rules we teach at the club, now take off your gloves," he said angrily.

Mary running forward helped her brother to a chair. She was crying as Skipper began to apply cold compresses to the bleeding nose. "He's a bully – he's a bully," she cried, "just showing off, why doesn't someone pay him back?" To Pimbo's surprise, Mary looked straight at him.

Pimbo got to thinking again. There was something in what Mary had said. They were both guests of the club, he in some way or other was the host. Peter had brought along a cycle which was to be his. To worsen matters Tich too was staring at him.

Pimbo looked across to Skipper then Silver. Having staunched the bleeding from Peter's nose, Silver stared back. The look seemed to say – well what about it Pimbo? Skipper, too was looking in a funny way. For the first time Skipper appeared to be wanting Pimbo to do something different, as though this was the day of reckoning. Perhaps Mr

Sanders had a more sinister motive in coming along to the club. The blooding of Pimbo seemed to be the wish of the entire club. This time the skinny legs, the impish face, would play no part in winning for Pimbo.

"All right Tich, I'll take you on, we'll still be friends – but somehow . . ." Pimbo found it difficult to finish the sentence. Tich was acting in a strange way, it somehow didn't fit in with his usual behaviour.

Smilingly, Silver stepped forward. "It had to come to this, Pimbo," he whispered, "but I won't let things get out of hand."

Whilst Pimbo stood having his gloves put on, he noticed a feeling of expectancy running through the boys. Bobby Watson had so far kept out of things, he was watching from a distance, but the look he gave Pimbo was one of sympathy, and yet of admiration. Skipper came over and massaged the top of his shoulders. "I'm sorry Pimbo, but I know you wouldn't have me stop it – do your best, I'll explain later."

At the start Pimbo made certain of not making the same mistake as Peter. Tich, making a similar burst, found Pimbo side-stepping away from the clumsy lurch forward. Pimbo had always been capable of quick movement, and the work done on him by Mr Sanders in teaching correct breathing stood him in good stead, as Coulson made another attack.

This time Pimbo pushed out his left allowing his opponent to run into it. Although devoid of weight, the blow caught Tich between the eyes, and the impetus of Coulson's charge caused the surprised boy a distinct smartening of the eyes, the tears flushed down from the unexpected blow.

All at once Pimbo realized the position he was in, he was actually on trial amongst his own friends. Something had happened in the club, beyond even the control of Skipper, which forced him to show once and for all exactly what he was made of.

Skipping lightly to one side he found himself staring at the exposed midriff of his opponent. In his many evenings at the club's boxing sessions Pimbo had noticed a reluctance of boys to punch to the body – somehow the done thing seemed always to punch to the head.

Taking a chance Pimbo inhaled a deep breath as taught by Mr Sanders, he mustered every ounce of power into a final swinging blow. Being shorter than Tich, his swinging right landed exactly where he intended – smack in the centre of Coulson's midriff.

As the air left his body, Tich's cheeks pouted out. Regaining his balance Pimbo swung his left in a smiliar arc to that of the first blow. The effect was astonishing – Tich collapsed in a heap on the club floor.

Shouts of, "Good old Pimbo, we knew you could do it," filled the club room. Mary was jumping up and down clapping and shouting.

Silver immediately worked on Tich Coulson helping the boy back to normal breathing. Feeling sorry for Tich, Pimbo walked across laying his gloved hands around his opponent's shoulder: "I'm sorry Tich, I never meant this to happen."

Shrugging his shoulders, Tich showed no malice toward his previous opponent. Looking up at Silver, he forced a smile. "I guess you're right, club rules are more important than my feelings – I'm sorry."

Coming over to congratulate him, Skipper was all smiles. "Trust you to pull something extra out of the bag, you weren't meant to win. I just wanted you to show the club that you weren't afraid to have a go."

Pimbo felt in no mood for wasting words. "But I don't understand, Skipper. What's it all about? I've known nothing all evening, it seemed that the whole club ganged up on me – but why?"

Skipper sat down. "You're right Pimbo, the club were ganging up on you, through my fault – not yours. They heard about the May Ball, the marquee banquet, and the Neals. They reckoned that you were having favours shown – remember Pimbo that they are all club members."

"But I didn't want it that way," said Pimbo, "I only wanted Jennie to get better, remember at the marquee you said I was thinking about my friends . . ."

"Of course you do Pimbo, but those things aren't always allowed for in life. When Peter brought you the cycle, Tich lost his head. He didn't know about the cycle that you gave Jennie – he was jealous, and tried to take it out on Peter – the only way out was for you to prove yourself."

Pimbo stared at his club leader. "But I thought the club was going to be great, everyone friendly – I didn't think that I would be fighting a friend."

Skipper stood up, "The club is great, Pimbo. Where else could you have a Dean's son taking on the club's best boxer, and the club's weakest boy, prove himself a veritable David. Now we'll have tea and cakes – this time it's all on the club."

The club had now settled down. Having produced tea and cakes Blackie was prompting the singing of well-known camping songs. Between mouthfuls of cake Peter and Mary joined in the singing as lustily as the boys of the club.

Remembering his promise to visit Jennie, as the choruses came to an end, Pimbo called Peter and Mary for the visit to Brown's Yard.

On the way, as he wheeled the cycle which Peter had brought Pimbo, balancing one foot on the pedal scooted slowly along. He couldn't wait to go out riding with Jennie.

At the top of Brown's Yard the youngsters found Alf Smith and his wife teaching Jennie the art of riding a cycle. Mrs Smith was holding the saddle with one hand, and guiding Jennie's arm with the other. He father walking in front admonished her occasionally for not looking straight ahead. "You must keep your eyes away from looking down at the wheel . . ." he was saying, then catching sight fo the youngsters he moved forward and halted the cycle, lifting his daughter gently to the ground. "A cup of tea for each of our guests," he said happily.

Pimbo was pleased at Alf's remark, he thought at first that they might be too nervous to invite Peter and Mary into their home.

Jennie ran immediately to Mary and clasped her hand. "Oh, I'm so pleased to see you, I haven't forgotten the handkerchiefs – I've a little present for you, come in."

Jennie was looking much stronger, her convalescence with the Neals had added weight to her small frame. Running upstairs she returned quickly carrying a white box. Opening it in front of

a wide-eyed Mary she produce a beautifully coloured scarf.

"I told Mrs Neal about you," said Jennie, "she
sent this as a present from us both, the colours rep-
resent your father's college."

Jennie was puffing as she finished her speech,
laughingly she said, "Mrs Neal made me learn the
speech off by heart, I thought half-way through I
might forget what to say."

Sitting at the table drinking tea Pimbo looked at
the change Rose Smith had brought into the little
kitchen. He remembered his being called in by
Jennie's father concerning Miss Cowell and the
worn shoes incident. Since then Alf had pulled his
weight, several places showed signs of recent paint
or distemper applied by none other than Alf.

In turn Jennie's mother too, had made a fresh
start. Where possible second-hand furniture had
replaced the old tattered pieces. Peter and Mary
sat contentedly talking to Jennie. Looking across
at her husband, Rose Smith felt proud to see her
daughter holding her own with the dean's children.

Pimbo rose suddenly from his chair. "I'm afraid
we must get back to the club, Mrs Smith. Skipper
likes us to be present at the closing session."

With good-byes and promises to come again,
Peter and Mary left their newly-found friend at
Brown's Yard.

# CHAPTER 21

## Pimbo's test of nerve

Pimbo kept up the weekly routine of fetching coke for Mrs Parker. Of late, the old lady had been acting strangely. Several times she had offered to pay him twice on the same day, at first he thought she was testing his honesty, but somehow Pimbo felt there was something happening to the mind of the old lady.

"Your dad was killed in the war," she was saying, "your mother died of T.B., doesn't Mrs Freestone ever tell you about your real parents?"

Having been asked a similar question many times by thoughtless neighbours, Pimbo had ready his stock reply. "Perhaps Mrs Freestone doesn't like to talk about things that are long past – she might not wish to worry me," he said kindly.

"Place isn't the same since the war, no one's friendly any more – you're the only one I have visit me," said Mrs Parker.

The boy stared at the old lady. "But I thought you had a daughter, you told me about her, you said that she told you that boys are nosey and tell their parents about you."

Mrs Parker nodded, "She doesn't come any more

since my husband was sent to the lunatic asylum.
Molly always said it was my fault, that I drove him
there."

Pimbo was beginning to feel out of his depth, he
felt suddenly that he shouldn't be listening. The old
lady seemed to read his thoughts. "I know that you're
only a boy, but you get mixed up in all kinds of
trouble. I saw you through the window with a policeman and Mr Brown, have you been spying on me?"

Pimbo could scarcely believe his ears. In Leeke
Street is had been common knowledge for many
months that during a stroke poor Mr Parker had
attacked his wife with a chopper. For the safety of
Mrs Parker and himself, he'd been removed to the
asylum. It was also rumoured that due to his habit
of attacking nurses, he would most likely remain in
the hospital for the rest of his days. To avoid
annoying the old lady, Pimbo answered softly. "Of
course not Mrs Parker, you've been very kind to
me, I wouldn't spy on you."

Suddenly her face took on a strange change.
From the kindly old lady she had always been to
Pimbo, she seemed transformed into a kind of
witch. Moving quickly to the kitchen door she
turned the key, depositing it down her blouse. "You
won't leave here unless you tell me the truth. I've a
poker here which you'll feel the weight of – now it's
up to you my boy."

Wondering what to do next, Pimbo began thinking
that sometimes he'd involved himself too much in
many things and people. He had paid a big price for
his illness, everyone was saying how it had turned
him into a man – it was a kind of magic in some
people's eyes. But here he was a boy of eight at the

mercy of a confused old lady with a poker in hand,
and a locked door to prevent him running away.

"You know me well enough, what harm can I do?
What notice would be taken of a boy, even if I were
a spy? What could I find out about you?" Pimbo
tried to pacify the old lady.

Mrs Parker leant forward brandishing the poker
in Pimbo's face. "You drove the old ladies from the
sweet-shop, kind dear old souls were Mabel and
Lucy, as soon as you showed your face in Leeke
Street – trouble began."

Feeling hurt at the old lady's words, he wished
suddenly that Skipper might appear. Skipper
should be helping people like Mrs Parker, now he
realized how important colleges were; working
people were too busy working, they had no time to
learn about psychology, the old lady had something wrong in her mind – Skipper would know
what to do.

"I can get a friend to help you," Pimbo said
kindly, "he runs our club, he's a gentleman, knows
all about old people."

Mrs Parker scowled. "He knows enough to keep
away, doesn't he? I don't hold with high faluting
words, give me good old commonsense – my husband will be home in a minute, he'll soon show
him."

Now Pimbo was feeling afraid, holding the poker
firmly in her grip the old lady moved closer to him.
The mention of her husband's coming made it clear
to him that her mind was rambling more than ever.
"I'll go now Mrs Parker, my mother asked me not to
be too late home – do you mind?" Pimbo tried a last
moment thought.

The words were lost on the old lady. She sat
motionless staring at the boy as though no words
had passed his lips. Rising quickly, Pimbo tried to
follow his request with action. As he was about to
make for the front room, she brought the poker
down hard on his wrist, a crackling noise and a
sudden sharp pain ran up the length of his arm –
his fingers felt numb as though they were stricken
with pins and needles.

"That'll teach you, sit there or you'll get another." It seemed unreal to Pimbo that this old lady
was the same person whom he'd met when seeking
a job for his picture money. Her eyes glared as she
stared him fully in the face.

He tried to move his arm and fingers, thinking that
he might be able to play on her sympathy, he pointed
to the bruise and swelling already evident on his wrist.

"You've hurt my wrist, Mrs Parker, you may
have broken it. You're so kind, usually – what's the
matter? You're not well really?"

Again Mrs Parker seemed oblivious to the situation, she sat rigidly staring into space.

The boy pondered carefully over his next move.
Mrs Parker needed help, it seemed that she had
worsened since his arrival. Skipper once told him
that old people could change overnight, he called it
a stroke or something – he supposed it was why Mr
Parker had attacked his wife – he hadn't meant to
be cruel, he didn't think Mrs Parker did either.
Skipper also said that one day he would organize
things so that old people would have more visits,
they would not be left alone to die. He said that the
1918 war had made people think – things were
going to get better.

Looking through the kitchen window into the little backyard, Pimbo remembered the first day he'd called on Mrs Parker. He thought of the large brown rat which had startled him – a sudden idea sprang to his mind. "Quick, Mrs Parker, there's a rat underneath your chair, give me the poker, I'll kill it for you."

Jumping from his seat, Pimbo held out his hand to receive the poker. For a moment the old lady seemed not to have heard, her face remained emotionless. Then to Pimbo's relief she slowly held out the poker for him to grasp. Pretending to cuff about him with the poker, he rattled the weapon against the legs of the chair. After a time he stopped, pretending the rat was dead he picked up a newspaper from a near-by table, and went through the motions of wrapping the dead rat inside the paper. "I've killed it, I'll put it in the dustbin for you – give me the back door key," he said softly.

Producing the key from her blouse she handed it over to the elated boy. Somehow his successful ruse was short lived, now he was feeling sorry for the old lady as she sat still, staring into space. He could see in Mrs Parker thousands of similar old ladies, each in their own little street, each with their own tragedy. He wondered why he had to worry about it, how he got into such places. Mrs Neal had said, "Just carry on looking after your own kind"; it seemed that it was to go on for ever. Suddenly he wanted to cry, he thought of the sweet-shop, Jennie, Old Jack, Jimmy O'dell and the chimneys, and his recent fight with Tich Coulson, all came rushing into his head as though they wanted to explode out of the top.

The tears came slowly at first, then in fitful cascades of sobs and hiccoughs, reminiscent of a small frightened boy. He sat holding his head between his hands, and sobbed and sobbed. After a time the welling up inside him gradually subsided, as though he were drained of all burdens.

Mrs Freestone appeared suddenly at the kitchen window, knocking it sharply she shouted to her son. "I could hear you crying from my window, open the door – or I'll smash the window.'

Pimbo got up and let her in through the back door. "It's Mrs Parker, she's not well, Mum. I've been trying to help, you'll have to fetch a doctor."

Mrs Freestone threw her arms around his slight frame. "Oh, Pimbo, it's cruel, why on earth must I pick a son who decides to take on the whole world. You've been doing too much, I've tried to pluck up courage and stop you – but now it's all worked up inside you. You're only a child – I knew that one day this would happen."

Mrs Parker sat slumped in her chair, head bowed, with a trace of saliva oozing from her bluish lips. "Mrs Parker's had a stroke, Skipper said that's what happens when old people don't know what they're doing – are you going to call a doctor, Mum?" Pimbo's voice was now firm and steady.

Running back to number ten Maude arranged for her husband to ring a doctor. Meantime Mrs Bruce had wandered round to see what help she could offer.

"What's it this time, Pimbo? Helping old ladies in distress, eh? I must say that you're a marvel for ferreting out trouble. I'm sorry I was rude the last

time I came round, I've heard a lot of good about
you since then," she said gently.

Nodding his head, Pimbo replied. "I always visit
her, it was a good thing I was here – I hope she'll be
all right."

Mrs Bruce folded her arms. "I've seen it all
before, son. It'll be Chesterton workhouse for her,
she'll never come back. Nice little home, nice furniture. Worked hard all her life, she and her husband; tells everyone that she's got a daughter – but
it's just all fancy. Poor old girl – it'll be Chesterton
for sure."

Dr Roberts, who had attended Jennie, stepped
suddenly into the little kitchen. Feeling Mrs Parker's pulse, he then placed a stethoscope on her
chest. Shrugging his shoulders he looked up at Mrs
Freestone who had just returned. 'I'll have to get
her to Chesterton, can you help get her ready?"
Glancing at Pimbo, he noticed the boy's swollen
wrist and the heavy bruising running up his arm.

"I must look at the boy afterwards – his wrist
may be broken," he added hurriedly. After seeing
the old lady comfortable and prepared for the coming of the ambulance, Dr Roberts attended Pimbo.
Manipulating the boy's wrist skilfully he eventually diagnosed no breakage of bone. "Lucky for you
my boy, there appears to be no sign of broken
bones," he told Pimbo cheerfully. "I'll bandage it for
you and pop on a sling."

Arriving back at his home Pimbo found his
foster-father preparing a pot of tea, biscuits were
laid out on a plate. "You've had a bad time, eh son?
Your mother gave me all the story, now you must
forget all about it."

Handing a cup of tea to Pimbo, Bob noticed the determination that remained in the lad. Somehow it didn't seem possible that his tiny frame could put up with so much pressure. People from Barnwell, having heard stories of Pimbo's exploits, would ask, "How's the old boy getting on – what's he been up to now?"

Since his return from Papworth, Bob would smile at the reference to a small lad being called 'old-boy', it seemed a proper Cambridge expression. He some-times felt guilty at not seeing as much of Pimbo as he might have. Around Barnwell the name of Pimbo seemed to be turning into a symbol of everything a boy stood for, he as foster-father could only stand in the wings and watch his lad perform.

"Why don't you keep with kids your own age Pimbo? You seem to run into trouble by hobnob-bing with older people."

As Bob spoke the sound of an ambulance passed the door; walking to the window with his son, they both watched the vehicle draw up outside Mrs Parker's home.

"What's it like in a Union?" Pimbo asked, "Mrs Bruce said it isn't very nice."

Bob frowned, "People who never have to go, might think it nice. But I've seen friends who've finished their days in the Union – I wouldn't say it was nice, Pimbo."

"But why isn't it nice – there must be a reason?"

"I suppose it's because of ending up as nobody. You own nothing, you wear workhouse clothes. Everything you've done in life is finished – but let's talk about other things, you've had enough for one day Pimbo – I've got good news for you."

Bob smiled as he watched Pimbo's face brighten. "Mr Neal has offered me a full time job, I shall be earning two pounds a week, when you're older he wants you to work in the shop on Saturdays."

The ambulance was moving away from Mrs Parker's door, the small crowd was dispersing gradually. Mrs Freestone came through the front room into the kitchen and ran towards Pimbo. "You've done it again, Pimbo. What do you think has happened? Mrs Parker has left you some money."

Staring unbelievingly Pimbo looked across to Bob, who asked his wife, "But how do you know so quickly?"

"It was Dr Roberts, apparently he has attended Mrs Parker for many years. The old lady's husband died in the lunatic asylum three years ago, he left a large sum of money. Mrs Parker gave full concession to the doctor to handle her affairs as far as was legally right." Maude paused for breath. "Knowing her health was failing she asked the doctor to arrange that if ever she were taken into hospital – Pimbo would receive this sum of money. She stipulated that as you were her only visitor she wanted to make sure that you would receive something for your kindness."

For the second time that day, Pimbo cried. He remembered Captain Woods saying of Old Jack, "Miracles sometimes happen". He cried to think that his foster-parents might now to able to get things they'd gone without. He cried, too, for Mrs Parker who in her delirium had struck him with a poker – but in her sane moments had thought so kindly of him. He cried when he thought how lucky he was that these things still happened to him.

# CHAPTER 22

## Pimbo changes school

In order to allow his arm to recover Pimbo was away from school for a few days. The school clinic gave massage and heat treatment, and gradually his arm and hand recovered from its injury.

Skipper visited him for a chat, telling Pimbo not to worry about the incident of the poker. Mrs Parker had died on the way to Chesterton Union Hospital; a solicitor, helped by the doctor would shortly draw up a legal document which would benefit Pimbo to the tune of three hundred pounds.

"I'll see Mr Neal," said Bob Freestone, excitedly when hearing the news, "he'll be able to fit Pimbo out with new clothes – we won't know our Pimbo – shall we Skipper?"

Mrs Freestone hugged her foster-son. "It'll be shoes now, Pimbo. Shoes for best, what do you think of that, my boy?"

"I won't want other boys to make fun of me, they all wear boots. Shoes are for toffs, they'll laugh at me," Pimbo replied.

Maude hugged him again. "Just like you, Pimbo. But you musn't think that way. You'll feel better in nice clothes – you earned the money. While other

boys were out playing, you were thinking of someone. Besides I've never seen you in a pair of shoes, I
always reckoned that you were too good for boots."

Skipper and the Freestone family, after a long
discussion decided to allow Mr Neal to handle the
money left to Pimbo. On Skipper's suggestion the
master tailor would be allowed to invest the money
which would then be allocated to Pimbo when
reaching maturity. Meantime should a plan which
might be of greater benefit to Pimbo come to light,
this could easily be rectified.

Next morning Pimbo met Jennie on the way to
the school dinner centre. Jennie, who was filling
out, seemed happy. In Fitzroy Street they stopped
to window gaze in the large furniture store owned
by Laurie and McConnell.

"Mum and Dad's saving up for a new sofa," said
Jennie, "they reckon if ever we have a party, it'll be
just the thing for Peter and Mary to sit on. They
like Mary and her brother, Dad said that they
weren't stuck up."

"Do you like school dinners? What's your dad
think of your going?" Pimbo asked.

Jennie turned away from the store window. "Dad
said if he can get more overtime, I needn't go
because Mum will be able to buy more food. The
school board man told Mum that Oxo cubes weren't
enough for a growing child".

Reaching the bottom of Eden Street the children
turned and made their way towards the dinner
centre. By now other children, coming from different directions had joined Pimbo and Jennie. Pimbo
noticed how easy it was to identify a dinner centre
kid.

Boys had run-over-at-heels boots, torn jerseys, a collar too big, turned back by a large safety pin – or no collar at all, patched trousers, pale wan pinched little faces, and usually a sniffling cold.

Girls wore frayed dresses, usually much too long. Worn, tatty lace-up boots, their hair not only matted, had also a 'wet' look suggesting a soaking in parafffin to rid the hair of lice. Each child seemed well aware of the furtive glances given by better off passers-by.

The dinner centre itself was all rattle and bustle. Meals were served between noon and one-thirty, allowing the children to return to school in time for the afternoon lessons. A majority of the servers were ladies from the Women's Voluntary Service, who treated the youngsters with a kind of austere respect.

Jennie and Pimbo sat together. The smell of the cooking reminded Pimbo of the two urchins depicted in the Bisto kids advertisement poster shown in the window of Lucy and Mabel's sweet-shop. In this case, he thought, there was no fear of a child's staying outside – this was a free-for-all.

Grace was said at the beginning and end of the sitting. There followed a mad rush for the doors, where outside in Eden Street, the children split up to go their various ways back to school.

As he was due to leave school on the following day, Miss Cowell called Pimbo into her study. She sat thoughtful and kind looking as he entered. "Good afternoon, Jackie Thompson, or shall we refer to you as Pimbo?" she opened up brightly. "So you will soon be leaving us? I've been reading your record, first at the top of your class – are you pleased, Pimbo?"

"Yes, Miss Cowell, I wanted to please you, you've been very kind," replied Pimbo nervously.

Miss Cowell leaned forward. "A good friend of yours, a Mr Adamson, is a new member on the Voluntary Welfare Board for deprived children, we meet occasionally. He's told me a great deal about you, Pimbo. One thing being that you resemble a pollinating bee, affecting everything that you come in contact with – is that correct, Pimbo?"

"I try Miss, I'm not that good though, I'm lucky in that I seem to be in the right places at the right time – that's all."

Miss Cowell smiled at Pimbo's reply. "The nineteen-twenties are bad years for children, Pimbo. Mr Adamson also tells me that your health is improving – keeping up your malt, eh? I'm putting you forward for a place at the Central School for Boys. Mind you, you'll have an examination to pass – but I think you're capable of doing almost anything, Pimbo."

Pimbo was unable to think of words to say in reply to the headmistress's wonderful proposition.

"I believe you know a good deal about Jennie Smith, young man?" Miss Cowell said smilingly. "I'm keeping her here for another year – since knowing you she has come along wonderfully. By the way I was checking her composition the other day, she was writing about the May Balls, do you know that to Jennie it must have seemed like a real fairyland."

Rising from her chair the headmistress led Pimbo gently to the door. Pausing for a moment she looked down at the boy's inquisitive puckish face. "We have a book in the school library called

*What Katy did next*, I shall be awaiting the day when we have another, *What Pimbo did next*. I'm sure it will require a great deal of imagination. Good-bye Pimbo, good-bye," she said kindly.

Outside the door Pimbo felt tears about to come. Rather than face the class or teachers, he veered away from the classroom into the direction of the school' s toilets.

In the toilet he thought back on the happy days he'd spent at the little school. He wondered whether adults really knew how small boys felt when about to leave their old school to start afresh. He supposed that people like Skipper and Miss Cowell did. They studied children. Jennie's composition might have been read by many teachers. Bread and dripping, Oxo cubes for dinner, newspapers for table clothes, pawnshops and rows, that's what kids put in their compositions. Skipper was about things like that, he reckoned that he would like to do things the way Skipper did, he hoped that one day he might. Drying his eyes Pimbo returned to his class.

As Pimbo was about to go out of the school gate for the last time Miss Meakin called him back. She was clasping a small brown parcel. "It's for you, Pimbo, from the rest of the teachers," she said softly.

"Thank you, Miss. It's very kind of you all,' he moved away – after thanking the teachers who stood around watching the little ceremony, he felt again the urge to cry.

Outside the school he opened the parcel. Inside was a wrist watch. It was the first watch he'd ever owned. Strapping it on he found that the leather strap required adjusting. Being a short distance from Mr Cash's harness shop he asked the old shoemaker to adjust it for him.

"What's it this time, young man – not stolen property, I hope?" Mr Cash's eyes sparkled as he took the watch from the excited boy. Making a new hole in the strap he handed the watch back to Pimbo. "There, try it now," he said confidently. It fitted perfectly.

"Thank you Mr Cash – it's a present from the school."

"I know it is, I knew weeks ago," the old man laughed at Pimbo's surprised expression, "one of my customers is a jeweller – he remarked on what a funny name Pimbo was, said something about the name being inscribed on the back of the watch he was supplying for the school presentation." Mr Cash looked at Pimbo mischievously.

Pimbo stared at the back of the watch, the inscription read, 'To Pimbo, from the teachers at River Lane Primary School.'

Bob and Maude Freestone felt proud when Pimbo excitedly displayed his present. "If you do as well at your new school, well then you're half-way to passing your scholarship," said Bob. "You might have to cut out a few of your escapades, though," laughed Bob, looking over to his wife.

Maude smiled, "You may as well try and stop him breathing, I reckon he can do it and still have time to set the Cam on fire – eh Pimbo?"

Pimbo started his new school with a determination to do well. Young Street school was situated in a street bearing the name of the school. It was a very old building enclosed by six feet high railings.

On the first morning he found the playground overcrowded and noisy. The usual game of tennis-ball soccer was in progress and Pimbo felt self-conscious about his new shoes against the heavy boots of the other boys. With relief he heard a shrill whistle heralding assembly time.

The headmaster, Mr Legge seemed a kindly but firm man. He welcomed the new boys with a speech embracing integrity, trying hard, and playing the game. Pimbo felt strange in his new clothes, he wondered whether too much might be expected of him. Then he thought of Mrs Parker who, before her stroke would have been pleased with his smart appearance. Somehow this thought helped his determination to do well.

The classrooms were divided off by large glass-panelled walls, these ran on rollers and were pushed into position. Pimbo's teacher was Mr Mallett, a genial looking middle-aged man of immense proportions.

"So you're from River Lane eh, my boy?" he greeted Pimbo, "You've come with a good reputation, I hope that you live up to it. One thing though, don't get mixed up with the wrong crowd – they'll pull you down if they get the chance."

To his surprise at playtime Pimbo spotted Tich Coulson, he walked over to him. "I'm sorry about the fight," said Tich, "I was jealous of Peter. Do you think you'll like it here? Dad said it's my last chance to break away from my old habits – he wants me to try for the Grammar."

"Me too, I want to do well, my parents have been so good, and I don't want to let them down," Pimbo replied.

He found most lessons were well within his capacity for learning. The classrooms were much airier than those of River Lane. Mr Mallett turned out to be a patient teacher with a profound sense of humour. During a short break for a change of subject he walked over to Pimbo. "Most boys who come from River Lane primary say that they miss the girls – do you?" he asked jokingly.

Pimbo smiled, "In a way, but I think girls hold you up, I reckon boys learn more quickly than girls, Sir."

"Not a bit of it young man, it's the other way round – you'll find out as you get older."

"I think it's because girls want to marry and settle down," Pimbo replied. "They don't bother about learning, only cooking. Jennie Smith wants to be a good cook – but she's a poor reader."

The teacher smiled at Pimbo. "Jennie Smith will have to read well if she wants to be a good cook, otherwise she'll be unable to read her recipe. That's what we call motivation, once you make up your mind you can achieve anything you desire – that's what we try to teach."

"You mean it's a special way of teaching that will help poor kids?" Pimbo asked.

"I've been teaching for twenty-five years. I started at a public school, then at a private school, and on to the elementaries – in fact I've done the lot. In a school like this most kids come from poor homes, their parents never had a chance but boys are boys the world over – give a boy a reason to learn, then he'll learn."

Looking around the classroom Pimbo noticed that most boys were doing something; moving

books from their desks with heads tucked away
behind uplifted tops. Somehow he felt guilty at
receiving so much attention from Mr Mallett.

"It's all right my boy. I know what you're thinking. I'm not wasting my time on you. Every boy will
get his turn. I've seen a boy make it in engineering
because his granny gave him a train at Christmas.
One lad became a veterinary surgeon – just because of his love for animals."

"That's what Skipper does," broke in Pimbo, "he
finds out about a kid's background then gets to
helping them. I want to do something like that – do
you think I might, sir?"

Mr Mallett placed a hand on Pimbo's shoulder.
"Your friend Skipper is well known in Cambridge.
Perhaps I've got a head start because you see,
Pimbo, I know all about you and your interests in
helping all kinds of people. You're only ten Pimbo,
we must not allow you to think too far ahead. We
must teach you to be a boy for a while – then, hey
presto the rest will follow."

Glancing once more at the hard, tough looking
lads in the classroom, perhaps being a boy for
awhile longer might not be a bad thing after all –
Pimbo thought.

# CHAPTER 23

## Pimbo receives a toast

Skipper came round to see Pimbo at the week-end. He was carrying official looking documents under his arm, and smiled warmly as he greeted Pimbo. "A day of reckoning my boy, some good news, and a lot of planning to do."

Removing a document from the file he showed it to Pimbo. It was a report from the lad's recent X-ray examination, giving him the all clear. Pimbo was no longer required to submit to further tests, and provided he was sensible in both diet and exercise, there would be no concern with regard to future health. "You've been very lucky Pimbo, Dr Phillips will be writing a letter to your foster-parents. Not many boys come through as you've done – I always reckoned on you being that bit special," finished Skipper.

Pimbo nodded. Being involved had left little time for worry about T.B. Making friends with Bobby Watson, meeting Skipper and his friendship with Jennie had given him something to live for. His foster-parents too, had meant so much. Knowing someone loved him gave him a confidence he'd lacked at the Holt Sanatorium.

"What's the planning you speak of Skipper?" he asked suddenly.

"I shall be leaving Cambridge in a week or so for my vacation. I've been thinking that we've so many things to celebrate, that a real slap-up party should be arranged – what do you think Pimbo?"

Pimbo looked a little surprised. "What things do you mean, what things are we to celebrate?"

"Well in the first instance it's your tenth birthday. Then we have the success of the club, not one boy in Barnwell has been in real trouble since forming the club. Jennie Smith had been promised a party after her wonderful recovery from diphtheria. Captain Woods tells me that your friend Old Jack is still doing well and wishes to be remembered to you. I could go on Pimbo, there's Jimmy O'dell who no longer climbs inside chimneys, there's Tich Coulson – isn't that enough?" Skipper asked.

"But what's so special about those things, it happens all the time – everywhere?" said Pimbo.

Skipper smiled. "Pimbo this is 1924, a war just gone by has turned the country upside down. Unemployment, poverty, means tests have eaten the soul out of men who fought in that war. Their children such as you were born with nothing. In years to come someone will want to know how you kids got by, what made you tick – that's how we can help build a better future. You're only a kid Pimbo, but you're in on this, you and your friends."

"You mean the party will be at the club – everyone will be invited?" asked Pimbo brightly.

Skipper nodded his head in agreement. "Right, enough talking – I'm leaving it to you to tell Jennie

Smith and her parents, you may invite whom you wish.

The next club session was spent in a general cleaning of the premises. Skipper, Blackie and Silver recruited the services of Mr O'dell the sweep. Mr Sanders came along, and Mr Brown, although handicapped, managed to find something useful to do. The place was soon looking spick and span. Coloured streamers were sent along by Mrs Neal with a promise of more to come. Windows of the club were cleaned to a sparkling pitch.

"You see what I mean?" laughed Skipper during an interval for tea and biscuits. "A few months ago none of these people ever thought of getting together – now they can forget poverty a while."

Bobby Watson who had borrowed a large brush from Mr O'dell was making a noble effort at sweeping a reluctant cobweb from the ceiling. His efforts caused a merriment of laughter from Jennie Smith, who was busily making something out of the streamers.

Skipper's college had sent along lashings of good things, sandwiches, cream buns, and many other small sundries. Mrs Freestone was busily setting up the catering side of the party. During a lull in the work she called Pimbo into the little side room. "I suppose you've heard the good news?" Maude said warmly. "Your friend Skipper has followd up all your X-ray reports, he had been allowed to do this on account of his social studies. I wouldn't have been able to tell you any bad news – you understand, Pimbo?"

Pimbo nodded happily, he'd enjoyed a wonderfully mutual relationship with both his new parents. Behind the scenes they both had fretted about his welfare, worrying that one day they might lose him. Skipper had become their champion – what better than a sociology research student looking after Pimbo outside the home.

Maude held Pimbo's hand. "One thing I must tell you, you've reached the stage when you must know. Your father's identity has never been established, about your mother it is true that she died of consumption. We think that your knowing too much about either might not be good for you. During the war lots of things happened which shouldn't – but from now on Pimbo you're our son. From tomorrow the Children's Welfare has drawn up new papers in which your name will be changed to Freestone – how do you feel about that?"

Bob Freestone who had been standing by listening to his wife, broke the silence. "I'm not much of a hand when it comes to speeches and sentiment, but Pimbo Freestone sounds good to me, I've got something to be proud of – a good regular job, and a real son."

Looking into their son's face both parents read a complete answer.

The club was getting well under way, Mr Neal had sent along the Union Jack which now hung proudly over the entrance door. Jennie Smith, looking very sweet in a pretty party dress, had been surprisingly joined by Peter and Mary whose father the Dean had driven them to the premises.

Jennie was staring admiringly at the food tables set by Mrs Freestone, it reminded her of the banquet in the marquee. Jennie's mother was happily setting out little napkins supplied, too, by Skipper's college.

Captain Woods and his wife opened the celebrations with a short prayer. Several members from the Citadel were present, including Mr Dryden, Pimbo's cornet playing friend.

Skipper's opening speech was short but to the point. He stressed the importance of providing an outlet for youngsters, at the same time they must be guided through difficult times. Skipper related a few of the events which had brought about the club's foundation. He explained how Pimbo's fight against bad health had ended so triumphantly. An inference about Pimbo's tenth birthday brought the speech to its close with a rousingly sung 'Happy Birthday'.

Old Jack, looking sunburned and fit emerged sudenly from the crowd, pressing a pound note into Pimbo's hand. "For your birthday Pimbo – for what you've done. Remember the one way trip? Well, I think I've made it."

Suddenly all activities were stopped by Skipper, who had Jennie standing by his side holding a slip of paper tightly in her hand. It seemed that something unusual was about to take place. There was a whispered hush as all eyes focused on Jennie. Alf and Rose Smith stole admiring glances at their daughter as she stood in the centre of the club room.

Placing her feet tightly together she read from the note in a nervous voice. "Ladies and Gentlemen, this evening we have two special guests, many of you will remember the well-loved characters – I announce the presence of Mabel and Lucy Gray."

A little door at the rear of the club opened suddenly, revealing the smiling faces of the sisters. As they moved forward they were immediately snowed under by happy youngsters anxious to renew acquaintance with the former sweet-shop owners.

After a time the sisters walked up to Pimbo who had stood back allowing them to receive their rapturous welcome. "A real surprise for you, eh Pimbo? Skipper has kept in touch with us all along. When he told us about your X-ray reports, your tenth birthday, and of course the party – well we just couldn't stay away," said Mabel.

Pimbo stood timidly by as Mabel and Lucy hugged and kissed him.

The sisters seeming not a day older since their departure to the North, turned to address the rest of the party. "We have another surprise for you, there's a young man waiting outside – shall we ask him to come in?" beamed Lucy.

A hearty chorus of "Yes" filled the club room.

A tall smart looking youngster, dressed in a neat suit with shirt and tie to match emerged suddenly into the room. Pimbo stared unbelievingly – the unknown guest was Dollar Smith.

Remembering the words of his now legal mother, "Going into an approved school – either killed or cured," Pimbo thought at once that in Dollar's case a cure had been effected. Dollar seemed a changed boy as he gazed warmly at the two sisters.

"We've been keeping in touch with this young man," Lucy said in an effort to put Dollar at ease, "and he's not let us down, so we thought it nice to bring him along. Dollar has more than paid for his silly behaviour; he volunteered to help us at home, chopping wood and running errands. The Boys'

Approved School was just a short distance from our home, so we arranged for Dollar to be allowed out on good behaviour."

Moving into a crowd of his former friends Dollar was soon embarking in a flurry of hand shaking, Pimbo was amongst the first to shake his hand.

The party soon got under way. Musical chairs, musical parcel, postman's knock, and other popular charades were gone through. Mr Sanders, using Pimbo to show off his newly-found athletic prowess gave a shortened version of his favourite escape routine.

Mabel and Lucy each gave a turn on the violin, giving all present nostalgic memories of the old sweet-shop.

Jennie sat next to Pimbo during dinner, with Bobby Watson on one side, and Peter and Mary on her left. "I miss you at River Lane," Jennie was saying, "Miss Meakins says I'm improving my reading and doing well at cookery classes. I'll bake you a cake, one day Pimbo," she finished warmly.

Pimbo remembered telling Jennie about the poor girl who cooked well and won a handsome husband. He saw no reason why she shouldn't cook well and yet marry a poor husband, as long as they wanted each other. He glanced at Bobby Watson, thinking what a grand friend he'd been. It was through Bobby that Pimbo had taken such an interest in becoming strong. Looking back at Jennie, he decided that once he too could ride a cycle, he would take Jennie for long cycle rides.

After dinner Skipper, Blackie and Silver came over and watched as the boys sat listening to the music from the gramophone brought along by Peter.

"In a year's time you'll be sitting for a place in grammar school," Skipper said to Pimbo. "I'll have left Cambridge by then, as will Blackie and Silver. There's something special to tell you, and I want Silver to do it for me."

Moving away from the club leaders, Silver sat down beside Pimbo. " Well here goes, Pimbo, but remember a lot of people had a hand in this – I'm only the spokesman. The money left you by Mrs Parker, with the permission of your parents, has been put in a special trust towards a scholarship for you. The Educational Board, provided you do reasonably well at your new school, has allowed special grants to be made, giving you a chance to study sociology. Mr Neal has agreed on the new change of plans."

Pimbo looked happily across to his parents, then to Jennie and Bobby.

Silver went on. "You see Pimbo the interest you've shown in other people has paid off. Everyone had a good word to put in for you – sociology might seem a big word to you, Pimbo – but all it means is understanding people – you'll have a head start over many others."

"A toast, let's drink a toast to Pimbo," everyone was shouting. Bobby's father again provided drinks for the adults, but this time had not forgotten the youngsters. Bottles of Stone's ginger beer lay piled on the table.

With a glass of ginger beer at his lips, Pimbo smiled at his parents, then at Jennie, as he awaited the toast to be proclaimed.

"A boy's will is the wind's will – and the thoughts of youth are long, long, thoughts." Pimbo still couldn't remember the words, but he was thinking of scholarships, his parents and above all Jennie.

"A toast, a toast to Pimbo," said Jennie, as she smiled at her young friend.

CHAPTER 24

*Pimbo meets old friends Billy Sparkes, Bert and Emma Todd.*

# The Exodus

Some time later, coinciding with Pimbo's departure from East Road School, came the removal of
house into the new Council estate of Darwin Drive.
Maude Freestone was agog with excitement as she
journeyed down town to collect her key from the
Housing Officer at the Guildhall. During school
holidays, Pimbo had listened to gossip among the
neighbours and it seemed that not only his street,
but many others were joining the welcome exodus
into new homes that contained bathrooms, inside
toilets, coal sheds with concrete bases, and worthwhile garden space.

"We won't be able to keep chickens – or pigeons"
Chub Whitehead was saying over the fence to Bob
Freestone. "Only proper sheds and they must be of
a certain design approved by the Council!"

Glancing around, Pimbo smiled as he took in the
pathetic attempts at shed building that most residents had aspired to. Corrugated iron, once new
and shiny, was now incapable of reflecting the rays

of the sun. Red and rusting it stood out like a sore thumb. Cheap tea chests were used as sides and doors buckling under usage, it left gaps, and the well known tea firm Brooke Bond received a rather dubious spate of advertising space. Tate and Lyle sugar boxes, vied with the tea firm's commercial status – the fact that both firms were responsible for the production of the numberous cups of tea gulped down by the residents, afforded a kind of neutrality.

As each neighbour received their key, hand carts of all descriptions were to be seen lining the kerbs of the street.

"I'll get my lino down first!" Maude said excitedly "you'll help me Pimbo, as Bob's chest won't stand too much strain!"

Borrowing a handcart from Kidman's, a building store on East Road, Maude, with the help of Pimbo and Billy Sparkes, managed to load up the cart with enough lino to lay in the front room and one bedroom.

"It's not inlaid" she was telling Mrs Whitehead, "but there's not so much tread in the bedroom. I reckon that with my money for next week's work on the houses I can afford to get a square for the kitchen – Pimbo's bedroom can wait a while longer.

To many, the move from small houses which had been handed down by their mothers, into a large spaced council house was a major event in their lives. Pimbo had heard Maude say that people would miss the low priced rents. Some were paying as little as two-and-sixpence a week – the sudden rise up to ten-shillings would have to be found somehow. Then, too, extra bus fares would take their toll. But somehow on this sunny summer morning Pimbo, his friend, and Maude set out with light hearts and a hope for the future. It was as though they were entering a new phase of life – it was another Empire Day, without the flags.

Darwin Drive was a long winding street running off Histon Road. The brand new red tiles of the houses seemed to offer warmth and welcome as they entered at last into their new locality.

Empty handcarts, solitary at the kerb, told of the few others who had already made the journey. Whitewashed windows in lieu of curtains blotted out prying eyes, as furniture of all standards was manipulated into nooks and crannies. Mattresses, hastily covered, were scampered from cart to bedroom. Those lucky enough to be blessed with a visit from the Gas Company were able to boil welcome cups of tea.

Lucky new residents, whose house furnishings could stand scrutiny, proudly invited new arrivals in for a cuppa. Maude and her two young helpers worked hard in order to get most things done to allow a further return journey for a second load before dark. On the way back Maude related to Pimbo how many of the old homes in the back streets of Cambridge would gradually be run down.

Dobbler's Hole, Smart's Row, Gas Lane, all might come under the hammer. Small cul-de-sacs such as Brown's Yard, Shelley Row, and Staffordshire Gardens, would be boarded up ready for the demolition squad. The promised homes for veterans of the First World War had now more

than a mirage aspect about them. Maude said
there would be many a tear shed as Grannies,
having lost their husbands, would follow their
grown-up children into new areas with the possi-
bility of having to start all over again.

Back at Darwin Drive again Maude, with ster-
ling work from Pimbo and Billy, soon had things
shipshape. Bob Freestone was occupied in salvag-
ing little ornaments from a large tea-chest. These
usually occupied a place on the mantelpiece above
the fireplace.

"Hold it Bob!" Maude said suddenly "things are
changing, antimacassars are out nowadays; man-
telpieces and ornaments don't fit in with new
Council houses. We'll put 'em on the sideboard in
the front room – and be careful, a pair of those
belonged to your Mum!"

While Bob and Maude attended to the little
fiddly-bits as Pimbo called them, the two boys
walked outside the house to study the garden.
Small wire fences separated each home with a
wooden creosoted fence at the bottom of the
garden. Two doors away was a one-bedroomed
flatlet, one of a few dotted at strategic points
around the new estate. A large red faced old gentleman was carrying a tin trunk into a small brick
shed at the side of his flat.

Glancing at Billy, Pimbo decided that the old
man might need help – together they walked the
short distance to the flat. "Want any help, Mister?"
asked Pimbo brightly. As the man turned the boys
noticed that he was the possessor of a very large
red nose, Pimbo thought at once of the film com-
edian Schnozzle Durante.

"That's nice of you boys, perhaps you could fetch along the other trunk alongside my back door – it's not too heavy, but my ticker isn't what it was!" The old fellow's voice was warm and friendly. Having done their job, the lads were invited into the flat by the old gentleman.

To Pimbo's amazement the room was a clutter of old newspapers, magazines and large leather-bound reference books.

"You'll be finding out soon enough!" the old man said suddenly "they call me 'Old Cherry-nose'. Well anyway they did in my last place – I suppose boys are the same everywhere?"

The two boys, while 'Cherry-nose' was talking, took in as much of the room as possible. An old typewriter stood proudly on a small table under the window. Newspaper cuttings were pinned willy-nilly around the four walls. Pens, and pencils, lay strewn around the two large desks as though the old man was afraid of drying up for writing equipment.

"Well, I suppose you know by now. That's it, I'm a journalist, free-lance, they call me. Getting too old for regular hours, I like my lie-in in the mornings."

"What do you write?" asked Pimbo.

"Anything!" replied Cherry-nose "weddings, funerals, special events, unusual stories, about unusual people. I can look out of my window, and watch the Estate grow. It'll be good around here, watching people come from tiny back street homes, see how they adapt, watch the youngsters grow. I reckon there'll be a story in every home – what do you think, boys?"

Billy, ever at a loss for words glanced at Pimbo.

"Dad says as how a lot of people might not be able to afford the rent. Some will take a long time in settling down, especially the old people who will miss their friends!" said Pimbo, not wishing to let his pal down.

A shout from outside broke up the conversation. It was Bob Freestone. "Come on you lads!" he taunted good humouredly "you're supposed to be helping your own kin – what about it, or I'll stop your beer money!"

Cherry-nose, smiling broadly, slipped the lads two-pence each. "Come round when you like, I'll have a little job for you, chopping wood, or running an errand!"

Back home, Pimbo was surprised to see the change that his parents had brought about during his absence. The furniture, spread over a large area seemed to have taken on a new look. Maude had polished and shone, and utilised every space. "I've got twenty more houses to finish – with the money at half-a-crown a piece, I'll get a table and chairs. Pimbo, my boy, it's taken me nearly a lifetime to get a home together, but it's been worth it, what you can do by your own efforts gives greater pleasure!"

That's what old Cherry-nose would write about, thought Pimbo. Bert Todd was always on about a place fit for heroes to live in. He reckoned that being in the War entitled him to it. Emma Todd wouldn't be able to afford to fit out a new Council house. She'd have to put her stuff in as it was, it'd be swallowed up and Bert couldn't do anything about it. It was a good job Maude was able to clean the Council houses and earn extra money. Pimbo wondered how it was that the free-lance journalist knew about people such as they to write about. But he supposed being old, Cherry-nose must have come across something like it in his own life – you couldn't just guess about things – they had to be real.

Before going to bed Pimbo watched from his neat little bedroom window. It overlooked Gilbert Road which was a long winding road stretching from Milton Road and on to Histon Road. He remembered Bob, who was reading from a newspaper, mentioning that some of the well-to-do, whose homes overlooked the Council estate, had written into the Cambridge Daily News deploring the fact that working class homes would soon be defacing the scenery around their posh area.

With the wind blowing in apparently the right quarter, Pimbo could smell the lovely fruity smell of the distant Chivers jam factory. Well, anyway thought Pimbo, people who lived on the Council estate might get a job at Chivers. He supposed that the toffs from Gilbert Road ate jam – so the poor from Darwin Drive would be allowed to do something about making their breakfast table more appetising.

Craning his neck Pimbo could just see the flag of Cambridge Town Football Club. Their ground was a short distance away and he looked forward to seeing Cambridge play their "Derby" match with Hitchin Town. With a few more days of the holiday left he was looking forward to seeing Jennie and taking her around his new house – perhaps she might come with him to the football game. Then he would be starting his new school, the Central School for Boys, with new friends to make. But he

would keep in with his old pals, Billy Sparkes,
Bandy Banfield, Roger, and visit Bill Westley and
Cracker.

His mother proudly placed her new rent book on
the sideboard, so it would be conveniently near the
front door in response to the rentman's insistent
knock. It was Maude's habit to place her rent
money straight into the rent book as soon as her
weekly allowance came to hand. "If you can't pay
one week, you can't pay two!" was a maxim handed
down from her mother.

The council had a nasty system of giving notice
to any tenant whose arrears surpassed that of one
week. Just a formality, the anxious to please rent-
collector would say — but Bob reckoned that being
on the Council's book was a step nearer to class
warfare, but there it was, a new house was something that hard working mothers had cherished
since the birth of their first offspring.

Pimbo next morning helped Maude in putting up
new curtains. She had bought a box of Drummer
dyes and steeped a pair of sheets given by Mrs.
Neal from St. Barnabas Road. "Not too bad!" said
Maude, holding them up to the light "they'll do a
turn until I get round the sales. I'll bet the dye will
run when I wash them — but beggars can't be
choosers!"

His own little room windows were rubbed over
with a piece of whiting ball which was part of his
payment from a Tom King excursion into the Lin-
ton area. A peep out of the window would mean
rubbing away the whitewash, and a failure to
replenish some would bring a sharp rebuff from an
indignant mother.

A few days later to Maude's delight Emma Todd arrived, and was allocated a house a little way up the drive from the Freestones.

"Birds of a feather flock together!" exclaimed a jubilant Emma, "with your old man's asthma, and Bert's lungs, I reckon we women stand a good chance of always getting the last word".

That's one good thing mused Pimbo. The Council seem to have a policy of grouping similar types of tenants together. Perhaps it was for them to give each other moral support. Bob had reckoned that people who were unable to keep their homes clean were lumped together in whole streets – anyone not residing in such areas could be considered on a high status level.

From a distance Pimbo could hear the unmistakable chanting of boys from the nearby Akeman Street estate. Opening his window made the chanting more discernible. "Old Cherry-nose, old Cherry-nose" it went on, and on. Running downstairs, Pimbo went out into the street, and up to the old man's flat. A crowd of boys were mingling outside the journalist's gate. The boys were of the same age as Pimbo, but there were at least a dozen of them. One boy threw a small pebble, and this action was quickly taken up by others, suddenly the old fellow was being hit from all angles.

Unseen by the boys, Pimbo walked over to the freelance's front door, and gave several hearty raps on the knocker. Then moving into the path leading to the garden where the old man was defending himself as best he could, shouted. "It's a policeman, Sir. He's called for your report – he said not to worry, he'll come round to the garden!"

Without bothering to look around for the presence of the policeman, the boys bolted, as only
young boys with a fear of the law – could scarper.

Cherry-nose walked slowly from the garden to
the door of his flat. "Thank you boy!" he said
gratefully. "I think it's time that you knew my
name, I'm Mr Palmer. Your helping me has placed
you out of the Cherry-nose category. I haven't
heard my name spoken by a boy for some years – I
reckon that I'm a natural – that is, for baiting
purposes. It was quick thinking, that bit about the
policeman – how'd you think of it?"

Pimbo smiled. "I've had the police on my side,
and I've seen them in action against my friends. I
reckon you can use them to suit your own purpose.
Sometimes you can use them to a better advantage
when they're not there – it worked, and was worth
a try!"

"You called me, Sir, too. That was nice, I know
that you couldn't very well have shouted my nickname – but 'Sir' coming from a boy was extra good!"

Mr Palmer for the second time invited Pimbo
into his flat.

From a large trunk in the corner of his living
room he pulled out a coloured mass of folded material. Unwrapping it he held the material up for
Pimbo's scrutiny. "Curtains. I've collected them
over the years. Women take pity on me, bring them
along – I reckon many of them were trying to hang
up their hats. But I wasn't having any, being a free-
lance means flexible hours, women don't like a man
to be away from home!"

Handing the bundle to Pimbo, the old man
smiled "Give them to your Mother, I'm sure she'll

find good use for them – tell her it's my thanks for your good help today!"

Pimbo reckoned at once that the curtains might well fit his bedroom, and perhaps have some left over for other use. "But what about your rooms, can't you use them, it seems a pity –?"

The old man, with a shrug, stopped Pimbo going any further. "Men don't bother. If I put them up I'd never notice when they needed washing. Better no curtains than dirty ones – that's me boy. But there's one thing though, perhaps you can help me. My old pride keeps nagging at me, I'm always on the look out for a story, before I get too old to wield a pen – but anyway did you read this in last night's news?"

Picking a folded copy of the Cambridge Evening News he pointed out a small column to Pimbo it read: "Reports of strange apparition at Coe Fen. Ghost like figure seen amidst the trees. Weird noises heard by passers-by. Could there be a phantom of the Fen?"

Shaking his head Pimbo stared at the journalist. "I didn't see it, in the move I suppose Mum hadn't time for evening papers. But a ghost, how can I help you? I've been over to Coe Fen swimming, but I don't know much about the place!"

"You seem just the boy to me. Poking your nose in everything; I mean that in a kind way, hasn't anyone ever told you that you seem a rare one for ferreting out trouble – perhaps this time you may be able to ferret out a ghost?"

It was true, mused Pimbo, people many times had pointed out his habit of sniffing out complex situations – but ghosts?

"Well, you're game then?" Mr Palmer said confidently, "you can bring your young friend with you. I'm well used to tracking, I'll take all the risks, I need you as eye witnesses. You might be thinking why not take an older team? But boys your age are sincere, they speak the truth and the public will sit up and take notice. Then, too, I'd have difficulty in convincing an older person to take on the job – boys relish adventure. Go home and talk it over with your parents, then let me know as soon as possible!"

On the way home Pimbo decided on the method he would use to break down his parents into consenting to the rather wild-sounding scheme – he would use the curtains as a peace offering!

## Cambridge Past and Present

Cambridge, of memories sweet,
Characters in every street,
My friends lived there;
Who, over the passing years,
Helped mop my tears,
With loving care.

Lion Yard, oasis of glass and stone,
Casts out antiquated tone,
The Lion looks down;
As cobbles give way to mosaic,
Buskers fill in lunch-time break,
Shoppers, wear constant frown.

The Kite flies high – but wide,
Plans flow as ebbing tide,
A loyal 'mayor' proclaims;
But, open scars of once proud homes,
Lay, now, as flesh-picked bones.
Councillors, play waiting games!

Harrassed motorists park their cars
in stone mansions, with concrete bars.
Price of fuel, droops their head;
Tourists, gaze at gargoyled wonders,
politicians, hide their blunders,
try out fresh fields – instead!

School-leavers eye future – most foreboding,
Jobs, mortgages, health-care eroding,
but youth will have its fling;
Cambridge, august seat of learning
challenge youth, with all its yearning,
the bacon, home to bring.

Some say, the old die young,
their feats remain unsung,
Cambridge – must be bold;
a little of its famous past,
mixed with present – may hold fast
our heritage of old!

Fred Unwin

*The arguments concerning changes in the 'Kite'
(Fitzroy Street area) went on for several years. Fear
of change gave birth to Pimbo's 'Cambridge Past
and Present'*

## East Road College

St. George's school stands out proud,
Amidst East Road terraced houses.
Street vendors cry their wares aloud,
Some pupils wear patched trousers.
Its soccer teams win many games,
Ellis, Bullen, Bell and Palmer ("Cherry")
And many other illustrious names;
Such as, Cornwell, and Herb' Merry.


Mr Kingdom, is Skipper of the school,
What rival can come near him?
The lads are happy in his rule,
And most applaud and cheer him.
For those that cannot play a game
There's metal, and also woodwork;
Mr Taylor, helps the duck that's lame
To form life's solid bulwark.
Believe it, or not, the dear old place,
In those distant far off days,
Boasted, a science-room – of no disgrace,
Where lads could learn their trades.
St. George's, will ever lead the way,
Intact, through countless ages,
When poverty, and worse, held sway,
And boys grew up in stages,
Into men, whose memories today;
Hold dear to East Road school
That helped them in a vital way
To Live the Golden Rule!

*The author attended the above school, and has happy memories of those days. The following teachers will be remembered by many ex-pupils: Kingdom, Coleman, Mallett, Duckering, Price, Stubbings, Baldry and Miss Perry! God bless them all!*

CHAPTER 25

*Roger, the student, gets Pimbo's friends to form a Fellowship to help old people.*

# A shock for Jennie

One Sunday, a few weeks later, Jennie visited Pimbo at Darwin Drive. Maude and Bob had prepared everything in a shipshape manner. Dressed in a pretty summer frock, Jennie shyly made her way to the back way of number thirty-seven, a number which, Maude pointed out, was similar to that of her Father's first dwelling place after he was married. Pausing at the back door for a moment, Pimbo pointed out the freshly dug vegetable garden, and how Roger had talked Bob Pilsworth and his friends into joining the Fellowship.

"They came along and dug a bit for us, then went along to Emma Todd's" Pimbo said. "With Dad's bad chest it would have been too much for him – he would have worried about what the neighbours might say at a derelict garden – and him at home all day."

After tea Pimbo suggested that they take a walk around the estate, he would show Jennie the new home of Bert and Emma Todd and perhaps call in to see Cherry-nose.

Passing the journalist's gate on the way to Emma's, Pimbo noticed that his half-pint milk bottle had not been taken in. Knowing that Cherry-nose was a man of regular habits – it seemed strange that Mr. Palmer was not around. The two youngsters unable to get a reply at the back door of his flat, went round to a little window at the side of the house. Peering through the dingy lace curtains Pimbo was unable to see any sign of the old gentleman. It was a warm afternoon and suddenly Pimbo noticed something that caused him more than a little concern – a group of large bluebottles were buzzing around a corner of the room which he could only surmise might be Cherry-nose's bed. Bert Todd had told Pimbo a great deal about bluebottles, and the First World War. The old soldier at times had laid it on thick. It was usually after a big battle, rotting corpses, stench, and hot pitiless sun – like a swarm of bees! Bert had spared no punches. Putting two and two together, Pimbo began to fear the worst. He remembered the journalist saying something about his "ticker", perhaps the excitement at Coe Fen had been too much for the old fellow?"

A small ferret-faced woman suddenly appeared at their side. "I'm his next door neighbour, isn't he up yet? It's a bit late for him even allowing for his Sunday morning lay-in!" Poking around in her apron pocket, she produced a latch-key.

"The girl had better stay behind, you can come in with me as witness – I want no argy-bargy from the Police. It's funny, he was all right yesterday. I'd given him some curtains – said I'd help him to put

'em up – but he seemed quite determined to manage himself."

Walking in front of Pimbo the woman stopped a
few feet from the bed. Turning to the boy she held
up her arm as though in protest. "It's all over, no
need to come any further – he's as dead as a door
nail!"

Turning quickly, Pimbo spotted Jennie who,
with curiosity getting the better of her, had walked
a little way into the room – she was staring white-
faced at her young friend.

"It's the first time!" Jennie said quietly, "I've
been to funerals – but never anything before the
funeral!"

"You can get out quickly – my little madam!" the
woman said sharply. "Kids nowadays have got to
be in everything – you're Mum won't thank me for
letting you stay. Your face will stay like that, that's
what'll happen – your boy, here, won't want you
then, will you boy?"

Anxious for Jennie to leave, Pimbo nodded. "You
might dream, Jennie! Stay outside, I won't be a
minute!"

"I'll fetch a doctor, boy!" the woman said quickly.
"I'll straighten his arms and legs – but I haven't
touched anything, no money or nothing – now you
know that? – and don't you touch nothing neither!"

Left on his own, Pimbo got to reckoning again.
Poor old Cherry-nose had thrown a lucky seven –
that's what Bert Todd had called it. Bert said that
some men had an inkling that they were about to
die. It was like dying with your boots on, getting a
story, making new friends. Glancing at the table
which housed the old man's typewriter, Pimbo

could see a fresh length of typing paper had been inserted. On the top of the paper read "Coe Fen Hoax". Maybe, the thought of ghosts had made Cherry-nose over excited?

It was the first time Pimbo had made friends with someone, without that friendship growing into something tangible, whereby he could benefit from a period of experience of happiness. Now poor old Cherry-nose was dead – he supposed that Bert Todd had been through many such experiences during the war – but this wasn't war, and Pimbo felt cheated out of something special.

The little woman who had gone to fetch the Doctor, no doubt looked on the old man as someone for whom her motherly instincts, long since gone, might be dragged to the surface. Strange it was, he thought, that poor people looked after their own kind. He remembered Mr Twinn reciting something about "Let the dead bury their dead" – he wondered whether the present situation might be fitting to the text.

Now the woman was back with the Doctor. To his surprise it was Dr Webb from Maid's Causeway, who had visited Bert Todd at Gas Lane. Recognising Pimbo, the Doctor smiled. "Oh, it's you again, eh? I'm afraid you're too late this time, my lad. You are too young to be hanging around on such errands – now away with you, into the sunshine!" Catching sight of Jennie lingering outside the door, he smiled mischievously at Pimbo. "Next time I see you, it's got to be a wedding, a baptism, or Confirmation class – no more sorrow!"

With a last look at Mr Palmer, whose body the thin little woman was now covering up again,

Pimbo joined Jennie outside in the afternoon sunshine. At Cherry-nose's gate, they ran into Bob Pilsworth and his three pals. They were carrying spades and forks and seemed prepared for a busy gardening session. Noticing Pimbo's set expression Bob stopped and touch Pimbo on the shoulder. "What's it this time – don't tell me let me guess – the old fellow's had a heart attack? Just as we were about to set his garden straight!"

Pimbo and Jennie followed the newly formed Fellowship as the members passed the back door into poor old Cherry-nose's vegetable patch. The gang had cleared a goodish space. An onion bed, straight and firm as a die, stood out among the hefty clods of an old potato patch. "Me old man spent a long time on his allotment, taught me a wrinkle or two!" said Bob, knowingly. "I reckon allotments are marriage savers, every time he'd had a row with Mum – it was up the allotment. Gave him plenty of time to cool down – by the time he was home again with a good clump of beetroot, Mum had forgotten what the row was about!"

The screech of an ambulance caused the youngsters to stare out into the street, new neighbours, some with furniture remaining on the Kidman's hand carts, paused in their unloading to observe the goings-on.

Bob Pilsworth had something more to say. "Me Dad told me once about a village near Bottisham, Quy I think it was. They built new council homes in Quy, and the old churchyard was full up of graves – so they opened up a brand new graveyard – just as though it was for the new Council estate. Me Dad

reckoned they opened up a grave in the first week –
a baby's it was. Every day after, me Dad used to
watch out for new diggings – he reckoned they
were fairly regular at that!"

Pimbo smiled at Jennie in an effort to divert his
young friend's thoughts away from death. It
seemed funny, though, that on Bob's first consignment to break away from the dole it had to end this
way. Digging graves, digging vegetable patches,
reminded him of Mr Twinn giving a sermon on
planting potatoes, how the old seed died before the
new potatoes could grow. The old die that the
young might live, only Mr Twinn had called it
"being born again".

Suddenly, they were carrying the old journalist
away. The thin little woman after locking the door
came round the back to the boys. "You can pack up,
now!" she said tartly. "You've done a good job. I
suppose the Council will be letting again – three
months it takes to fumigate and distemper the
walls. P'raps you'll get another old fellow to do for –
anyway it keeps you off the streets and out of
mischief – I must say. The Doctor says to give the
boy and girl a tanner each, now off you go!"

Pimbo was left suddenly alone with Jennie. "What's
a journalist?" she asked. "I heard someone say he was a
journalist – does that mean he had to travel?"

Smiling broadly, he squeezed her arm, gently.
"Of course not. Mr Palmer wrote for classy papers,
like the Times and Telegraph. As he became too old
for a regular column he sent out articles all over
the place – freelance, that's what they call it!"

Looking puzzled, Jennie said "Why is the Times
classy Pimbo?"

"Well, people really like it. They fold it up, and carry it about under their arms. Only certain people read it, it's about money and deaths, and long letters from retired people. We have the Daily Mirror, but people like us only peep at the pictures, and just read the headlines, it's like someone telling us what to do, the headlines is just like a Schoolmaster watching over us when we have left school. The Times don't really have headlines – they call it Editorials, I suppose people who read the Times don't need telling what to do!"

"Poor old Cherry-nose!" replied Jennie. "You liked him, didn't you Pimbo?"

'I can't make it out!' blurted Pimbo. 'He's the only one who has died on me. Mr Adamson told me that everything leads to something but with Cherry-nose it seems a dead end. Somehow I thought it was going to lead to big things, him being here on the estate, all new and that. He said that he was going to watch us all grow up – write about us, and that I could visit him and tell him about things"

Jennie suddenly became all serious, as she had about cooking, and one day marrying Pimbo. "If it hadn't been for Mr Palmer, Roger wouldn't have met Bob Pilsworth. There would have been no Fellowship Club, and no gardens dug for invalid people. Cherry-nose started it all – and no-one knows how it might end. It won't be in the Times, for sure it won't, but if it were we wouldn't see it anyway! But we know it's true and that's the main thing!"

Pimbo couldn't help laughing at Jennie's serious little face. He remembered telling her at the Fair about how she could say big words and talk about nice things. She didn't waste words – not Jennie!

Then, too, hadn't he said "The ghost is dead – long live the ghost!" Well then, he would say "Cherry-nose is dead – long live Cherry-nose!" Perhaps the digging and the Fellowship Club might grow into bigger and better things. He would see the old journalist in every new venture, so indeed Jennie was right again – Cherry-nose would never die – that is – once and for all!

"It's enough about death" Jennie said suddenly. "Let's have a walk around the housing estate, it will be my first look at so many new houses."

Darwin Drive wound its pioneering way in a kind of horse-shoe pattern, which led into Akeman Street. The two youngsters eyed with anticipation the names of the traders whose proud signs stood triumphantly over the top of their respective shopfronts. Mr Sanders the baker once had a shop in another part of the town. Bob Freestone had spoken to Pimbo of the master-baker's hard working hours. Up at 3 a.m. baking until 8 a.m., then a quick breakfast, and serving in the shop until closing time.

Pimbo got to wondering whether the new tenants might run up bills in a similar fashion to that of their pre-move environment. Someone had said rates payable from the new proprietors left little room for much of a profit margin – they couldn't afford to allow too much credit!

Bateson Road, at the bottom of Akeman Street displayed a grand show of green in front of its shining new homes. Pimbo noticed that almost every house had a pram either at the front or rear of the house. "It's the Council!" said Jennie, brightly "they keep all young families together, the new school at the bottom of the road will save bus fares, that's what Mum said!"

A young man stepping from a small blue van attracted the youngsters' attention. Walking to the rear of the van he pulled out an armful of clothing which, having eased into a carryable position, he carried round to the nearest home.

"It's the Tally-man!" explained Pimbo. "Dad says they keep you poor. By the time you've paid for whatever you buy the things are worn out and you have to start over again."

Jennie smiled. "But poor people couldn't get much any other way. Mum told me that you just have to be careful and not have too many things. She knew a woman who paid out nearly all her money on a Friday night, and never had enough left over for her rent!"

"They're like vultures" Pimbo put in, "the van moves from home to home, right up until late in the evening. But some salesmen are good, they won't allow a poor family to run up bad debts – others, for the sake of extra commission pile it on, but they lose in the end because the families that owe money, drop out!"

Reaching his home Pimbo invited Jennie in.

Maude and Bob seemed more than a little concerned that Pimbo was feeling the death of Mr Palmer too deeply for a small boy. They realised that to Pimbo a new friend must play an important part in all the futuristic episodes of his young life. As he entered the little kitchen Maude looking across to Jennie, smiled. "I hope that you've been keeping my son busy, and his mind away from things that a small boy ought not to be enraptured in – what's he been up to this afternoon?"

"We've been looking around the estate!" Jennie answered brightly. "Pimbo reckons that anything that happens from now on will have the blessing of Cherry-nose – he reckons newspapers have power, and that his friend has started off something big. Poor people have a right to be included in stories about life, after all some people write about animals!"

"What's that to do with Mr Palmer, are you getting high-faluting ideas Pimbo?" his father put in.

Pimbo shrugged. "Of course not, Dad. I just couldn't forget the way Mr Palmer showed such interest in the way we live; his little room, the typewriter, all seemed permanent factors which fitted into this moving into the new flat and mak-ing friends with us all – I'm not worried about him any more, I just know everything will turn out O.K. Roger and Skipper would have said the same!"

Pimbo walked the short distance with Jennie back to her home. Noticing her thoughtful look, he squeezed her hand tightly. "You're not afraid, are you Jennie? I mean about Mr Palmer – I'm sorry that you had to become involved – but death's funny isn't it, it makes you think?"

"We're growing up, we've got to know about things. I thought at one time that people died only from Consumption or Scarlet Fever. We've got to learn together, it will do us more good than harm. I'll bet Mum and Dad don't even know too much nowadays – why shouldn't we know. My teacher told me that I must swot up more about history!" Then looking at Pimbo, Jennie laughed, "my teacher would be cross at me for learning about things that are nothing to do with King Alfred's burning of the cakes – and yet she expects me to attend cookery class to learn how not to burn cakes!"

Pimbo laughed back. The two youngsters turned into Auckland Road from Midsummer Common. A great white tent was being erected by a group of swarthy muscular young men. The name Chipperfield stood out in contrast to the white of the tent, the great red letters seemed to scream out the Circus's function as 'the Greatest Show on Earth'.

Trailers of barred coach-like contraptions were scattered at great intervals over the Common. Pimbo visualised the tigers and lions, monkeys and perhaps performing bears, that might be lurking inside.

Suddenly they were youngsters again, the thrill of the Circus, the animals and the clowns, pushed away their slightly morbid interest in death. Somehow Jennie and Pimbo knew that the old journalist would not have objected.

During Pimbo's boyhood, the Cambridge Daily News was sold on street corners. Buffetted by wind and rain, the news-sellers looked, at times, a bedraggled bunch. Thanks to Ron Bishop, an ardent employee in the News office, who had campaigned for years to have kiosks erected, they now sell their papers in warmth and comfort. Hazel, the little lady in the Petty Cury kiosk, has recently completed 25 years service. Mr Bishop keeps an expert eye on them, arranging transport and supplying them with newspapers. Cherry-nose, would have done the same.

# CHAPTER 26

*Pimbo records his adventures whilst undergoing training at Fulbourn Hospital. Jennie joins him as she considers taking her entrance exam for the hospital. Both are now in their late teens.*

## Pimbo's training at Fulbourn Hospital

The Intermediate Examination was held at Addenbrooke's Hospital. Taken after a year's nursing, it entailed a written paper on a broad spectrum dealing mainly with questions relating only to the first year. Pimbo felt fairly confident as he had taken copious notes during his sessions in the nurses' training school.

George Andrus, a first year student who had failed in his first attempt and was also taking the exam, arranged to cycle the short distance with Pimbo. Both cyclists took the short route by Tennis Court Road at the rear of the hospital. Leaving their cycles in a rack outside the Blood Laboratories they made their way to the examination hall.

"I'll show you a short cut," said George confidently. Amidst a maze of corridors and tunnel-like passages. Pimbo noticed suddenly that they had only five minutes in which to make the examination admission regulations.

"I'm going back to our starting point – at least I've some idea where to go from there," said Pimbo firmly. To his surprise George carried on stubbornly down the labyrinth of corridors.

Breathless and not a little anxious, Pimbo found himself at the hall entrance confronted by a stern matronly examination steward. "Not a good start, Nurse. Another minute and you would have been disqualified – you're from Fulbourn, aren't you?" she rapped as Pimbo meekly handed over his credential card.

There was no sign of George Andrus. Pimbo thought immediately of the psychology attached to such behaviour. George had once failed the exam – was this an histrionic attempt to justify another failure? Sometimes Pimbo hated psychology, it made one presume all kind of things against one's best friend.

Inside the hall were little desks adroitly placed to make it impossible for the passing of notes. Exactly in the centre of the room was a large clock. In the silence of the austere atmosphere it seemed to be ticking out a message, 'Do your best, do your best'.

Pimbo had enough courage left to glance round at the participants. Rosy-cheeked little general nurses, trim and neat in their starched uniforms. He saw no other male nurse – George had not made it! After a formal short talk from the matronly-type head – the examination began.

It was then and there that Pimbo lost his identification. He was now Student Nurse J. Freestone, the nick name Pimbo no longer existed. It was amazing how the name had caught on at Fulbourn Hospital, he supposed it was easy around the tongue. Glancing down at the questions he thought of the tutor's advice – "Read them thoroughly, then get stuck into those you are confident of doing."

Pimbo wrote industriously and thoughtfully for some time. Between pages he couldn't resist having a peep around the room. Opposite him was a flustered looking girl simply staring into space, at the corner of her eye was welling a tear. After a whispered encounter with the head steward she was whisked away into a side room. Some girls wearing confident smiles were hammering away with their pens in a dedicated attempt to carve out their nursing careers. Others to gain inspiration were biting the end of their pens. Pimbo thought of Jennie, who one day would be doing likewise. The questions were now biting a little deeper, he had used up the gift questions. Was 'hypo' – less or greater than 'hyper'? – He remembered a little code he had devised, 'Hypo – low' and breathed again.

He wondered if he had written enough, the time was getting on and there was still the essay to complete. Mr Langton had said, "Go to town with your essay. You might stand or fall by it. Open up your heart – it'll make up for the loss of an odd question. You've two more years; they want to know whether you'll stay the course – what you write in the essay might go a long way in making up their minds."

He chose 'What I Discovered in my First Year of Nursing' from three other subjects. From the corner of his eye he could see another weeping nurse escorted from the room. He lowered his head and scribbled away: he wrote of the discovery of what had gone before and how through the haze of past mistakes was emerging a brighter hope.

Of what it takes to become a good nurse, the pitfalls, the late night parties which eat away efficiency. He mentioned hierarchy visits where a scurry around to present a false picture was gradually being pushed to where it belonged – back in the Dickensian days.

Pimbo wrote of the paradoxical atmosphere evolving around many family admissions into hospital. He often thought that in a few cases the wrong partner was admitted. The frail woman who had carried on against her husband's antics of pub, football, plus the occasional philandering, had finally broken down, exhausted in both mind and body. The husband remained at liberty to carry on. Usually social workers were too willing in writing off husbands, as having anything to do with their spouse's breakdown.

He had discovered a crying need for a fresh look at the situation concerning the role of the husband. It was old-fashioned as in the case notes he had read, where the husband was considerd just a bread winner – and no more. Social workers must take husbands into their confidence; more than that, they must explain that times are now changing; the husband should have an equal share in the domestic scene. Pimbo knew young married friends where changing nappies, cooking and using the washing machine was now a chore shared by both partners.

Pimbo paused from writing for a moment's reflection. He wondered whether examiners might think the essay too deep for an eighteen year old student. Then again he thought how true it all was. Hadn't he discovered these points? At group meetings where such points were hurled across the room, interlaced with choice language, the pictures of family strife had been built up. It was in the first year curriculum. In remedial drama buried under the play acting was a real life cameo going on. Different characters, new names, but still something in their lives being enacted all over again.

Back to pen and paper he explained how knowing all this was in no way turning him into a wise old owl. When faced with a problem of his own he remained as indecisive as ever he was. One of his many discoveries during the first year at the hospital was of not knowing himself. The mirror he was holding to the world had no reflection of himself. Sometimes as he watched patients go through a crisis, he actually envied them. He was afraid that in a like circumstance he would be unable to match up to it.

The austere lady tinkling a bell told him that there were only five minutes to go. Several examinees were writing furiously, some with a smug air of confidence signed their papers and left the hall. On the stroke of time Pimbo handed over his document, tip-toeing from the hall.

Outside, as Mr Langton the tutor had warned, he experienced an awful feeling that he'd written a load of rubbish. On his return to Fulborn he found Jennie Smith awaiting in his room at the nurses' quarters.

"How'd you get on – did you do well?" she asked earnestly. "I thought of you at ten, then when I saw George Andrus return at eleven. I wondered if anything had gone wrong."

"George messed about, and must have missed the exam. He nearly got me doing the same, he'll have to sit later. But I think I did all right, it's funny I thought about you too: I reckon you'll be O.K. when the time comes, Jennie – it wasn't too bad."

Jennie smiling, commenced making a pot of tea. She knew her way around Pimbo's room, soon a pot of tea with buttered scones was taking the edge off her friend's exam ordeal.

"I'll bet you've not remembered about tomorrow night," asked Jennie mischievously, "now have you?"

Pimbo smiled. "Don't worry Jennie. I've got the tickets, no one misses the Nurses Dance. It's only once a year, we all want to get the hospital out of our hair once in a while. I'l pick you up at eight o'clock."

As they sat drinking tea he looked across to Jennie, who somehow seemed to have grown a little older. It was a long way from the days of Brown's Yard, poor kids' dinner centre, and dresses held together with safety pins. Jennie had grown up with Pimbo, shared the poverty of between-war years, was now prepared to share with him the excitement of psychiatric nursing.

"Do you think you'll take to nursing?" asked Pimbo.

Jennie shrugged. "It's stretching me to the limit. The old ladies' wards at times seem so depressing.

They scream and shout, mumble about things of long ago, throw food on the floor, fight and scratch each other – I marvel how the nurses stand it. Do you know, Pimbo, in spite of all that, I've actually seen nurses kiss these noisy, quarrelsome old women. The public think such things don't exist – but they do Pimbo."

Her young friend nodded. "A sister once told me how easy it was to love old people. She said that knowing an old lady had no one in the world to care for her, made it easier. But I suppose as nurses put them to bed, get them up in the morning, feed them, bathe and share the day with them – they're like mothers of small children really. How many mothers find difficulty in kissing their child?"

Jennie smiled at Pimbo's way of putting it. "Sometimes it's not as easy as that. My sister in charge is furious with one of the voluntary workers. He's a new chap, been on the ward about three times, stays for an hour. It seems that he wrote an article in his group's magazine, real negative stuff. Wrote of patients sitting staring into space, bored stiff. Of how some were made to go the the toilets against their will. He considered colour television, green lino, coloured furnishings, fish tanks as artificial items still reeking of institutionalization.

"What's she say to you about it all?" asked Pimbo.

"Said as how most patients where possible are given something to do. She reckons amateurs expect too much from old chronic geriatrics. A mother with a few months old baby expects it to be incontinent, expects to have to feed it, doesn't expect the

baby to be older than its years. It's really like that
with some of her patients, however noble you talk,
however idealistically you view the situation there
comes a time when certain old people reach a stage
where just sheer maintenance is the only thing
that can be done. An old lady of ninety, worn out
bodily, was confronted by one such amateur. "I'm
going to teach you how to play Ludo, my dear," said
this well meaning person.

The old lady threw the dice and Ludo board
across the room. "My dear, I never have liked
playing Ludo. I don't want to play at my age. Has it
ever struck you that some people simply want to sit
and remember their youth – I wonder what you'll
be doing when you reach my age?"

Pimbo smiled at Jennie's sincerity. "You're
right, Jennie. Some patients can do more than
others. It's not fair to generalize. There's a
rumour that staff integration is on the way. Very
soon I might be working with you on female
wards – and you with me on male wards – what do
you think of that?"

"Would you be a hard task master?" teased Jennie again.

"Of course not, by the way it's getting late, you
must be off. Before you go, since you've been talking of nurses kissing objectional old ladies – do you
think we might manage a kiss between us?"

Jennie blushing at Pimbo's request, said
quickly, "Psychiatric nursing does something to
one. Maybe helps shed inhibitions, working together is like – well, knowing each other."

Walking with her to the door, Pimbo turned and
kissed her full on the lips. He saw in her smile

something which said that their friendship was deep enough to keep both from having misgivings about becoming nurses.

The Nurses Annual Dance was held in the main hall. Most of the entertainment for both nurse and patient took place in this vast room. Throughout the years many changes in construction and decoration had taken place. At each side of the room were the shells of the old-fashioned fireplace. These had been replaced with fashionable storage heaters. From the ceiling hung a magnificent chandelier, where coloured bulbs strategically placed, gave when lit an impression of a cascade of precious stones.

A local band was providing music. Sitting perched on the stage they looked authoritatively down on the scene below. Jennie and Pimbo, as junior staff, felt at times rather over-awed by the occasion. Senior staff, a few in evening dress, kept together in little gossipy bunches. Pimbo perked up as he recognized several of his contemporary nursing friends gradually permeating into the large assembly.

Jennie was wearing a pretty dress loaned by a cadet friend. She sat close to Pimbo as though afraid of being swept on to the floor. As he glanced at the older staff, Pimbo realized how easy it was to get lost, and tucked away, in the bowels of the geriatric side of the hospital.

It seemed that the admissions section of the nursing staff regarded the other half, that of long stay patients, as the cinderella of the hospital. He laughed almost openly at his thoughts, as he looked over to Jennie, and realized what a lovely little Cinders she made, and anyhow they were at the Ball.

With the floor full, and the band warmed into a tune they both knew, Pimbo and Jennie took to the floor. They became lost as swirling dresses of the wives of senior staff fluttered around them. Jennie was smiling up at Pimbo and seemed happier than ever he'd seen her before.

During a lull in the dancing Pimbo spotted Mr Langton, the tutor, coming towards him.

"Good evening, young man. Mr Freestone I believe, isn't it? Let's see, you took your Inter the other day – how do you feel you've done?"

Pimbo blushed. "Oh good evening, yes that's right. I'm pleased about it. I took your advice and put all I could into my essay – I think that I might get through."

Mr Langton smilingly sat beside his young student. "And what did you write about, something about 'My First Year' I warrant?"

"I tried to remember most things, but since then I realize that I might have included a lot more."

"Such as?" asked the tutor, winking at Jennie.

"It was about the corridors, how much change in one
year the corridors show of the hospital's progress."

"The wind of change, blowing through the corridors – you could say, my boy," put in a twinkling Mr Langton.

Smiling at the pun, and realizing the tutor was trying to put him at ease, Pimbo went on.

"I see patients who once were never allowed to leave their wards, in the corridors, on their way to purchase from the canteen, with money that once was tightly governed by red account books. Patients who would make a dash through a half open door, now walk contentedly along brightly painted corridors." Pimbo paused and thought he would put in a little light relief of his own.

"I see strange contraptions in the corridors. Equipment which looks as though it came from strange planets. No scrubbing brushes, no pails of dirty water. Cables spread about and uniformed personnel placing warning notices of 'Work in Progress' at each corner. The new domestic army has moved in leaving nurses with more time to deal with their patients. They are infiltrating into the wards with suction machines, humidifiers, electric polishers. Strange plastic containers marked with '305' and '608' as though the liquid is a strange formula sent by the government in its fight against enemy agents – that's what I call progress. I wish now that I'd remembered to put it in my paper," finished Pimbo ruefully.

The tutor rising, patted him on the shoulder. "Enjoy your dancing. It's enough that you've told me. Look after your partner, I'm afraid we've been talking shop for too long."

Jennie, after he had gone, took Pimbo along to the buffet. Alongside was a fully-fledged bar manned by white-coated barmen whom Pimbo recognized as porters. Ham rolls, sandwiches of all description were on display. Collecting cardboard plates, they filled them with what they could eat, retiring to a quiet corner as the band began playing soft music.

"Tomorrow is Open Day on the ward I'm working on, care to come?" asked Jennie. "It'll prepare you for the day when we integrate."

"Anything for a quiet life, Jennie. What about us forgetting work for a change? What about your parents, do they visit, do you go home occasionally?"

Jennie sighed. "They're afraid to come to Fulbourn. You see Pimbo, they belong to the old school of 'yellow tickets' and the old word 'Asylum'. It was only because of you they let me join as cadet nurse – even then I had a job to convince them."

"But don't they watch telly, see the papers; there's always documentaries and articles about the new changes? Surely they must know things are different from the olden days?"

"Mum and dad were brought up fighting authority. Fulbourn to them will always be a place where the working class, when they lose their reason, are put out of the way of society. They don't realize that middle-class people and University dons have similar problems. To them Fulbourn conjures up strait-jackets, locked doors and hard cruel attendants – they don't believe anyone at Fulbourn is a real nurse."

Pimbo rememberd Alf Smith, Jennie's father. When Pimbo first called on Jennie to walk with her to school, Alf had shown his antagonism against authority. One day he might go home with Jennie and talk about the changes in Fulbourn with Alf. He could take pictures and the new literature, perhaps Jennie's parents might visit her more and attend Open Day.

George Andrus suddenly appeared and sat beside the young couple.

"What happened after I left you?" inquired Pimbo.

"I was a pig-headed fool, I went on and on, finished up at the stoker's furnace," replied George. "Now they're saying I funked it, they reckon I did it for the purpose – got lost so as to miss the examination."

"And did you?" asked Pimbo kindly.

"Yes and no. I wanted to scare myself into believing that I was doing it for that reason, then at the last stage I would make a dash and arrive in time to take the exam. Something went wrong, I really did get lost – but I didn't mean to involve you, that's why I let you go on."

"Well then, all is not lost. You can have another go, then you can prove them all wrong. Now forget it – by the way, haven't you a partner?"

George blinked. "I just came for a break. I like the music and the pretty dresses. Sometimes I get frightened thinking I'm a loner. Do you think it silly of me, do you think I'll ever make a good nurse?"

Jennie butted in. "I've been telling Pimbo that I feel psychiatric nursing does something to you. Makes you keep looking into yourself, then when you look too deep you don't like what you see. I suppose it might be dangerous should you overdo things – what say you, Pimbo?"

Her student friend nodded. That's right, George. I suggest that you have a chat with Mr Langton. I'm sure he'll get you going for that Intermediate. I remember in training block Mr Langton telling us that we all have a minor neurosis which we just have to live with – now what about a dance with Jennie?"

As the evening wore on, Pimbo and Jennie met several friends, they were mildly surprised at the number of people they got to know during a year at the hospital. Jennie promised that she would take him home to see her parents if he in turn did likewise with his parents.

Pimbo knew it would not be difficult. Bob and Maude Freestone, his adopted parents would be pleased to visit and call on Jennie at the hospital. Bob, who suffered from asthma had recently undergone a very bad bout, resulting in hospitalization at Papworth Hospital. For this reason he'd not been able to see much of them. Now with Bob coming home he would invite Jennie to visit with him.

With the playing of 'Auld Lang Syne' the dance was brough to a conclusion. The young couple had thoroughly enjoyed themselves. Pimbo had learned one important lesson – how very difficult it was for psychiatric nurses to avoid discussing work at social functions. Then he supposed it was the same for everyone. Jennie didn't mind and this time kissed him good-night without his asking.

# CHAPTER 27

## Kent House

Pimbo received a letter from the General Nursing Council informing him of his success in passing the Intermediate Examination. He felt good about this, and phoned Jennie Smith to arrange a small celebration. His new ward was that of acute admissions, this augured well for new experiences – Pimbo with a year's work behind him felt ready to move into a more intricate sphere of nursing.

The charge nurse, Ronald Burton, was a double-trained nurse, with motivation for experiment and change. Pimbo was given an early opportunity to experience Mr Burton's calibre.

A new admission named Klug, came in early one morning. His diagnosis was that of a psychopath. He came from a well-to-do-family, his father was head of a large industrial firm in Norway. According to his sparse case note history, Klug had apparently been in several mental hospitals dotted all over the country.

Klug, after going through the normal preliminaries of admission began to unpack. Large suitcases filled with expensive clothes had to be tabulated by Pimbo. During a short intercession, Klug received visitors with whom he walked airily over the whole area of Kent House, acting as though he was a hotel guest. In a final act of exhibitionary swank, he swung an expensive camera, complete with rare leather accessories, over his shoulder, stating, "I'm just showing my friends around the grounds – I suppose we'll take a few snaps."

Pimbo, being the senior nurse upholding to the Charge, lost little time in describing Klug's strange antics.

Mr Burton listened intently as Pimbo went through the gamut of Klug's behaviour.

"And what do you think about him? What do you think I should do?" asked the charge nurse.

Pimbo blinked. It was strange to hear his opinion being sought. It gave him a nice feeling that somewhere along the line his training record was not amiss. "I'd kick him out, I think that he's an imposter. I'm sure there's someone with more priority waiting for a bed."

An hour later whilst making a bed in a small dormitory facing the entrance to the hospital, Pimbo noticed a well-dressed figure striding down the gravelled path, carrying a heavy suitcase in each hand, assisted by a retinue of friends, whose contribution to Klug's discharge could only be expiated by the carrying of a large amount of luggage.

Klug had indeed turned out to be a typical psychopath, travelling from one psychiatric hospital to another. Rather than put his head down to assist in his father's business, Klug chose an easy way out – Mr Burton's fesh outlook had made certain that Fulbourn Hospital was to be very low in star ratings in the A.A. Handbook.

Terrace Ward was full of interest. With Pimbo's ever increasing knowledge he was able to extract the most out of the dullest looking case histories.

Harold Rhodes afforded the young student nurse with some exciting moments. His schizophrenic traits had begun with the death of his father. The mother, missing her husband's attention, had doted her whole being on the life of her son. Harold's sister led a normal young girl's life. Four years older than her brother, Katie had a nice boy friend with whom she spent a considerable amount of time.

Harold during the winter months rarely left the house, and spent his time doing out of character tasks such as dusting and cleaning for his mother. Religion had begun to play a big part in both their lives, Harold's interest being mainly due to the dominance of his mother. Gradually the young man became more and more inhibited, until the schizophrenia and the newly acquired religious fervour had bitten deep into the son's personality. Katie, sensing something wrong in her brother's behaviour, wrote to the hospital which eventually led to Harold's hospitalization.

Pimbo found the young man very pleasant, with a typical twist of conversation atttributable to a schizophrenic. Harold related to the student nurse an unusual story of whilst dusting for his mother, of knocking the hand off of Christ's figure emblazoned on a Crucifix statuette. For this he felt that he owed a penance to Christ. Pimbo tried in vain to persuade the patient to think differently and to accept the fact that Christianity taught love and forgiveness.

It was during the first hour of his early morning shift that Pimbo received a further insight into the mind of a schizophrenic. It was customary for patients to use an electic-shaver, for this a special socket was fitted in the washroom. A group of toilets was next to the plug point and Harold used the buzz of the shaver to hide the noise whilst he committed one of the most bizarre actions ever to have been achieved at Fulbourn Hospital.

During a lull in the shaving a nurse heard a peculiar sawing noise coming from inside one of the toilets. On investigation, to his horror, the nurse discovered Harold almost unconscious, having amputated a hand by the primitive use of a bread knife. The schizophrenic, in a cold calculating manner, had also provided himself with a tourniquet, and had succeeded in stemming any dangerous flow of blood.

After a while, in complete composure, Harold was taken to the casualty department of Addenbrook's Hospital.

"It was a form of expiation," he told Pimbo on his return from Addenbrooke's. "You might call it an eye for an eye, a tooth for a tooth. It's written in the Bible – so now I'm satisfied. I shall rehabilitate myself in the use of an artificial hand, and carry on as though my debt has been paid."

Harold was true to his word. He turned out to be one of the physiotherapist's most apt pupils. After a few months' hard grind in the workshops, Harold was able to turn out work with his new hand which might easily have put an ordinary limb to shame.

The nursing staff however realized that Harold, underneath, still remained a danger to himself, and a worry to his widowed mother.

After several weeks, Harold was allowed home

on long leave. It was strange too, that Pimbo was on duty a few days later when the telephone rang in the charge nurse's office. It was a call from the Mental Welfare Officer. Had Harold been seen at the hospital? It seemed that he'd left home clad only in shirt and trousers, presumably to return to the ward. The time of his departure was reckoned to be about 2 a.m. – as it was now 10 a.m., a disturbing gap was evident in the fairly short trip from home to Fulbourn.

Two days later Harold's body was found in the near-by river. It seemed that deep down, Harold's expiation had not been complete. It was probable that deep in the Bible lay a text which interpreted by the young man's poor sick mind – demanded another sacrifice – that of his life!

Pimbo thought deeply about the experience. It proved without doubt that paranoid delusions were the most dangerous aspects of schizophrenia. No amount of talk would budge a patient from such set ideas, it turned him into a would-be murderer, a suicidal danger, or an unpredictable menace to society. In some cases a Home Office order had to be made on this type of patient to protect both public and patient.

A few nurses believed that given a proper setting where perhaps an aspect of histrionics prevailed, a delusion could be broken, that is by a persistent pointing out of its incongruity in relation to facts.

Pimbo, ever anxious to learn, found an opportunity to try this theory out on a new patient. This man, a college student, was coming up for vital examinations. The undergraduate went around the ward insisting that he was Jesus Christ. It was done in very dogmatic tones, almost aggressive, and to Pimbo there seemed an air of artificiality about it all.

During a quiet spell Pimbo managed to engage this patient in conversation. Remembering his Salvation Army days Pimbo pointed out the humility of Christ, the love He spread and the purpose of His coming.

"The way you go about things is entirely wrong. You're not showing love. Jesus by his actions, pointed out that He was the Christ. Shouting out a name as you do – merely gets on people's nerves. You're certainly not anyone resembling Christ," finished Pimbo.

The patient became very thoughtful and to Pimbo's surprise made no attempt to challenge. From then on he stopped the impersonation, using other means to justify his admission to hospital as being anything to do with academic finals and the fear of failure.

Coming on duty one early shift Pimbo found a broken coffee table standing on one side in the patients' lounge. As he read the hand-over book, he found the breakage had been caused by a young epileptic's fall during the evening.

The patient was considered a pseudo-epileptic, a bad tempered spoilt child who was given to histrionic outbursts, manipulation, and almost psychopathic tendencies. He was in hospital mainly to define whether his personality change had been due to genuine epilepsy or that probably there might be a brain lesion which, despite numerous X-rays, had not been detected.

Pimbo after reading the reports went down into the dormitory to supervise patients preparing for breakfast. The epileptic had made no effort to rise but pointed to the bottom of the bed. "It's my toe, Nurse. It's sore, I can't walk on it; can I stay in bed until the doctor sees it?"

Lifting the bedclothes, Pimbo scrutinized the patient's toe. It was very red, swollen, and to his reckoning might well be broken. "O.K., you do just that. I'll get a bed-cradle to take the weight off it until the doctor comes."

Walking down to the clinic he met the shift's staff nurse, and asked if he might have a bed-cradle, explaining the situation.

"Now look here, don't tell me he's caught you. Always up to his manipulations – tell him to get up." The staff nurse's voice was firm as he walked briskly away.

Realizing a sense of injustice somewhere along the line, Pimbo spotting two more nurses approaching the patient, with an irate staff nurse behind, decided that he'd done enough, so moved away to the far side of the dormitory.

There was instant chaos. A furious scuffle ensued, bed clothes were strewn everywhere and the epileptic was locked in combat with two nurses who seemed intent on his getting out of bed. Suddenly the appearance of Mr Burton caused a cessation of hostilities.

"What's all this then?" demanded the charge. "Anybody know what caused this fracas?"

The staff nurse looked over to Pimbo. "It was Freestone, Ron. He fell for his usual line – bed-cradle and all."

Mr Burton stroked his chin. "Looks to me like a case of failing to read the hand-over book. Isn't it possible that the patient has hurt his toe, or didn't you notice the broken table? Get him back to bed at once – Nurse Freestone fetch a bed-cradle and set it up, I'll have the doctor along after breakfast."

The charge nurse called Pimbo into his office immediately after breakfast. "It was a case of leading the pitcher to the well once too often – or 'crying wolf' as they say. The staff nurse, being late on duty, met you in the corridor before reading the nurses' report. It's a lesson to us all never to take things for granted. Don't get a swollen head over your part in the proceedings – you'll get caught yourself one day. By the way, the fellow's toe is broken, he'll have to go for X-ray later this morning – you can go as escort, seems he had a lot to say in your favour."

During his short break, Pimbo thought over the mornings' event. It worried him that he might have fallen foul of the staff nurse and others. Nursing on Terrace Ward was an exacting duty. Sometimes at the end of a stint he felt emotionally drained. Team work was most essential, it had been said that becoming involved with physical attacks by patients with a timely rescue by nurses made the attacked nurse 'one of the team'. In Pimbo's case it seemed that this theory had been put in reverse. His thoughts were broken by the arrival of the staff nurse, who this time was smiling warmly at Pimbo. "I'm sorry boy," he said, "I acted badly, my biggest mistake was not reading the hand-over book. It can and will happen to the best of us." Joining Pimbo in a cup of coffee the staff nurse went on. "We had a patient here once, an old schizophrenic, always complaining that the rats were eating away his stomach. One day at a doctor's meeting I put forward a suggestion that there might be something more to it than the stock delusion. The doctor ordered stomach X-rays and it was discovered that the patient was right. A carcinoma was actually eating away his stomach."

Many of Terrace Ward's admissions were patients who it was thought, returned when the domestic side of life was becoming a bit too much for them. Ronald Burton's 'new look' policy decided that in future this type of patient would be sent immediately to the old block. Kent House in itself certainly looked an inviting place, rather on the lines of a hotel. Beautiful drapes, coffee tables in liberal supply, television, and a lounge furnished with settees and chairs all of which were top class furnishings.

An excellent dining-room, separate tables, with choice of menu, piped music, and again with furniture of top class. Patients attended a ward meeting at 9 a.m. Here, they could discuss themselves, each other, criticise both doctors and nursing staff. During the evening dances, socials, films and games were at their disposal. Also a large art therapy room staffed by qualified staff could be used at any time of the day.

It is small wonder that the mention of the 'old block' to a returning patient was received coldy. One such patient, not bothering to unpack her bags, immediately called a taxi and returned home.

Life was very fast moving, one morning Pimbo helped in the admittance of a University professor. The unfortunate man was suffering from a recurrent attack of hypomania, which is the active part of a manic-depressive. Before hospitalization the professor had 'organized' a spurious trip to the Antarctic. Boots the Chemists had been inundated with orders for a thousand hot water bottles and numerous other articles which might have been required had such a trip existed.

Friends of the professor had received letters, perfectly typed and grammatically correct, inviting them to participate on the expedition, both physically and financially. The patient spent much of his time in a side room sending off countless letters on new ventures, and had they been despatched, would have caused disruption amongst the social circles of the professor's wide acquaintances.

A further problem caused by the patient's illness was the pacification of his wife. On each admittance she threatened to leave him, but due to the exuberant spirit brought about by his malady, the professor found difficulty in taking his wife's threat seriously – making matters worse.

However, with electro-convulsive-therapy, plus medication, the University man was returned to the safety of the college cloisters until his next mood swing.

Hypomanic symptoms amongst the working class patients, however, brought different problems. Much of this was in the category of sixth-form pranks. Pimbo, one early shift while making beds near a window, saw what looked like a hedge moving. Knowing that Charlie Meadows, a 'hypo' had been reported missing, Pimbo immediately informed the nursing office of his suspicion; it seemed that a coloured hat just visible above the hedge was one usually worn by Charlie.

A junior nursing officer picked Pimbo up in his car and set off towards the moving hedge.

As the officer sped along the road towards Cambridge, Pimbo out of the corner of his eye spotted a figure walking towards the hospital carrying an enormous bunch of flowers, corn stalks, and hedge-growth of every description. The bundle was so high that Pimbo realized how he'd mistaken the patient for a walking hedge. Charlie had been waving down the car in order to attract attention.

With a screeching of brakes the nursing officer turned the car round and drove slowly up to Charlie.

"What the hell game do you call this?" demanded the officer. "A merry dance you've led us. We've had the police out since midnight – and here you are carrying a load of rubbish."

In true manic style Charlie replied, "Why are you so mad? It's a lovely morning, the sun's shining, I'm celebrating the beauty of the day by gathering God's flowers. Anyway, I tried to stop you going by, had I not waved, you'd have been half-way to Cambridge. Why bother me? I'm happy – it's you that needs cheering up."

The fact that Charlie had picked the flowers from private gardens, snatched ears of corn from the harvest fields meant nothing. He was happy and the world had to know it.

Another of Charlie's little tricks was to drive a double decker bus away from the depot and leave it parked outside the Main Reception Office at Fulbourn.

In deeper trouble, Charlie once managed to enter a room where a group of senior nurses were having a discussion, and steal a cash box containing fifty pounds. Only with the aid of police dogs was the money recovered, Charlie had buried it under the window of the chief nursing officer's block of offices.

As most hypomanics do, however, Charlie went a little too far in an escapade at his work's factory. This involved the police and Charlie's name appeared in the local press. Pimbo met his wife one afternoon while Charlie was undergoing legal proceedings away from the hospital. Mrs Meadows was a brave little woman, pretty, with a typical countrywoman's complexion.

"I'm nearing the end of my tether, Nurse, this time Charlie has dragged the family into it. They laugh at the children in school, somehow I can't face the neighbours any more. At first they seemed to understand – but now – ?"

Pimbo could only nod in sympathy. It was the same old story. It seemed so unfair that the wives should suffer so. There were many patients with Charlie's complaint dotted over the hospital. Some had been in for years, been from ward to ward. New doctors, anxious to impress, had tried experiment after experiment – but still the only hope lay in remission. Each admittance was like the sea eating away at the cliff edge – in Charlie's case the crumbling away had reached the size of an avalanche.

"I'm sorry," said Pimbo. "It's an illness, the doctors do what they can. Charlie has little control – he needs support, you're the only one, once he leaves here, that can give it him."

Jennie Smith came along in the evening to help

celebrate Pimbo's success in passing his examination. She seemed happy and well; Pimbo offered a
sherry and took one himself.

"Here's to the first leg of your nursing career,"
said Jennie as she raised her glass level to that of
her young friend. "Mum and Dad send their best
wishes, and hope you will visit them when next you
come home."

"I'm waiting for your turn. Just think, at school
together, nursing together and perhaps one day we
will be fully trained together – and then?" Pimbo,
perhaps with the help of the sherry, had gone deeper
into Jennie's future than ever he'd done before.

"And then – what?" Jennie lost no time in slipping into the opening which Pimbo had offered.

"Fulbourn's a big place, Jennie. We two can be
lost in a world of schizophrenias, depressions, and
other mental illness. It's not fair, we give out all the
time. It's expected of us; the other day a tiny little
Chinese nurse, in England for only a week, was put
on a ward with aggressive psychopaths, she was
thrown to the ground, and her hair was tugged
almost from the roots – 'and then' is my way of
saying we must stick together Jennie, you and I.
We've come a long way together and there's something in it for us – there must be."

Jennie clasped Pimbo by the arm. "I'm glad you
said that. Sometimes I'm afraid. When I think of you
it makes me feel stronger. If you weren't in the
hospital – I couldn't stay. When I hear the old ladies
screaming I ask myself if I can see it through. Some
nurses leave, but I want to stay. The home sister said
I've the makings of a good nurse. She said my room's
so tidy – but she doesn't know that it's because I

daren't let her see it otherwise. Do you think I'd make a good nurse, Pimbo?"

Pimbo thought of the nurses he'd met so far. The intellectuals whose opinions usually outshone their deeds. The youngsters who really wanted to become nurses. He recalled how fate decreed that the intellectuals passed their exams, whereas sometimes the latter type fail. Somehow he knew Jennie would get by, he would see to that, he would help her – and then, he smiled at the same words cropping up again. But this time he knew 'and then' would be that one day he would marry Jennie.

Jennie looking on somehow sensed his thoughts. Filling his glass and her own, once more she raised a toast. "To 'and then'," she said laughingly.

Kent House, Terrace Ward and its occupants, were far from Pimbo's thoughts as he clasped her close to him. "Of course you'll make a good nurse – and a good wife, too," he said warmly.


## Varsity Drug-Addict


My thoughts were as the wind, to wander
More curious than a cat to find,
Something, beyond the intellect or reason,
Wherein I may enhance an average mind.
A no-man's land of fantasy to enter,
Barbs of positioned wire, dip in my soul.
Tear at health, wage war against society,
Of reputation take a heavy toll.
Labyrinths of twisted thought meandered,
Through cul-de-sac of grandiose tinted dreams,

Alas, my college days, now over,
Distintegrate long thoughts of youth, it seems!

Fred Unwin

*During his days as a psychiatric nurse at Fulbourn
Hospital and hostel-keeper at King's College, the
lament of the above student gave cause for the
writing by Pimbo of 'Varsity Drug-Addict'.*

## The Attic Room

Room of mine, viewed with awe,
Slanted beams, the dark stained floor.
My very books seem to despair,
To emulate who once was there.
Through the window, on roofs I see,
Birds, that seem to mock at me.

I sit and ponder, wonder why?
To pass exams, I ever try.
Last term's occupant, fared so well,
Tutors, try my despair to quell.
Through the window, on roofs I see,
Birds, that seem to mock at me.

Terms pass by, exams are done.
My degree obtained, with honours won.
Parents come, with pride and joy,
Praise the efforts of their boy.
Through the window on roofs I see,
Birds, I swear, that sang for me.

*Pimbo's poem, concerning the ruminations of an
anxious student.*

# CHAPTER 28

# Training school

Pimbo was due for a week in school. Apart from an initial six week training stint, the rest of the training schedule was split up into two-weekly and weekly blocks. On the first morning a lively discussion was taking place on the merit of punctuality.

"I think that a nurse who turns up punctual at every duty stint is likely to be a little on the neurotic side. She worries herself sick lest she be late, and the other nurses' opinion on her is more important than her punctuality record." The junior tutor started the ball rolling.

"On the other hand, you get a nurse a few minutes late who comes in all smiles and apologies, and seems better balanced, in that she cares not what her colleagues think about her."

Pimbo listened to heated replies on the tutor's examples. It seemed to the young nurse the psychology at times could be very misleading. One morning when unavoidably late he noticed the disappointed look on the night nurse's face when she realized that she had missed her bus through his lateness. Stability and neurosis was not a factor the nurse was interested in – she just wanted to get off the ward after a hard night's work.

Then too, this logic might well apply at any time. One morning whilst surveying an excellently kept ward by the outgoing night nurse, Pimbo heard the day sister remark, "What's she trying to prove?" The good work done by this conscientious nurse had been belittled, for what reason?

Pimbo thought that may be this sister had found difficulty in coming up to such a standard. "What's she trying to prove?" could well be a remark made out of jealousy.

Bringing out this example, Pimbo obtained scant respect for his analysis by the remainder of the class. Some suggested that the night nurse was in the same category as the nurse who was always punctual. This nurse was more afraid of her image than not daring to leave a ward less than excellent. Few gave her credit for doing a good job of work. Pimbo reckoned that should this policy be adopted, nursing would consist of hard faced neurotic nurses doing excellent nursing, and carefree lackadaisical nurses with lower standards being considered the acme of the nursing profession.

This argument led into the awkward question, what is a good nurse? One member of the class pointed out that a charge nurse, now retired, told him of a nurse's report being returned to him with a note inside, 'No nurse can be that good'. The report had been full of glowing reports about this nurse, whom the charge had considered an excellent student.

The tutor stepped in. "It could be that this particular nurse had been good in so far as she had achieved. This would make her less than whole. In the next phase of her training it might well bring out weaknesses which had not been highlighted. This could apply vice-versa to a nurse who had not shown initial excellency, but improved during further training."

A general argument ensued on the merits of the intellectual nurse against that of her more practical colleague. Most thought the former was inclined to be lazy, but generally managing to talk her way into the good books of people that mattered.

Pimbo thought at once of a student who whilst the charge nurse was present, practically bristled with ideas and talk of improvements. Left on his own, this young man was hard pushed in doing the most routine of tasks, these he left to the 'practical' nurse, whilst he read up a few case notes. It was finally agreed that a rare combination of both intellect and practicability was the ingredient more desirable for producing a good nurse.

Case note jottings and over-sweeping statements came next under the hammer. A nurse pointed out an unusual case where the patient and the patient's father were well known to him. The patient, a man of very low I.Q. or mental capability, was the eldest of a large family. The father, now a prosperous businessman had worked his way up from the lowest rung of the ladder. During his climb, the father had done everything possible in helping his sub-normal son. He had tried him out in different departments, in each case the son had caused havoc to the business, doing enough damage at one stage almost to bring the business to an end.

The son bullied his brothers and sisters, finally bringing things to a climax with an assault on an elderly neighbour. This brought about his hospitalization at Fulbourn Hospital.

The father made regular visits to Fulbourn and usually stayed with his son for several hours. The nurse in question pointed out the sincerity of the father's feelings for his son, which came out in conversations between the two which took place outside earshot of the patient.

One day to his surprise, whilst reading up the patient's notes, he read the following entry by a psychologist. 'This man shows more concern in building up his business, than he does for the welfare of his son.'

Mr Langton, the Senior, who now had taken over the sessions at the interval for coffee, looked around the bevy of eager young students. "The psychologist may well have been wrong, but you must remember he had only an hour or so to sum up the situation. It depends upon the father's attitude during the confrontation – some people are never at their best whilst undergoing cross-examination." He paused in order to allow his words to have effect.

"Nowadays, this sort of mistake is not likely to happen. From the G.P. onwards, and the covering support from the social worker, we should alleviate such problems – but always we must be on the look-out for cases which might slip through the net."

The tutor went on to relate how during his early days at another hospital, the old case notes showed how, due to immense numbers of patients and gross understaffing, mistakes of diagnosis might occur. A young doctor fresh from college noticed that a very old patient who was blind, had on his admission to the hospital been diagnosed as a G.P.I., an affliction due to syphilis. The case notes showed how a small red typed passage, worded in exact phrases as the initial entry, appeared with monotonous regularity year after year. The doctor queried the diagnosis on the grounds that there was no deterioration in the patient, no record of any more investigations, and that the patient, now ninety, was in excellent health. For some years he had worked in the hospital laundry, and his blindness was due mainly to haemorrhages at the back of the eyes.

The doctor's exposition achieved nothing towards putting the clock back, but the hospital superintendent ordered a careful check of all case notes which helped considerably in the prevention of further mistakes escalating year after year.

The policy of the training school, that of concentrating on practical demonstrations which had direct bearing on what actually happens on the ward, was brought out forcibly in the next session. A middle-aged patient had agreed to present herself for questioning by the students. She realized the implications involved, but had been so grateful for what the hospital had done for her, that this she felt was a way of saying thank you.

She had lost both parents at the age of seven. Her father had been killed in the Second World War, her mother died during childbirth. An auntie living some distance from the patient's home had agreed to bring up the young girl, the legal documents were thus completed.

During the students' questioning, Peggy brought out facts which pointed to her ensuing unhappiness. Gradually she found that she had to do everything two or three times, this exacerbated into a set number of times, and thus she found that the toilet chain, before she was able to leave the toilet, had to be pulled eight times. She became obsessed in everything. Had she turned off the gas tap? Was the door bolted? The light switch off? Until bouts of severe depression set in which finalized in her hospitalization.

"Did you ever feel at any given time where you might be able to say that 'this was the beginning', where suddenly you found a change in your outlook on life?" Pimbo's question caused Peggy's face to brighten for a moment. Then it clouded into a typical expression of the depressed patient, corner of the mouth dropped slightly, with heavy sad eyes.

"It was one day when my auntie must have been very cross with me. I was eleven at the time, and had been out to play. I was a little late, and to worsen matters had dirtied my dress. My auntie grabbed me by the shoulders and shook me – I shall never forget her face as she yelled at me, 'You little brat, you'll turn out just like your mother – no bloody good.'"

Peggy paused and to the embarrassment of the class began to cry. Mr Langton touched her gently on the shoulder, and arranged for a cup of tea and her departure into a quiet room at the back of the training school.

"Well, now, does anyone feel that the outburst from Peggy's auntie had anything to do with her eventual breakdown?" Mr Langton, despite the previous incident, spoke with a completely detached tone of voice.

Most students agreed that it could have been the straw on the camel's back. Some felt that Peggy would have broken down at some time anyway. She seemed the type that was born to lose, and had it not been auntie, well, it would have been something else.

Pimbo pointed out a case where an adopted child, who was unaware of her foster parents not being her real parents, was told by the next door neighbour of the real situation, which caused the child, aged eleven to become one of the most disturbed patients in the home to which she was forcibly sent, and now this girl aged nineteen, was in a female refactory unit of this hospital.

Mr Langton nodded his head. "You see people can only tolerate so much. Some people's tolerance level is higher than that of others. Each person reacts to a sudden shock, a disappointment, a failed exam, in the only way their personality dictates. It is said of Freud, to whom we owe so much, that one day when told of a colleague's slight disagreement of his thesis, that Freud fainted like an hysterical woman – and yet here we have a man presumably with all the answers. In Peggy's case we can only assume; remember that patients at times attribute a breakdown to something which happened years ago, a widely used excuse is that of stealing a coin from the collecting box in Sunday School."

"But why is nothing clear cut?" put in a student. "We argue and debate, yet psychology seems to be a medium in which anything goes. It almost seems an abstract art – small wonder that the psychologist's couch becomes the butt of newspaper cartoons."

"I welcome the day whenever it comes for psychiatric treatment and results to be clear cut. We shall be able to empty the hospitals. Remember in general medicine there is no absolute clear cut method of effecting cures for all ailments. I must tell you of a book I was reading about Judy Garland. The most eminent psychologists in the world were called in for her benefit. Each one after the first session would say confidently, 'All she needs is a little love' but one by one they dropped her case – almost frantic themselves. They had tried a little love, but the glory of bringing about a cure for this lonely superstar was denied them." Mr Langton smiled as he looked at the sea of serious faced students, "But don't let it throw you, keep trying, that's what keeps us all in psychiatry, one day there may be a breakthrough."

Next day was taken up with a visit to the mental welfare officer. Pimbo luckily won a draw for deciding which nurse would accompany the Mental Welfare Officer on his daily round. Mr Bulwinkle had been an M.W.O. for some years, graduating from a registered mental nurse into the realms of the Health Service.

"You'll have to take things as they come boy. Never had this in my day. The curriculum's improving year by year, but I'll try and find an easy case for you – we'll visit Perry Fulton."

Perry lived in a small sleazy street off Mill Road, Cambridge. He had been an in- and out-patient for some years. Simple schizophrenia, plus an obvious

low intelligence quotient had made a difficult issue
of controlling both the taking of medication and
Perry's attitude toward his family. In answer to Mr
Bulwinkle's knock, a furtive face appeared at the
window, it was that of Mrs Fulton.

"What do you want, snooping around? Who's
that with you? Wants to mind his own business –
he does."

The M.W.O. smiled at Pimbo. "She'll let me in, her
bark's worse than her bite. She's epileptic, spends
most of her time on the sofa. On phenobarbitone, but
takes an overdose now and again when Perry gets
troublesome. We have to get Perry in for six weeks,
on a maintenance dosage of largactil. This usually
does the trick, while Mrs Fulton gets three weeks in
hospital to dry out, and the Red House Council Home
take the three kids for a build up."

Inside the house Pimbo took stock. An awful
smell of stale urine prevailed throughout the room.
Old coats supplied the only bed linen for a broken-
down bed in the corner of the room. Mrs Fulton,
after opening the door, had apparently returned to
her previous position on the bed.

Perry sat in a filthy armchair with what seemed
like an old sack covering his lap. He was unshaven,
with unkempt hair, and just visible at the bottom
of the sack protruded the greasiest pair of suede
shoes Pimbo had ever set eyes on. On a dirty table
at his side stood two or three packets of cigarettes,
and two bottles which Pimbo recognized as containing largactil tablets.

"Been missing your tablets again, Perry?" said
Mr Bulwinkle. "Looks like you're due in Fulbourn
again if you don't buck up."

Perry mumbled incoherently about minding one's own business. Mr Bulwinkle took the prescribed amount of tablets from the bottle and stood over Perry whilst he swallowed them. A filthy-looking glass containing milk was half emptied in helping them down.

"It's a good thing the kids are at school, it means at least they get a dinner each day. During the holidays we arrange for their going to a dinner centre – but if Mrs Fulton's not doped up, Perry's too schitzy to do anything about getting them there. She seems to think kids can live on a small bar of chocolate."

The M.W.O. showed small concern at telling Pimbo family details in the presence of both parents.

"Apathy, you've got to see it to believe it. Nothing seems to sink in, no pride, no principle. In the winter they don't light a fire, the kids group together under a pile of coats in one filthy bed. We've tried everything."

"But what about the N.S.P.C.C.? Don't they look into the situation?" asked a surprised Pimbo.

"They can't get in. The Fultons seem to work up enough energy to bolt all doors. Legally, unless cruelty can be proven, the N.S.P.C.C. are powerless. Once the local superintendent managed to get a foot in the door and Mrs Fulton waved three bars of thin chocolate under his nose saying, 'As long as I feed them you can't interfere.' I checked on Mrs Fulton's parents, the father died of syphilis, and the mother committed suicide. A whole history of a similar nature was revealed throughout the family tree – they just don't seem to stand a chance."

On the way back to the M.W.O.'s building, Pimbo said good-bye and thanked the officer for an interesting morning. Mr Bulwinkle had one more thing to say, "Get it all down boy, the exams are getting tougher. In my day it was razor blades, sharp instruments, keys, choking over meals, and how to use a broom handle as a splint, 'the bundle of five' we used to call it – even then we had failures.'

Pimbo realized the changes which had taken place over the last few years. The training programme so far had covered everything. From a general nursing view, too, it had been on a similar vein. Dummy patients which almost wetted the bed, drip stands, trolleys and trays, with doctors from Addenbrooke's giving lectures, also scattered between training stints were symposiums of high quality involving consultants and senior registrars. It was not an unusual sight to see a psychiatric nurse on his way to a lecture carrying a huge volume of Grays Anatomy.

Mr Langton gave Pimbo an hour's tutorial on the following morning. He was checking on the young nurse's previous papers.

"You seem to have a preference for schizophrenia, not an uncommon pattern. But I suggest you take more interest in the other aspects of mental illness," he began. "Films, TV, and documentaries choose the schizophrenic field because of the dramatics. There's a lot we don't know about schizophrenia. Another thing, Nurse Freestone, I noticed that you use the term hypomanic, I know what you mean, but actually I prefer your pointing out the over active phase of manic-depression, otherwise the depressive part of this unfortunate malady might be neglected. Do you realize that sometimes it may be years before we see the depression side of a manic-depression patient?"

Pimbo realized how thorough the tutorial was in picking out points which matter. From discussion with other nurses he'd found that often a nurse would swot up a certain subject only to find it irrelevant in both ward and examination room.

Mr Langton seemed to be smiling at Pimbo's time off for reflection. "What are you doing about the brain, my boy? A student in last year's block had an unfortunate experience in the practical room. A doctor placed a skull in his hands and said, 'Now tell me all you know about this – inside and outside'. I hope that you aren't putting all your eggs in one basket?"

Pimbo got the message. "This woman, Mrs Fulton, whom I saw today, her face was blotchy and covered in red patches, why isn't she kept under supervision by her doctor? Her children suffer, yet nothing seems to be done?"

The tutor nodded. "Her red patches denote side-effects from phenobarbitone. Doctors nowadays have full surgeries. This woman I understand has her prescription fetched and carried, the doctor rarely sees her. More and more patients coming into Fulbourn are little more than social problems. The Health Service is now expanding to embrace such cases. Psychiatric nurses will soon be out in the community, you could say that Mr Bulwinkle might well be the last of a dying race."

"Fulbourn Hospital will have a new role to play – is that the coming thing?" asked Pimbo.

"There will always be the kind of patient that only Fulbourn can look after. It will take a long time to wind up the present system. Economy-wise, shortage of money, shortage of nursing staff will have much to say in the matter. To send nurses into the community means extra nurses, we still have our own house to put in order. Housing shortage, new changes in sexual liberation, produce stress. We have already said that a large percentage of new admissions come from social problems — so far we've done very little to alleviate this problem. You will do well to study this issue, examination questions, by the time you are ready for your Finals, will be built around the changing social environment."

The hour tutorial was finished, Mr Langton gave Pimbo a sizeable amount of written work. The young nurse felt the training week most beneficial. On the morrow, his day off, he'd planned to take Jennie home to tea. Jennie had looked in earlier and seemed full of good spirits.

# CHAPTER 29

## A day with Jennie

Jennie called for Pimbo early next morning. She looked pretty, wearing a flowered dress, new shoes, and a blue ribbon tied neatly to accommodate flowing auburn hair. Pimbo noticed how grown up she was, Jennie had an air about her, telling the world that she knew eactly where she was going.

"I'm taking my entrance exam next week," she said, as they boarded the bus for the short journey into Cambridge. "I shall be eighteen in three weeks' time – then I can begin training for the real thing. Do you feel different since passing your Intermediate?"

Smiling at her girlish frankness, Pimbo nodded. "Of course I do, do you know, some senior nurses seem to be saying, 'wait until you fail your Inter – that will take you down a peg or two.' After you've passed, well you're O.K. then until the Finals come along. But seriously, there's more responsibility, you get left in charge of a ward during staff shortage and you feel as though you're getting somewhere. But let's stop talking shop and enjoy the day."

The bus was swinging into Drummer Street, the young nurses purposely went the full journey to enable their walking into the new shopping centre, and then through the pleasant Christ Pieces. This eventually led them into Darwin Drive where both Pimbo's and Jennie's parents now lived.

Bob Freestone was in the garden as the young couple approached the house. An asthmatic over a period of years. Bob had recently spent a few months in Papworth Hospital, now looking much fitter he greeted the young nurses warmly.

"Well, bless my soul, two nurses for the price of one. It must be a cushy life, you're both looking well contented – but maybe it's because you're seeing more of each other, I always did say that one day you two would pair off."

Laughingly, he kissed Jennie on the cheek, patting Pimbo on the head, he called out, "Maude, they're here, put the kettle on – let's have a cuppa."

Maude Freestone, a large matronly type, came smiling at the entrance to the little parlour. She and her husband were Salvationists, and attended regularly the Citadel in Tenison Road. "Well, if it isn't my Pimbo, I suppose they all call you Pimbo, somehow you fit the name like a glove. And Jennie too, never seen her looking prettier – and she a skinny little freckled-face thing – it seems but a short time ago since you both were at school."

Over a cup of tea, Maude and Bob told Pimbo of the goings on in the little street where they had once lived for many years. Nothing had changed much, thought Pimbo. His parents' simple conversation about warm inter-relationships with ordinary working people seemed in direct contrast to his life at Fulbourn.

The questioning of motive, digging deep into personality traits at Fulbourn, it seemed that no one could really be normal. There, people had gone about their work, brought up families, and seemed to go on for ever without breakdowns. But then to be fair, thought Pimbo, it was only a little street and after all, didn't Mr Parker die in Fulbourn, he had once lived in that street. After a while, Jennie kicked his ankle under the security of the table cloth. Pimbo got the message, it was their day off and he supposed Jennie wanted to make the most of it.

"You'll be in for dinner, I'll get your favourite", said Maude, sensing the youngsters' impatience. "Then I suppose you'll have tea round Jennie's, her parents will want to see you Pimbo."

Jennie and Pimbo decided to walk along the River Cam. The day was warm and sunny and it seemed years since they as kids, armed with jam jars, stick, string and bent pins, went fishing for that formidable foe – the stickle-back.

Pimbo felt good. To be away from the intricacies of depression, schizophrenia, and other mind-sapping maladies gave him a new sense of freedom. It seemed that sometimes the intense involvement rubbed off on one's self. He watched Jennie as she swung on the toll gate, and allowed it to swing back, giving Pimbo the opportunity of passing through.

Instead, he jumped on, and together they swung backwards and forwards. Jennie was laughing as Pimbo had never seen her laugh before. They carried on until a frosty-faced middle-aged man broke the sequence.

"It's not a fair-ground you know – public property this is, no wonder rates go up. Wilful damage by hooligans – wouldn't have happened in my day, a good belt around the ear, that would have stopped you."

With a glare fit to kill, the man stomped his way past the young nurses. Pimbo realized at once his mistake in thinking that when clear of Fulbourn – a new life might prevail. In a group meeting the man's behaviour would have been put down as a mild depression, unhappy marriage, frustration, or simply a hatred of all young people. It seemed that Fulbourn and what happened on wards was just a prolongation of real life. People were people – in any language.

Jennie not to be outdone, continued swinging on the toll gate, determined to hold on to her happiness. Pimbo knew it was for real. At Fulbourn, both had gained a knowledge far beyond their years. 'Happiness is where you find it' was a well used phrase of Mr Langton's, 'and when you find it – hold on', this was Pimbo's added tag. Looking at Jennie's smiling features, he moved in closer. With the toll gate swinging, Pimbo said tremulously, "Jennie, I want to become engaged, I don't know whether you or I should ask – but what do you say? We can start saving right now." Somehow they couldn't stop the gate. It was as though the moving gate represented a speeding car bent on destruction, unless someone applied the brake the young couple would career headlong away from each other.

Jennie applied the brake by gently answering, "Yes, of course, Pimbo."

Pimbo's foot stopped, giving momentum to the swinging gate. It stopped at once with a clanging jerk. Stepping off the youngsters moved on to a seat at the river's edge. As they finished kissing they stared peacefully into the calm of the slow moving Cam. A duck, with its entourage of ducklings floated gracefully by, Jennie looked up at Pimbo, and smiled knowingly.

They both laughed. "Not as many I hope," said Pimbo, who despite the experiences at Fulbourn, managed a slight blush.

Jennie, throwing her arms around Pimbo, kissed him again and again.

"In the olden days it would be the boy asking the girl's father for the hand of his daughter. Nowadays anything goes, but I know my dad will say yes – he likes you and so does Mum," said Jennie, as the happy youngsters swung into the rear entrance of her parents' little house off Newmarket Road.

Alf Smith, Jennie's father, accepted the news of Jennie's engagement with a happy smiled. "Reckon you two have taken over the nursing administration of Fulbourn Hospital. Your mother tells me the letters you write home – well she never thought you had it in you. I know Jennie's got a good 'un in you, Pimbo."

Rose Smith clasped her daughter's hand, and kissed Pimbo. From inside her blouse she withdrew a small bundle of notes and pressed them into Pimbo's hand. "It's for the ring, to help toward it anyway. Jennie writes a good letter too. I've been reading between the lines, my daughter's had her eye on you for a long time – so I started saving."

At Pimbo's suggestion the happy party went
immediately to Bob and Maude Freestone, to break
the news of the engagement. This was celebrated
with a round of sherry, Pimbo had never thought it
possible to cram so much into one hectic day.

Back at the hospital next day, to Pimbo's surprise, Jennie was to spend a week with him on the
Deighton Centre. This was a large unit dealing
with occupational therapy for inmates and day
patients. The day patient was the brain child of the
new changes sweeping through the social services.
Hitherto, old people separated from their family
unit, and awaiting admission to hospital, would
spend lonely hours, sometimes unattended in their
homes until death overtook them. Then again in
changed circumstances, where the old person
needed only day time care until the arrival of a
daughter or son from work, the centre was ideal.

The patients resident in the hospital found the
Deighton Centre a great change from the olden
days where lines of apathetic patients sat pass-
ively between meals. Pimbo noticed before his allo-
cation to the centre the great spirit displayed by
these people as they made their way each morning
to this new found haven.

Pimbo, who had followed with interest all aspects of the First World War, remembered many
scenes shown in old films of the 'walking wounded'
making slow progress from the battle fields. The
plucky patients, on crutches, in wheelchairs, walking aids, and assisted by nurses, by grit, stubbor-
ness not to give in, reversed this picture in Pimbo's
memory – they were walking toward the battle
field.

The therapeutic value of this did wonders in rejuvenating worn limbs, stroke-ridden muslces, depressed minds, and giving gnarled fingers a new lease of life. Patients were stirred from chair-bound senility into a world of strip-lighting, coloured plugs, bingo, sing songs, coach outings, and renewed acquaintances with old friends and neighbours. The Deighton Centre, around ten a.m., was chock-a-block with nurse therapists, contract plug packing, radio emitting music for all tastes, visitors from other hospitals who were anxious to gain an insight into this new phenomenon, and an atmosphere reeking of honest endeavour.

There was old Mrs Whitmore, aged ninety, once a mother of eight strapping sons, one by one for one reason or another, they leave home. As the years take their toll, the old lady each day cooks for them. The burnt meal extricated from the oven by kindly neighbours, is replenished each day by the demented Mrs Whitmore.

"They won't be long," she says, as another journey is made to the butchers. Finally, the money runs out, along with the neighbours' patience. The old lady is taken to Fulbourn where no longer need she cook for eight phantom sons – meals are now cooked for her. The old lady enjoys herself at the centre, although her conversation bears no relation to reality, others listening in, seem to be on a kind of wavelength to her, and reply with enough sagacity to induce a smile to her care-worn features – no rational neighbour could accomplish that.

Then too there is old Mrs Grace. Years ago she lived in a nice little house with her husband. With

the marriage of her only daughter, and the advent
of her grandchild, life was indeed pleasant. Came
the death of her husband, with the moving away
into another city of her daughter's family, life came
to a halt for Mrs Grace. Loneliness, ill health, was
enough to bring about another admittance to
Fulbourn's mounting register.

But in her new environment, Mrs Grace hasn't
given up. "For my granddaughter" she says as she
knits solidly away at a string dish-cloth. "Number
87, Ditton Walk – that's my number – that's where
I live" The knitting seems to cause little tingling
electrons to run up her bent fingers and stimulate
her brain into memories which give enough
pleasure to make her ask for more. Pavlov, I'm sure
wouldn't mind the stealing of such pleasures.

Loreen too, hard as her life has been, now is
content to make her way on crutches to the pleas-
antries of the day centre. Years ago with a drunken
husband, small children, and very little money
coming in, Loreen found the handicap too much.
With one leg, she would stand on street corners
bemoaning her fate to passers-by. Now, fitted with
a new light-weight limb, Loreen when meeting in
the corridors a face she recollects, asks kindly,
"How's your family, my dear?"

The Deighton Centre use the best of the patients
in doing small tasks such as packing sterile dress-
ings, stripping plastic rawlplugs from their embry-
onic state, into a usable neatly packed commodity
ready for consumer use. For this, money is earned
and put to the advantage of the hospital patients.
At one stage enough money was available for a
sizeable contribution towards the purchase of a

coach specially equipped for accommodating physically handicapped patients on outings to such places as Woburn Abbey, and the seaside.

Jennie and Pimbo, working together, assisted patients from their various wards into the Deighton Centre. The consignment was made in order that when either nurse had been given a ward on completion of their training, they would have a good knowledge of the work done, the type of patient suitable for such work, and the varied problems presented.

On the Saturday, the centre closed. Pimbo and Jennie took the opportunity to go into Cambridge. Producing an envelope from a top drawer of a small chest-of-drawers in his room, Pimbo looked across to Jennie.

"Twenty pounds in all, counting your mum's and my mum's contribution. What do you say in choosing an engagement ring?"

Jennie's answer came in her usual expression of delight, her nose would wrinkle, she would rub hands one against the other, and ended in giving Pimbo a warm embrace and kiss.

Pimbo chose Otto Wherle, a small jewellers on the Market Square. The assistant, a kindly middle-aged lady with a knowing smile at Jennie's request, foraged at the rear of the window, bringing out a large velvet backed tray shiny and resplendent with dazzling rings. Pimbo left things entirely to the assistant and Jennie.

The assistant seemed to mother Jennie along. "No, I think not", "not quite your type", "you're a little too slight for that one", "suits your finger", "brings out the best of your hand – you've very delicate hands – are you a nurse?" At last one was chosen. To Pimbo it seemed that it must be the best one in the tray, and for that matter why shouldn't it be – Jennie was worth it.

He reckoned that not many childhood sweethearts made it in the long haul to the end. Jennie and he had known each other since both were tiny. The hospital somehow had helped cement their friendship. It was funny thought Pimbo, that to many it was the exact reverse. The hospital had in some cases broken up romances, perhaps it was meeting other nurses on different shifts, that brought about an attitude where it didn't seem to matter whether hearts were broken – or not.

Maybe it all depended on really being in love. Suddenly Pimbo saw the assistant and Jennie both smiling at him. "A lover's trance – my boy, aren't you going to slip the ring on?" The assistant winked at Jennie.

Pimbo didn't know the real ceremony attached to the business of becoming engaged. He did know however that a lovely ring was there for the placing. Jennie, too, stood little for ceremony. Placing the appropriate finger delicately, invitingly forward, she wrinkled her nose again and kissed Pimbo, as he slipped the ring past her small rounded knuckle.

The assistant smiled as though the engagement had been engineered by none other than herself. "And may you both be happy – somehow I know you will," she said as she watched the young couple leave the shop.

Deighton Centre was usually busy on Mondays. Fresh from a week-end's rest, most staff were anxious to get on with it. Day patients, having had the welcome attention of their next of kin, or near relatives, forsaking the loneliness of a silent home, were pleased to return to a welcome sanctuary, as their week-end came to an end

Pimbo remembered a song by Noel Coward, something about 'everything stops for tea'. It seemed that week-ends were in a similar category. Week-ends, no doubt a good old English tradition, were sometimes a bug-bear to the psychiatric nurse. It caused a distinct shortage in the hospital, threw a large burden of responsibility on junior stand-ins, and no doubt many old people on the day patient register dreaded the coming of the week-end.

"It would be a good idea for voluntary workers to try and fit in most of their grand work during a peak period such as week-ends, or after five p.m." said Jennie.

Pimbo nodded. "It's been brought up many times at meetings. You see, charity begins at home. Helpers too have families, sometimes old people, whom they are able to sustain at home by not working at times when the old people require most attention. It's a vicious circle and so far no one has come up with an answer."

Old Jim Wooders was a long stay patient in the hospital. Jennie's duty was to fetch Jim from his ward and wheel him into the Deighton Centre. Jim, an ex-miner from the north, had chosen to live with his daughter in Cambridge after retirement. He had one eye, one leg, one lung, his 'good' leg was ulcerated and seemed likely, due to a gangrenous state, to be amputated. If this wasn't enough, Jim had become almost stone deaf which had helped change his personality into that of a disagreeable, cantankerous, paranoiac old rascal.

Each day he would accuse his only daughter of stealing the money which he kept under his pillow in a tin box. A kindly neighbour who came in to help lift the old man into the bath, was entreated by Jim to help count his money. This cast a seed of doubt onto the daughter, who although consoled by her neighbour that she had no doubt that she, the daughter, would not touch his money and that the old man was not in command of his reasoning, eventually had to arrange for her father's commitment to Fulbourn – she had borne as much as she could bear.

Jennie, who like Pimbo had read as much as possible about all patients' life recordings, felt sorry for the old fellow as she wheeled him along. She pictured him as a hard working miner, who had torn his body apart in order to keep his family. It seemed ironic that now a mere hulk of his former self, he should have changed into such a character now his working days were over. On visiting day the daughter had spoken to Jennie about the heartbreak she felt about her father. She told of how her mind had reached a state where she felt that she might have to see a psychiatrist. Now when visited, her father seemed much happier, never spoke of money, and found the Deighton Centre a place in which he could go over old memories, see new faces, and not be lonely.

Pimbo and Jennie moved around the patients who were seated at a large table carrying out their respective duties. Little jokes were exchanged, and some patients who had been in for many years and might have been discharged had relatives been available to look after them, took a great deal of interest in the goings on.

"Give him plenty to do, the lazy old sod. Eats double helpings on the ward – then sits sleeping, I've done two boxes to his one," says Big Tim, a seasoned veteran.

"Mind your own business," says the patient in question. "I'm only resting my eyes. My work is grade-one. When you've gone, the therapists have to do yours again."

Pimbo would often marvel at the occasional lucidity of such remarks. To the lay person it might well seem that the patient making remarks so apt and to the occasion, should be capable of living outside the hospital. In some cases, indeed, it was so, and little homes had been started in which the better type of patient might live together under casual supervision – this was proving a great success. Jennie and Pimbo had gained much experience during their stay at Deighton Centre, and were now looking forward to their day of marriage.

## In the Shadow of King's

O, King's magnificent and proud,
Cloaks of learning thee enshroud.
Our City's monument of fame,
Filled with many famous names.
Schools of scholars, through the years,
Reach a zenith with their peers.
Solemn words, and these are they,
Never, shall King's pass away!

Amidst the rebels, and the sport,
Some, maybe, were never caught!
Whom, the Town regard as pests,
Bored with laughing at their jests.
They, among the cheese and wine,
Cry, O, King's, forever mine.
Some may go, others stay,
Never, shall King's pass away!

Oh demonstrations furious field,
Garden House miscreants yield.
As Leftists make a last lament,
Tizzy, folds his crumbling tent,
Smiling Provosts, thus acclaim,
Victory, to a worthy name.
Now, with patience, day by day,
Never, shall King's pass away!

Porters, bedders, staff, untold,
Toil within these gates of gold.
Speak in hushed, or bated breath,
They, will stay until the death.
Gaze, upon the illustrious name,
Ask themselvese 'What is fame?'
Fame, is but a slow decay,
Never, shall King's pass away!

                                        Fred Unwin

*Pimbo and Jennie, in later years, experienced the
behind-the-scenes life of a famous college – King's!
Hence the poem 'In the Shadow of King's'*